TENDER IS THE NIGHT

The Callaways #10

BARBARA FREETHY

HYDE
STREET
—PRESS—

HYDE STREET PRESS
Published by Hyde Street Press
1325 Howard Avenue, #321, Burlingame, California 94010

Printed in the United States of America

Cover design by Damonza.com

ISBN: 978-0-9961154-8-3

PRAISE FOR THE NOVELS OF
#1 NEW YORK TIMES BESTSELLING AUTHOR
BARBARA FREETHY

"I love *The Callaways*! Heartwarming romance, intriguing suspense and sexy alpha heroes. What more could you want?"
-- *NYT Bestselling Author* **Bella Andre**

"I adore *The Callaways*, a family we'd all love to have. Each new book is a deft combination of emotion, suspense and family dynamics. A remarkable, compelling series!"
-- *USA Today Bestselling Author* **Barbara O'Neal**

"Once I start reading a Callaway novel, I can't put it down. Fast-paced action, a poignant love story and a tantalizing mystery in every book!"
-- *USA Today Bestselling Author* **Christie Ridgway**

"In the tradition of LaVyrle Spencer, gifted author Barbara Freethy creates an irresistible tale of family secrets, riveting adventure and heart-touching romance."
-- *NYT Bestselling Author* **Susan Wiggs**
on Summer Secrets

"This book has it all: heart, community, and characters who will remain with you long after the book has ended. A wonderful story."
-- *NYT Bestselling Author* **Debbie Macomber**
on Suddenly One Summer

"Freethy has a gift for creating complex characters."
-- ***Library Journal***

"Barbara Freethy is a master storyteller with a gift for spinning tales about ordinary people in extraordinary situations and drawing readers into their lives."

*-- **Romance Reviews Today***

"Freethy's skillful plotting and gift for creating sympathetic characters will ensure that few dry eyes will be left at the end of the story."

*-- **Publishers Weekly***
on The Way Back Home

"Freethy skillfully keeps the reader on the hook, and her tantalizing and believable tale has it all– romance, adventure, and mystery."

*-- **Booklist***
on Summer Secrets

"Freethy's story-telling ability is top-notch."

*-- **Romantic Times***
on Don't Say A Word

"Powerful and absorbing…sheer hold-your-breath suspense."

*-- NYT Bestselling Author **Karen Robards***
on Don't Say A Word

"A page-turner that engages your mind while it tugs at your heartstrings…Don't Say A Word has made me a Barbara Freethy fan for life!"

*-- NYT Bestselling Author **Diane Chamberlain***
on Don't Say A Word

Also By Barbara Freethy

To my amazing mother-in-law Dorothy Freethy, thanks for all the support and love, and for being my first reader on this book!

One

❯❯❯❮❮❮

"Yes, he's probably cheating on you. No, you didn't do anything wrong. Yes, you should absolutely find out, and, no, you won't find anyone better than me for the job." Devin Scott ended his cocky monologue by sitting back in the worn leather chair behind his desk and giving the beautiful blonde in front of him a weary, cynical smile.

Although he was fairly certain he knew exactly why this woman had come looking for a private investigator, he couldn't understand why any man would want to cheat on her. She was one of the prettiest women he'd seen in a long time with shoulder-length, thick, wavy blonde hair, honey gold skin, and slender, athletic grace.

Then again, appearances could be deceiving.

As she stared back at him with a pair of intense, intelligent blue eyes that made his nerves tingle, he suddenly wasn't at all sure why she'd come to his office.

"You think a man would cheat on me?" She crossed her legs, revealing a bit more thigh under the cream-colored knit dress that clung to her curves. "Why?"

"Because you're looking for a private investigator."

"And I couldn't have another reason for coming to

see you?"

"Most women who show up here don't."

"Interesting."

He sat up in his chair, instinct suggesting he might have misjudged her.

"Do you want to know what I think?" She tucked a strand of shiny hair behind her ear and gave him a challenging look.

He had a feeling he didn't want to know what she thought, but since it had been a really long time since anyone had surprised him, he said, "Yes."

"I don't think you're anywhere close to being the best investigator in the business, because I don't have a boyfriend or a husband, and if I did, and if he were cheating on me..." She paused. "I'd catch him myself, and I'd make him very, very sorry."

Seeing the steel fire in her eyes, he had no doubt that she was capable of backing up her words.

"I'm also not here to hire you," she continued. "I'm here to help you."

He raised an eyebrow. "Help me? How?"

"It's my understanding you've requested assistance from the FBI."

His heart sank, and his stomach turned over. "Hal sent *you*?" He couldn't help but emphasize the word *you*, because when he'd asked Hal for help, he'd hoped for a seasoned agent or a team or anyone besides this young woman, who couldn't have been on the job more than a year.

She stared back at him, her gaze unwavering. "Why shouldn't he send me?"

"How long have you been working for the Bureau?"

"A year, but that shouldn't matter. I'm good."

He appreciated the proud glint in her eyes, but having

been a special agent with the FBI for almost a decade, he didn't think she had any idea just how good or bad she was. "No, thanks."

Her right eyebrow shot up in surprise. "Seriously? You're turning down my help?"

"Yes."

"You're not even going to give me a chance?"

He shook his head. "Nope."

"Why not?"

"Because you have no idea the massive number of things you don't know, that the Bureau didn't train you to know, and I don't have time to teach you."

"You have no idea what I'm capable of, what I already know," she retorted. "But putting my level of experience aside, here's the bottom line—it's me or no one. That's coming straight from Agent Roman. Apparently, you've used up whatever credit you had on account with him. I've been assigned to help you for five days."

"Forget it," he said, disgusted and angry with himself for actually believing the Bureau might help him solve the murder of his former partner and finally get justice for her death. "I'll take no one."

She folded her arms across her chest, drawing his eye to her beautiful breasts, which were more than a little distracting.

"Then apparently you're as stupid as they said you were," she said.

It took a moment for him to get his focus back, and he frowned at her blunt words. "Who told you I was stupid?"

"Some of your old buddies. They told me you were once a brilliant agent, but you got caught up in your emotions, and you were too stupid to realize that you were obsessed with a truth that didn't exist. Maybe they're right. Maybe you have lost it."

She made him feel like he was a hundred years old instead of thirty-four. "I'm still brilliant, and the only thing I lost was the illusion that the Federal Bureau of Investigation was actually interested in investigating the death of one of their agents."

"If they weren't interested, I wouldn't be here."

"Lip service," he said dismissively.

"I might be able to help you more than you think."

"How so?"

"My name is Kate Callaway. My uncle, Jack Callaway, is deputy director of the San Francisco Fire Department. My cousin, Emma Callaway Harrison, is an arson investigator with SFFD, and I have two brothers and a bunch of cousins who are San Francisco firefighters. The case you're working involves a serial arsonist here in San Francisco. Who on earth would be better to help you with that than me?"

She made a good point. "When you put it like that..." he drawled.

"Exactly. I'm certain Agent Roman sent me because he thought I could help you and not just to get you off his back."

He wasn't as certain of that as she was, but her contacts with the SFFD could be of value. Still, he hesitated.

The fire in her eyes, the sexy, confident smile, and her very attractive shape reminded him that there was probably an even better reason to send her away than the fact that she was a green agent. He couldn't afford to be distracted. It had been months since he had a good lead. He couldn't blow that now. But was he really going to send away a resource who was extremely well-connected to the local fire department and arson unit?

Contrary to what his former coworkers thought, he'd never been stupid, and he wasn't going to start now. "Fine."

"Fine?" she echoed. "That's it?"

"You can help me."

"I'm so honored," she said sarcastically.

"You're going to be a pain in the ass, aren't you?"

"I'd say you could count on that. So, do you want to read me in?"

"On the way," he said, his gaze catching on the clock on his wall. It was almost five thirty. He got to his feet and grabbed his keys.

"On the way to where?" she asked, as she stood up.

"The Allure nightclub. I have to catch a cheating husband on his way home from work."

"That can't wait?"

"No."

"Maybe I can meet you later—or tomorrow," she said, following him out of the office.

"We can talk in the car."

"Or we could start in the morning."

"We'll start now." He paused at the top of the stairs. "Let's get one thing straight, Special Agent Kate Callaway—I'm in charge of this investigation."

"You're not even with the Bureau anymore, Mr. Scott, so how can you be in charge?"

"Because I am. Because I've spent every day of the last eighteen months looking for the person who killed my partner, and I'm not going to stop until I catch them. If you want to stay, that's the deal."

"You shouldn't be calling the shots," she grumbled.

He shrugged. "Take it or leave it."

"If I leave it, you'll have no one. You'll be on your

own," she pointed out.

"That's true. And if you want to walk away from a case that could put away the murderer of a special agent, then you can walk away. God knows you wouldn't be the first."

She stared back at him with doubt in her eyes. "I don't believe anyone just walked away."

"Do you see anyone else here?" he challenged. "You can make excuses. You can tell me the Bureau believes the arsonist is already dead. You can say that terrorist threats and sex trafficking and any other number of other crimes have had to take precedence, but the death of an agent should never be forgotten or go unsolved. Samantha Parker gave her life to the Bureau, and until her killer is in jail, I will be working her case. Got it?"

Kate nodded. "Yes. I'll stay, and I'll follow your lead until you do something stupid. Then the deal is off."

He'd probably already done something stupid when he'd agreed to work with her. But it was too late to back out now. For better or worse he had a partner—for several days anyway.

—➤➤◄◄◄—

Devin Scott wasn't what she'd expected at all. While he might have been described to her as a burned-out ex-agent with a crazy obsession and a huge chip on his shoulder, no one had mentioned that he was also extremely attractive in a scruffy kind of way, with wavy brown hair, intense dark brown eyes, and a day's growth of beard on his jaw. From the way his jeans and knit shirt clung to his lean, powerful frame, he also appeared to be incredibly fit. Whatever he'd been doing since he'd left the Bureau, he'd obviously kept in excellent shape.

Not that she should be thinking that much about his body. He was a job—just a job. She'd worked with good-looking men before, and his arrogant cockiness was nothing new, either. She had three older brothers who were as alpha as they come, and as a woman in a predominantly male field, she knew how to hold her own. She just hadn't expected to have to fight for an assignment that she didn't really even want. The only reason she'd said yes was because her boss had asked her to do him a favor.

She probably should have walked away when she had the chance, but as soon as Devin Scott had looked down his nose at her and said, "no thanks," she'd felt compelled to do whatever it took to get the job. She'd always been that way. When someone told her she couldn't do something, she became determined to prove them wrong, no matter what the cost.

The cost now was at least a few more days in the company of one cynical, moody man who might be taking her on a wild-goose chase.

Agent Roman had told her he was ninety-nine percent sure that Devin was just letting grief and guilt cloud his judgment, but it was that one percent of uncertainty that had gotten her the assignment. Agent Roman had sent her to make sure that Devin didn't actually have a case, but she wasn't going to tell Devin that.

Devin flipped the locks on a silver SUV. He opened the passenger door and grabbed a sweatshirt, two empty water bottles, and a couple of books and tossed them into the backseat. She noticed two of those books were on fire investigation. She had a feeling he was an expert in the subject by now.

She slid into her seat and fastened her seat belt while

Devin got in behind the wheel. "So tell me about the case," she said, as he started the car.

"How much do you know?"

"Not a lot. I only got the assignment this morning. I did a quick read-through, and I know that your partner, Agent Samantha Parker, was profiling a serial arsonist when she died in a fire with the man believed to be the arsonist—Rick Baines, a wanna-be firefighter."

"Baines didn't do it," Devin said flatly, not a hint of doubt in his voice.

"There appeared to be a great deal of evidence against him."

"He matched a general profile, but not the one Sam was working on. He didn't do it," Devin repeated. "The real killer is still out there, and he's going to strike again."

She thought about his words and the other piece of information that Agent Roman had given her before she left. "I was told that you thought you had a lead eight months ago and that it didn't pan out."

He shot her a dark look. "That doesn't mean I'm wrong now."

It might not mean that, but it certainly hadn't helped his cause. "Why did you leave the Bureau?"

"I'm sure they told you why. I needed time to work the case."

"That's why you're now tracking cheating husbands?"

"Yes. It pays the bills and gives me the time and the freedom to find Sam's killer."

"Were you and Agent Parker involved?"

The anger that came off him at her question heated up the air between them. His intense glare instinctively made her edge toward the door.

"No," he said, his voice tight, as if he were fighting for control. "She was my partner and my friend. She was also a loyal agent, and she deserves justice."

Despite his words, she felt like there was a more emotional connection between him and his partner than he was saying. But she changed the subject. "Tell me why you're so sure the man who was found in the house wasn't the killer."

"Because Sam left me a message right before she went to the scene. She was excited about a new clue she'd discovered."

"What was that?"

"She didn't say, but she did say we'd been on the wrong track, that everything made sense now, that the profile we'd been working was completely wrong."

"That sounds very general."

"Unfortunately, yes. She said she would tell me more when we met. She gave me an address and said 'see you soon.'" He let out a heavy breath. "That was the last thing she ever said to me. I played her message for everyone to hear, but it wasn't enough to convince anyone that Baines wasn't the right guy."

"Maybe she got it wrong," Kate said tentatively. "Maybe Baines *was* the guy. He was there. He died with her."

His jaw tightened. "She didn't get it wrong."

"What aren't you telling me? You would need more than a phone message to go against the entire Bureau."

"There's a hell of a lot more," he agreed. "But it's going to have to wait. We're here."

He pulled into a parking spot across the street from a seedy-looking bar named Allure. But it wasn't just a bar, she realized; it was also a strip club. *Great. Just what she wanted to do on a Wednesday night.* "That's the place?"

"That's it."

"What are you going to do?" she asked curiously.

"Take photos of the cheater for his wife."

"And then what?"

"Give them to her in exchange for a nice wad of cash."

"I mean—what is she going to do with the pictures?"

He shrugged. "Don't know. Don't care. Not my job to ask."

"I can't understand how a man trained to ask questions wouldn't want to ask *that* question. What if she's blackmailing him? Or setting him up in some way?"

"She just wants to know if he's lying to her. And I can already tell you—he is."

"You've followed him before?"

"No, I ran his credit cards. He comes here twice a week, on Monday nights when his wife is at her book club and on Wednesday nights when she goes to Pilates. He's, of course, allegedly working late."

"Where does he work?"

"An advertising agency. He's an account manager."

"How long have they been married?"

"Seven years."

"Does the wife work?"

"She does. She developed a line of popular skin care products that she sells online. Apparently, her business is quite robust."

Kate thought about that. "It sounds like she's more successful than he is. Maybe that's why he's cheating. He can't stand that his wife is doing better than him. I know men like that."

Devin sent her a speculative look. "Are you speaking from personal experience?"

"Of course not," she said quickly, realizing she had let a little of her personal past creep into their conversation. "Just saying he sounds selfish."

"Most people who cheat *are* selfish."

"I suppose. But you don't actually know if he is cheating. He might be watching the strippers but not actually doing anything."

"I doubt it."

"You really think you know everything, don't you? Yet, you were wrong about why I came to your office."

He frowned. "For about thirty seconds."

She smiled. "You hate to be wrong, don't you?"

"I'm guessing you share the same attitude."

"Well, so far tonight you're the only one who has been wrong, so I don't actually know what being wrong feels like."

"You're wrong if you think chasing Sam's killer is a pointless exercise."

She met his gaze. "I haven't made that assumption yet. I'm still gathering the facts."

As he reached for the door handle, she frowned and said, "Wait. Where are you going? I thought we were watching the door."

"We'll wait for him inside. It's more comfortable, and I could use a drink."

"You drink on the job?"

"One of the perks of working for myself now. Come on, I'll buy you a beer." He paused. "You're not going to tell me you don't drink, are you?"

"Since I met you twenty minutes ago, I've actually been thinking a lot about having a drink—or two," she said dryly.

For the first time, a glimmer of a smile crossed his lips. "I'd like to tell you that feeling will go away once you get to know me."

"But it won't?"

"Looks like we're going to find out."

Two

Okay, so Kate Callaway was not only attractive, she was also quick-witted and a bit of a smart ass. Maybe the Bureau had finally decided to hire some people who didn't have to do everything by the book.

On the other hand, she could be playing him. Hal had obviously sent her to assess the situation as an impartial, objective party. Kate needed to make friends with him so she could determine if he was as crazy as everyone thought he was. While it might be amusing to crank up the crazy for her, he had more important priorities, like finding Sam's killer.

The darkness of that thought squeezed his heart. It had been a year and a half since she'd died, since he'd let her down, but the pain felt as raw and as real as if it were yesterday. Breathing through the sudden tightness in his chest, he opened the door for Kate and waved her inside the club.

She gave him a surprised look, as if that gesture of chivalry was completely out of character. Apparently, he wasn't the only one who'd made a quick judgment.

He led her over to a table at the back of the room. A

dozen or so people were in the bar, and mostly seated near the center stage, where a busty redhead was performing.

A quick scan of the room told him that the man he was waiting for had not yet arrived. Usually Russell Walton hit the club between six and seven, so he should be walking in sometime in the next hour.

"What does he look like?" Kate asked. "The man we're waiting for."

He pulled up a photo on his phone and showed it to her.

"Good-looking guy," she said. "I wouldn't think he'd need to come to a seedy strip club to find a woman."

"Maybe this feels more private to him. His friends probably don't come here."

"What's his name?"

"Russell Walton."

"What does his wife look like?"

He flipped through a few more photos and showed her one of the couple taken at a party. "This is Brenda Walton."

"She's attractive, too. Does he really think he's going to do better here?"

He shrugged. "Can't say."

"I don't get why Brenda came to you instead of just confronting her husband or following him herself."

"She thought she'd make him suspicious and then she'd never know the truth, but I think the real reason is that she didn't want to find him with another woman."

"That wouldn't be easy, but at least she'd know for sure what was going on," Kate said.

He slipped his phone back in his pocket as a waitress came over to take their drink order. He ordered a beer, with Kate doing the same.

When they were alone again, Kate said, "So, while

we're waiting…let's talk. How did you and Sam get on the arson case in the first place?"

"There had been a series of fires involving historically significant and federally owned buildings here in the city. Sam and I were called in to help with the investigation. Sam was a more experienced arson investigator than I was. She'd been working with that unit for several years."

"I was wondering how you got involved since before that you were working on domestic terrorism."

"You're right. I'd spent almost a year tracking a couple of terrorist cells around the country. We were finally able to put them away. It had been a long assignment, and I was looking for something different, a change of pace. Sam suggested I come out and work with her. At that point, there was some concern the fires were also related to terrorism, so she thought having me on the case would be helpful."

"Did you ever find a terrorist link?"

"No, I don't believe terrorism is the objective of this particular arsonist. And neither did Sam." He paused, needing Kate to understand just good Sam was. "Sam was one of the most intuitive people I've ever met. She had a sense for what made people tick. She understood motivation better than anyone. It made her a good profiler."

Kate sat back as the waitress set down two beer bottles and a small bowl of peanuts.

"Food, yay, I'm starving," Kate muttered, reaching for a handful.

"You want something else to eat?"

"This will do for now. We're not going to be here that long, are we?"

"We'll see how long it takes for Russell to show up."

"I'm surprised you take any time away from the fire case. Agent Roman told me you are very...determined."

He smiled at her careful choice of words. "Is that how he described it?"

She smiled. "He might have used a different word or two."

"I'm sure he did. I lived and breathed the case the first few months after I left the Bureau, but I had to wait for the arsonist to strike again, to come back out of whatever hole that they had crawled into. In the meantime, I had to pay my bills. So I became a private investigator."

"Why did you ask Agent Roman for help now?"

"Because the arsonist has resurfaced. Two days ago, there was a fire at a school. That's how the trio of fires always starts. They begin small; a fire in a Dumpster or a shed, not particularly dangerous but still destructive. The second fire has always taken place at a community center of some sort, usually within a three-mile radius of the school. It's bigger, bolder, hotter. The third fire is the grand finale and has always involved a structure listed on the historic register. There have been varying degrees of damage and some injuries, but the last fire took two lives."

"What does the local arson investigative unit have to say?" she asked.

"Nothing. They closed the case along with the FBI eighteen months ago. I've tried to get their attention since then. I've been down there several times. I've contacted everyone at every level in the department, and no one was willing to help. These days I can't get past the receptionist. They're not interested in what I have to say. Even after this latest fire, they wouldn't return my call. That's why I asked for Hal's help."

"Did you ever speak with my cousin—Emma

Callaway Harrison? She's an arson investigator here in the city."

"No. While Sam and I were on the case, our contact was Karl Benzinger. After Sam died, I also worked with Benzinger's boss, Mick Young."

"We should talk to Emma."

"If you can get me in the door, I'd be happy to do that," he returned.

"So now you can see how helpful I might be," she said, a small smile playing across her lips.

"I'm not in the door yet."

"I want to look through every file you have before we talk to Emma."

"I'll show you everything."

"I wish we didn't have to hang out here. I'm eager to get started."

He had to admit her words were a refreshing change. "Why are you so eager?" he asked curiously. "This can't be the kind of case you want to work on. If you work for Hal Roman, then you're not involved with arson."

"No, I'm not usually, but I'm game for anything, and when I get an assignment, I dive in. It doesn't matter what it is."

"You are new," he said with a sigh. It felt like a lifetime since he'd been that enthusiastic.

"I can't change my age or how long I've been on the job. So if you want my help, you need to get over that."

"I don't believe Hal really sent you here to help me. He just wants you to confirm that there is nothing to help with. And I'm sure he sent you, Kate, because he didn't want to waste the time of a more seasoned and valuable agent."

She winced at his direct words. "Thanks for that."

"Just telling it like it is. And you already knew that."

"You're very cynical."

"You will be, too, if you stay with the Bureau. If I could give you one piece of advice, it would be to get out now before you change into someone you don't even recognize, before you lose your heart and your soul in a job that in the end is nothing more than work. You're not going to save the world. You might not even be able to save one person. You think you're living the dream, but for most people it turns into a nightmare."

His words came out with a reckless passion that he wished he'd been able to repress, but there was something about her wide-eyed optimism that pushed all the wrong buttons.

She gave him a thoughtful look, then said, "I think we have something else in common besides our desire to always be right, Devin."

"What's that?"

"We're both bad at taking advice."

He had to give her credit for taking his curveball and hitting it out of the park. He tipped his bottle to her. "Nice."

She gave him a half smile. "Did I mention I have three older brothers, two sisters, and a humongous family who like to give me advice every time I turn around? You're not going to scare me away, not from this assignment or from the job I've wanted to do since I was eleven years old."

"Eleven, huh? What happened at eleven?"

"Nothing." She averted her gaze as she sipped her beer. "Two men just came in. Is one of them Russell Walton?"

He glanced toward the new customers. "No." He gazed back at her. "What happened when you were eleven, Kate?"

"I already told you—"

"No, you didn't," he interrupted. "You can't keep it from me. It's in your file. Everyone who goes through Quantico is interviewed extensively about their background and motivation for becoming a special agent. And even if it's not in your file, it still wouldn't take me more than fifteen minutes to figure it out. A little Internet research, and I'd come up with an answer. Something happened to you or to someone you knew when you were eleven."

She let out a little sigh. "Fine. I was walking home from school with my best friend, Melissa, when her father kidnapped her. He'd been beating up on Melissa and her mother for years, and her mom had finally kicked him out and gotten a restraining order, but there he was. Usually, there were plenty of people around, but not that day. I was right there when he jumped out of a van, grabbed her and threw her inside. I heard her screams in my head and saw her terrified face pressed against the window for a very long time."

His stomach turned over. He'd worked a lot of child kidnappings over the years, and the story never got easier to hear. "Was she rescued?"

Kate nodded. "Two days later. The FBI tracked them to a dive motel in Idaho. I remember when they brought her home. A female agent held Melissa's hand as they got out of the car. I was so happy to see her safe. The whole neighborhood was there. When that agent handed Melissa to her mother, I thought I'd like to be her. I'd like to bring a missing kid home, make someone's family whole again."

"So you've got a hero complex."

"I don't have a complex anything," she said with a frown. "That incident was the seed of my motivation, but over the years I took time to figure out what I wanted to do with my life."

"It doesn't sound like you considered other options."

"I did, but law enforcement called to me. It wasn't just Melissa's kidnapping that influenced me. The Callaways are big on public service. All the kids are raised with the idea that it's important to give back, to serve the community, and I thought the FBI would be a great fit for me. I wasn't wrong. I'm good at what I do, and I like it."

"So now you're living the dream," he said dryly, waving his hand at the striptease going on at the other end of the room.

"At the moment, I'm living your dream, not mine," she retorted. "Why did you want to be an agent, Devin? And before you say you had no reason, let me remind you that I could also probably figure it out in about fifteen minutes, too, so why not save me the time?"

"My dad was FBI," he said. "I went into the family business."

"Really?" Surprise filled her gaze. "I didn't know that."

"Hal didn't give you my file?"

"He only gave me the case file, not yours, and no one mentioned to me that you were a legacy agent."

"My father died when I was fourteen. That was twenty years ago. Only a few people at the Bureau would remember him now."

"And one of those few is Hal Roman?"

He nodded. "My father was Hal's mentor. They were good friends. Hal encouraged me to follow in my dad's footsteps."

"Now I understand why Hal wanted me to help you."

"If he really wanted to help me, he would have sent

someone more experienced." He lifted the bottle of beer to his lips, wondering how the conversation had gotten so personal. It was his fault. He'd pressed Kate for information, and she'd come right back at him. He'd learned one thing about her. Despite what she'd told him, she did want to be a hero and while that wasn't necessarily bad, sometimes it was dangerous, and sometimes he was guilty of the same desire.

Like maybe now…

He shoved that thought out of his head. He didn't want to be a hero. He wanted to get justice, which was completely different.

He straightened in his seat as his subject walked through the door. Russell Walton wore a navy blue suit, a maroon-striped silk tie knotted around his neck. He fit right in with the other businessmen looking for after-work entertainment.

"Is that him?" Kate asked.

He nodded, taking out his phone and placing it on the table, so he was ready to take the shots he would need.

Russell walked down toward the stage and took a seat at an empty table right in front. He ordered a drink, then took out a bill and placed it in the dancer's thong as she shook her ass in his face.

"Looks like he's here to play," Devin murmured. "Hopefully with someone besides the talent."

"What if no one else comes? Maybe he just comes here to watch the show and then goes home."

"If that's the case, I'll tell his wife that." He discreetly snapped a few shots of Russell at his empty table. "But I don't think he's going to be alone for long. His credit card receipts appeared to be for more than one person." He'd no sooner finished speaking when a woman walked into the bar. She hesitated in the dark entry as if she were looking for someone, and then she made her way down to Russell's table.

Russell got up, took her hand and kissed her on the cheek. Then they sat down at the table.

"Wow, that was hot," Kate said dryly. "I think I'm going to need another drink to cool me off."

He frowned at her mocking smile. "It's early yet." But as he watched the two talk, it struck him that there was something off about the way they were sitting, talking, smiling at each other.

"She's not having an affair with him," Kate said. "She's not acting intimate."

"Maybe she needs a drink to warm up."

"No, she's not looking at him like a lover—more like a conspirator."

"Which would back up an affair."

"Or something else."

As much as he hated to admit Kate might be right, he couldn't deny that his own instincts were telling him exactly the same thing.

"Women lean toward the men they're sleeping with," Kate continued. "They put their hand on their lover's arm or their leg. They give their man a little smile as if they're remembering what went on the night before or the last time they were together."

"Did they teach you that at Quantico?"

"They didn't have to. I'm a woman. I know when a woman is interested in a man in a sexual way and that is not the case with those two."

He wanted to disagree, but he couldn't. Instead, he snapped the woman's photo, and then ran it through an app on his phone for facial recognition. It wasn't as in-depth as what the police department or the FBI could do, but if the woman's face had been on the Internet in the past few months, the app would pick her out.

A moment later, he had more than one result. "Lily Holbright, owner of Lily Bright Beauty Products—whatever that is."

"It's a hot new makeup company. Lily Holbright is a former makeup artist to the stars. My sister, Annie, is a big fan of the products. She gives me something every year to encourage me to wear more makeup."

Looking at Kate's clear skin, bright blue eyes, and naturally pink lips, he didn't think she needed anything to enhance her beauty, but what did he know? Maybe it was all a makeup illusion.

Kate glanced toward the couple by the stage. "I wonder if Lily knows Russell's wife. You said Brenda Walton sells beauty products. They're in the same industry. But I still don't think Russell and Lily are having an affair. So what else could they be doing together? And why would they be doing it here?"

Kate's questions echoed his own. He had to admit she was a quick thinker.

As Lily got up and headed toward the restrooms, Kate said, "I think I'll use the restroom, too."

"Don't talk to her. I don't want you to scare her off."

"Don't worry. I know what I'm doing."

Kate was already out of her chair and walking across the room before he could think of a good reason to call her back.

He turned his attention to Russell. The man pulled out his phone and appeared to text someone with a smile of satisfaction. Then he set the phone down and smiled up at the woman seductively dancing on the stage in front of him. Whatever Russell was up to, the man was clearly enjoying the show. He didn't seem to be aware of anything but the half-naked woman in front of him.

Acting on instinct, Devin got up and walked toward Russell's table. Russell didn't even glance in his direction. It was child's play to pocket Russell's phone on his way to the bar. As he waited for the bartender, he glanced back at Russell. The man was so caught up in the woman in front of him, he hadn't a clue his phone was gone.

But his inattention was about to end. Lily was almost back to the table, Kate following a few feet behind.

Kate met his gaze, tipped her head and walked toward the door. He followed her out of the club and across the street to the car.

"So, I might be able to help you," Kate said, giving him a proud smile as he got into the car and closed the door.

"How's that? Did you hear something?"

"Yes. Lily had a conversation in the hallway outside the ladies' room. She said she had a deal and that by the end of the week there would be no more competition and that Brenda Walton was done. Maybe there's more information on her phone." Kate pulled out a phone and put it on the console between them. "I accidentally bumped into her on my way out of the ladies' room."

He raised an eyebrow. "You stole her phone? You think the Bureau would approve of that?"

"I don't know about the Bureau but you said we were operating under your rules tonight, so I didn't think you'd care."

"I don't." He put Russell's phone down next to hers. "I got his, too."

Kate stared back at him in surprise, then smiled. "Well, how about that? We might make a good team after all."

"Don't get carried away."

"Hey, I just broke a law to help you. At least, you can

say thank-you."

"We may not be able to get into her phone."

"Well, in addition to getting the phone, I also just told you what she said, that she and Russell are conspiring to destroy Brenda. That's more than you got by just grabbing Russell's phone."

"Fine. I can say this: You might not be the *worst* person Hal could have sent to help me."

She laughed. "Well, I can say this: You are *definitely* the worst person Hal could have sent me to help. You have been nothing but rude and ungrateful since I walked into your office."

"If your skin is that thin—"

"It's not. But that doesn't mean I can't call out bad behavior."

"Look, if you want someone to throw you a parade when you do something right—that's not me. But..."

She raised an eyebrow. "Yes?"

"Thank you."

"Was it really that difficult to say? And why did you take Russell's phone if you don't have a way to get into it?"

"Brenda gave me Russell's password just in case."

"Oh, well, that's a little too easy."

"It doesn't always need to be difficult."

He ran through Russell's texts. There were numerous messages between him and Lily, and it quickly became clear that Russell was sabotaging his wife's business. "Damn," he muttered. "They are trying to destroy Brenda's business."

"I told you they weren't having an affair."

"But he is definitely cheating on her," Devin replied. "He's selling his twenty-five percent of his wife's company to Lily Bright Beauty Products. In return, Lily is going to bring her multi-million dollar advertising budget to his agency."

"I guess we know why Russell and Lily were meeting in secret."

"And why Brenda knew that Russell was up to something," he said. "She was just wrong about what that something was."

"What a douche bag. He's selling his wife out for his own personal gain."

"He justifies it," Devin said, glancing down at the latest texts. "He sent a text to his lawyer saying that with the advertising revenue, he and Brenda will be better off in the long run. That giving up twenty-five percent of her company is nothing compared to what will be gained."

"I doubt Brenda will feel the same way. It's her company, not his. I can't believe he even has the right to do that without her consent."

"She obviously put too much trust in him."

"I'll say. And he doesn't care at all about his wife's business; it's all about him." Kate paused, frowning. "He literally tore her down to put himself up. What is wrong with him?"

"Probably more than this one act of greed. I've seen enough."

"What are you going to do?"

"Hand Brenda her husband's phone."

"Maybe we can give her Lily's phone, too," Kate said with a smile. "Even if she can't get into it, it will piss Lily off."

"Good idea." He started the car and pulled away from the bar, wanting to put some distance between themselves and the club before Lily and Russell both realized their phones were missing.

"That was actually kind of fun," Kate said. "And

hopefully with this information, Brenda will be able to stop Russell from selling his shares."

"Maybe, but Russell and Lily seemed celebratory. It could be too late."

"I hope not."

He shot her a look. "Don't get too invested in this. There's a good chance that Brenda will do nothing but cry and tell her husband she forgives him as long as he promises not to ever do it again."

"She wouldn't do that. This isn't about sex; it's about betrayal."

"You'd be surprised what people do when they're in love."

"That's not love; that's stupidity," Kate declared.

He smiled. "For once, I agree with you."

She met his gaze. "If you keep an open mind, you might find yourself agreeing with me more than you think."

"We'll see."

Three

⟶ ⇒≫⫷ ⫸⟵

They met Brenda Walton in the parking lot outside her Pilates class. Kate waited in the car while Devin got into Brenda's Mercedes for a private conversation.

She couldn't see much, but after a moment the woman appeared to break down in tears. She was angry, too, slamming her hand against the steering wheel a few times.

She felt sorry for Brenda. The woman had worked hard to build a business for herself and to have her husband go behind her back and show so little respect for her feelings or her hard work had to be incredibly painful. It probably would have been easier for Brenda to hear that her husband was having an affair.

Kate sighed, thinking that men might be more trouble than they were worth when her phone rang. She was thrilled to see her twin sister Mia's name flash across the screen. "Hey bride-to-be," she said. "How are you doing?"

"It's getting a little crazy," Mia said with a laugh. "It's not easy planning a wedding in San Francisco when I'm hundreds of miles away."

"You could have gotten married in Angel's Bay," she

reminded her.

"It would have been incredibly difficult to get the entire family down the coast. Ria is eight months pregnant and Sara is having a ton of morning sickness with the start of her second pregnancy."

Kate smiled to herself. Her cousins and their wives were definitely adding to the family tree. "There must be something in the water with all these pregnancies. What about you? Are you planning to have kids right away?"

"No. Jeremy and I want Ashlyn to feel a part of our marriage, our family, before we add any more children into the mix. I also love my work at the art gallery here, and there's so much to do. I have free rein with the exhibits, so I'm enjoying my job again."

"That's great. How does Jeremy like being a police officer?"

"He likes it more than he thought he would. It's not a fast pace, but after his years in special ops, I think he was ready for a break. At least for now it's good. If that changes, we'll adapt. As long as I'm with Jeremy and Ashlyn, I don't really care where I live."

She could hear the contentment in her sister's voice, and she felt both happy for her and a little envious. "You've got it all, Mia. You're going to be a wife to a great guy and a stepmother to an adorable little girl."

"I do have it all, and it scares me a little. I don't want to jinx it."

"You can't jinx it. You and Jeremy are perfect for each other."

"Who would have thought I'd be the first to get married?"

Since Mia was a few minutes younger than Kate, Mia was officially the youngest of the six siblings. "I'm actually not that surprised. You've always been the one most interested in building a nest."

"That's true. Probably because I spent a lot of time in the nest that Mom and Dad created. All those years I was sick and fragile, home was my safe place. I want to give Ashlyn that same safe place, not just with a house, but with a family, with parents who love her and who love each other. Anyway, here I am rambling on...how are you, Kate?"

"I'm great."

"You're going to make the wedding, right? No last-minute assignments?"

"I'll be there."

"By Wednesday," Mia said. "I want you and Annie and me to have dinner together before all the events start on Friday."

"Don't worry. I have the schedule."

"Yes, but I know how you are with schedules and how assignments suddenly take you to the other side of the world."

Which was one reason why she'd agreed to help Devin. This assignment would take her right up to the wedding festivities. "That's not going to happen."

"Okay, good. I can't get married without you, Kate. You're not just my sister; you're my twin. For these big life events, we both have to be there. We're connected in a way that no one else can understand."

"I know." She and Mia were very different in personality, but their twin bond could never be broken. She heard Mia blow out a breath. "What is wrong, Mia? Why all the anxiety?"

"I had a bad dream. You were in danger. You were running and then you disappeared into this really bright light, and I couldn't see you anymore, but I could hear you screaming. I woke up in a sweat. It felt so real."

She shivered a little at her sister's words. "That sounds awful, but I haven't seen any bright lights."

"You're not in danger?"

"Not at the moment. I'm sitting in a car."

"Doing what?"

"Waiting for a guy."

"A hot guy?"

"Good body but bad attitude."

Mia laughed. "He sounds like every guy you dated in high school."

"I'm not in high school anymore."

"But you're attracted, aren't you?"

"It's not a date. We're just working together on something. And even if I were interested, he's not. He doesn't like me much at all."

"I can't believe that's true."

"Trust me, it is. He's been trying to get rid of me since I got here."

"Got where?"

She hesitated. She really didn't want to alert her family to her presence in the city just yet. "I can't say."

"You and your classified secrets."

"It's part of the job. I have to go, Mia. Stop worrying. This is a happy time."

Mia laughed. "You're right. Go back to your hot guy. We'll talk soon."

Kate ended the call just as Devin returned to the car.

As he slid behind the wheel and turned to look at her, her chest tightened and a little flutter ran through her stomach. Damn Mia for making her look at Devin as a man and not as an assignment. And damn her stupid body for responding to him in any way.

As she'd told her sister, she wasn't in high school anymore. She wasn't a teenager who let her hormones take her across lines she shouldn't cross. She was a federal agent and she was not going to forget that, not where Devin was concerned.

"What?" he asked, a quizzical look in his eyes.

She realized she was staring at him. "Nothing. Just wondering how it went with Brenda."

"Not great. She got worked up. I really don't like it when women cry. I am not good with tears. Thankfully, she got angry, too. When I got out of the car, she was on the phone to her lawyer. Russell is going to get a big surprise when he returns home."

"Good. So now we get to work on the real case?"

He nodded. "We'll go back to my office."

Her stomach rumbled. "Any chance there's a pizza place on the way? I haven't eaten since early this morning."

"Gianni's is down the block from my apartment. Why don't you order, and we'll pick it up on our way in?"

She looked up the number for Gianni's on her phone. "What do you like?"

"Anything and everything. I'm not picky."

"Not with pizza—only with partners?"

He smiled but ignored her question. "Make sure you get an extra-large. I'm hungry, too."

Devin's office was in the living room of his one-bedroom apartment, which filled the second floor of an old Victorian house in the Marina. The first floor was a boutique vintage clothing shop.

When Kate had first arrived, she'd been more interested in making contact with Devin than taking note of her surroundings.

The office was sparsely decorated with only a desk, two chairs and the usual computer and printer setup. But at the back of the flat was a den with comfortable leather couches, a big recliner and an even bigger television screen. There was a guitar resting against one wall, an exercise bike in the corner and a bookcase filled with books.

The most interesting item in the room, however, was on the wall. It was a large blown-up map of San Francisco with colored thumbtacks creating an interesting pattern.

"Are these spots where the fires occurred?" she asked as Devin came out of the kitchen with plates and napkins and set them on the rectangular wooden table next to the extra-large pizza box.

"Yes," he said, walking over to the map to join her. "Green signifies the school fires, blue the community centers, and red the historical structures."

She studied the pattern, thinking there was something about it that felt familiar, but she couldn't say exactly what. "And you're positive that all these fires are related?"

"The SFFD wouldn't agree with me, but I believe they are. There have been sixteen fires set in the last five years. It's possible that there were fires before that, but if there were, there was a gap in time of at least several years."

"What theories have you drawn regarding the significance of the locations?"

"If the arsonist is fueled by revenge, then it seems that the places being burned are some sort of a sore spot. The person could have been bullied at school."

"As well as at a community center," she mused. "Both places are where people go to learn or get help."

"And where people can feel marginalized," Devin added.

"What about the houses?"

"That's where the revenge theory gets hazy and turns to something else. The fact that all the houses are listed on the historic register is obviously important to the arsonist, but I haven't been able to figure out how or why."

"Maybe something bad happened in an old house," she suggested.

He nodded. "Or revenge isn't the motive at all. It could be about thrill-seeking, which is common for arsonists. Schools and community centers by nature involve lots of people, whether they're all present or not. The historic structures might also feel more important to the fire starter. He's not just burning a house but a structure that's valuable to history, to the city. And as you know, two of the houses were on federal land, which is also why the Bureau was brought into the case."

"In the Presidio, right?"

"Yes. The houses were originally part of the Army base there."

"Interesting." She wanted to know more, but the aroma of garlic and onions was calling to her. She sat down at the table and opened the box, pulling out a large slice of pizza loaded with vegetables and sausage.

Her first bite tasted like heaven, and she finished off the slice in record time, digging in for a second one while Devin was still working on his first. He raised an eyebrow, and she shrugged. "Second youngest of six kids. You learn to eat fast."

"You can have half the pizza, even if you slow down," he said dryly.

"Three slices is my limit. It should probably be two since I have to fit into a bridesmaid's dress next week. But I'm really hungry, so maybe three, and I'll just run a little farther tomorrow."

"Do you like to run or do you just do it because it's part of the training?"

"I like to run. I ran cross-country in high school. Running gives me time to think and burns off the extra energy I always seem to have. What about you?"

He tipped his head. "Same."

"Really? Something else we have in common. Hard to believe."

"Not so difficult. We both do the same job, or used to," he corrected.

"Are you really happy being a private investigator, Devin? Chasing down cheating husbands? You obviously could do so much more."

"I like my freedom, and right now it works for me."

"What about after you get justice for Sam? Will you go back to the Bureau?"

"I doubt they'd have me. I burned some bridges there. But if they did—I'd have to think about it."

"Because you lost your faith when they closed Sam's case?"

"I did. Although, to be honest, I lost a little faith before then. I don't like bureaucracy and politics. You think you joined an agency that will fight for truth and freedom, but within that agency there's not always truth or freedom."

"I don't believe that."

"I didn't believe it when I was your age, either."

She frowned. "Exactly how old are you, Devin?"

"Thirty-four."

"So not exactly ancient," she said dryly. "I'm twenty-seven, so you've only got seven years of wisdom on me."

"In the world we work in, seven years is a lot."

She finished off her slice and took a sip from the bottle of water he'd given her. Then she reached for her last slice. "You can have the rest."

"So you said your sister is getting married?"

"A week from Saturday. She's my twin sister, so I'm the maid of honor."

"Is she also in law enforcement?"

"No, she's an artist. She runs an art gallery in a small town down the coast called Angel's Bay."

"I've been there," he said with a nod. "Charming town."

"Very. Beautiful, quaint, and small. Everyone knows their neighbor. My aunt lived there for a long time. After she died, Mia—that's my sister—went down there to clean out my aunt's house and wound up falling in love with the guy next door. He's a single dad and has a daughter, Ashlyn. Mia is going to make a great mother. She's very patient and nurturing. And Ashlyn is going to be my parents' first grandchild, so she's already being spoiled."

"Your voice softens when you talk about your sister," he commented.

"I love her, and I miss her, but our lives are probably going to be in very different places for a long time."

"It doesn't sound like you and your twin are very much alike."

"We're not, but we're still connected. When she hurts, I hurt, and vice versa."

"Are you talking figuratively or literally?"

"Both. We seem to have a sixth sense when one of us is in trouble."

"I'm betting you're usually the one who's in trouble."

"Another snap judgment, Devin? You're not exactly batting a thousand."

"Am I wrong?"

She wished she could say he was, but her impulsive

curiosity had gotten her into a lot of bad situations. "Maybe not completely wrong."

"I didn't think so," he said with a cocky smile.

"I doubt you were an angel growing up."

"I definitely was not an angel. But I did try to stay behind the line before my dad died."

"And after?"

"I obliterated the line. I was reckless and stupid. I was lucky I didn't end up in jail."

"It's not too late. You may end up there yet if you keep butting into investigations that you're not a part of."

His smile faded. "Is that what Hal told you?"

"It's what he told me to tell you," she said pointedly. "He's worried about you, Devin. He thinks you threw your career away. He's hoping that once you've gotten over your grief you'll realize that you're chasing air and that you'll come back."

"Chasing air," he echoed. "That's exactly what he said to me. There was a time when Hal would have done exactly what I'm doing."

"Really?" she asked, thinking that her boss was one of the most rigid, controlled men she'd ever met. "Agent Roman is definitely not a loose cannon."

Devin shrugged. "Years ago, he was more of a rebel, but it doesn't matter what Hal thinks or has to say. I know what I'm doing. And I will prove all the doubters wrong."

She set the last half of her pizza on her plate. "Tell me about the most recent fire, the one that got you on the phone to Agent Roman."

"It happened on Monday at St. Bernadette's, a Catholic high school. It started in a half-empty Dumpster that had been moved against the building, next to the windows of the counseling office. The fire was estimated to have been set around one o'clock in the morning, which fits the patterns of all the other school fires."

"But that isn't significant," she countered. "I suspect stats would prove that most arson events happen after midnight."

"A good percentage," he agreed, "but still a common link."

"So there was no break-in?"

"A brick was thrown through the window of the counseling office. No fingerprints."

"It sounds to me like an angry student."

"That's what the fire department believes," he said evenly. "Do you want to stop there? Go back to Hal tomorrow and tell him I have nothing?"

She frowned. "Hang on. I'm not rushing out the door. I'm just processing the information. I've only been on this case about five minutes. If you weren't following a pattern of fires, you would have made that as your first suggestion, too." She paused, seeing something in his eyes that told her she didn't have the entire story. "What haven't you told me yet?"

"There was a St. Christopher's medal found near the Dumpster. At two of the other school fires, and one community center blaze, a St. Christopher's medal was found near the scene."

"That's a little more interesting. What's the time gap between fires?"

"Four to seven days between first and second fires. Three to six days between second and third fires, but all three occur within a three-to-four week period from start to finish."

She sat back in her chair and sighed, feeling a little weary, not just from her cross-country flight earlier in the day but also the last few weeks of intense investigative work. She needed to think and sleep and then think some more. "All right."

"All right—what?" he echoed.

"I'm in. I'll help you."

"Isn't that what you were ordered to do?"

She made a face at him. "I was given some latitude, just in case you turned out to be completely crazy."

"So you think I'm sane?"

"I didn't say that," she said, meeting his gaze. "I don't know you well enough to make that determination, but I want to know more. What's your next move?"

"I've been trying to get a meeting with the local fire investigator on the school fire, but every time I call, he's in a meeting."

"Who's the investigator?"

"Paul Bilson. Do you know him?"

"I don't, but I can call Emma and see what she knows."

"If she's willing to talk to you, that would be great."

"She'll definitely be willing to talk to me. I don't believe anyone in the fire department is deliberately letting a firebug roam free in the city. I grew up with firefighters. They risk their lives every day to protect the community from fire."

"I understand the service of the fire department, and, on occasion, their sacrifice," he said, meeting her gaze. "My anger overshadowed some of my common sense in the immediate aftermath of Sam's murder. I'm sure I said some things that were based more on emotion than anything else. Here's what I believe now. It's about resources and odds. They don't want to open up a case they think is solved. They have enough open cases to work on. Arson is hard to prove. There are only so many investigators to go around. I understand bureaucracy, Kate, but I don't have to like it. And I do believe that in the early days some people made mistakes, and it's possible others covered them up or just believed the wrong conclusions, but that doesn't matter. I'm not trying to find a scapegoat, I'm trying to find an arsonist—an arsonist I believe is still alive."

For the first time he sounded completely reasonable, which gave her some hope that he wasn't letting guilt and loyalty cloud his judgment.

"All right. I'll call Emma in the morning." She got to her feet. "I need to go. I've been up since five this morning, and it's been a long few weeks."

Devin stood up. "Where are you staying?"

She hesitated. "I'm not sure yet. I think I'm going to crash at my brother's place. But that depends on how persuasive I can be."

Devin smiled. "I doubt very many people say no to you."

"Trust me, it happens a lot. You said no to me earlier," she reminded him.

"Yeah, and look where we are," he drawled. "Somehow that no turned into a yes."

"Because I'm good."

"Someday I'm going to need actual proof to back that up," he said, a small smile playing around his lips.

The look that passed between them was far more personal than it should have been, and the memory of that look followed her all the way out to the car.

Four

---◆◆◆◆◆---

"I won't be any trouble," Kate told her older brother Ian, a half hour later. He had responded to her request to stay at his apartment with a decidedly irritated frown.

Ian ran a hand through his dark brown hair and blinked the sleep out of his blue eyes. "You're always trouble. What the hell time is it anyway?"

"It's only ten. Were you asleep?" she asked, pushing past him.

She put her carry-on suitcase against the wall and let out a breath as she looked around the simply furnished and very neat apartment. She'd definitely made the right decision in picking Ian's place to crash at. Her other brothers—Dylan and Hunter—were slobs. But Ian had always had an orderly mind, which was probably why he was such a renowned scientist.

"Rough month," he said, closing the door behind her. "What are you doing here? I thought you weren't coming until next week."

"My plans changed."

"Why aren't you staying at Mom's?"

"Because she has all the out-of-town cousins arriving

soon for Mia's wedding, whereas you have this beautiful new condo, and an extra bedroom." She wandered over to the window, impressed by the view of San Francisco and the Golden Gate Bridge. "This place is awesome. You must be making some nice cash these days." She gave him an inquisitive gaze, which he pointedly ignored.

"Why are you in town so early?" he asked. "Did the FBI kick you out?"

"Hardly. I haven't had a vacation since I started last year. I was due."

He moved over to join her at the window, but his thoughtful eyes were on her and not the view. And like always, Ian saw too much. "You look like shit, Katie. When did you sleep last?"

"On the plane out here," she said, not bothering to mention that before that she hadn't slept for three nights straight. Which was one reason why her boss had sent her out to San Francisco early. It wasn't just to do him a favor and help Devin; it was because she needed a break from the intense treadmill she'd been on.

"Why do you really want to stay with me?" Ian asked. "Truth."

She should have figured he wouldn't accept her explanation at face value. She'd never been able to get anything past Ian. "I have to check in on something work-related while I'm in San Francisco, and you know how nosy Mom can be. Plus, Hunter and Dylan's apartment is disgusting, and Annie has two roommates, so there's nowhere to sleep." She gave him a smile. "But this place is beautiful and quiet, and you have an extra bedroom, right?"

"It's my office, but there's a couch in there you can sleep on."

"So I can stay?"

"Do I have a choice?" he asked, running a weary hand through his hair.

"No. Speaking of people who look like shit...what have you been up to?"

"I'm working on something that's involving some long nights, but if we can make it happen, it's going to save a lot of lives."

"Can you tell me more about it? You're always so cagey about your job."

"I'll tell you when it happens."

She sighed. "Fine. Be secretive."

"Look who's talking," he returned.

"Do you have anything to drink?"

"Juice or something stronger?"

"Juice sounds good."

She followed him into the modern, gourmet kitchen, looking through his cupboards while he poured her a glass of orange-pineapple juice. She pulled out a box of cereal and grabbed a carton of milk from the fridge.

"Make yourself at home," he said dryly.

She gave him an unrepentant shrug. Growing up in a family with five siblings, it had always been every man for himself. Both her parents had worked so she and her brothers and sisters had learned to take care of themselves.

"So what's this work thing you have to do?" Ian asked, giving her a speculative gaze. "You're going to get me into the middle of something, aren't you?"

"No, of course not," she said, pouring milk on her cereal, then taking the bowl over to the kitchen island.

"Why don't I believe you? When you're around, things tend to get exciting."

"Not anymore. I'm much more thoughtful now that I'm a special agent."

He laughed. "I doubt that. How do you like working for the FBI? Is it what you thought it would be?"

"It's not at all what I thought it would be. Every day is different. Sometimes I'm doing nothing but boring paperwork or spending hours on surveillance, and other days I'm in the middle of the action, breaking down doors, searching for terrorists, calling in bomb experts."

"That sounds dangerous."

"There have only been a few scary moments. Most of the time it's pretty routine." She paused. "Enough about me. What's up with you?"

"Just work."

"What about women?"

Ian shrugged, folding his arms across his chest as he leaned against the counter. "Who has time?"

"Most healthy, young, single men under the age of thirty-five. What about Vanessa?" she asked, referencing a woman he'd been seeing the year before.

"She said I wasn't fun anymore," he replied. "She wasn't wrong. I've had my mind on other things, important things. She and her friends do nothing but bar hop on the weekends. They start drinking at ten in the morning and are wasted by dinnertime. I'm just not in that mode anymore."

"Not that you ever were." Ian was thirty-two and the second oldest of her siblings. He'd always been the most responsible one in the family. He was just too smart to do all the dumb things the rest of them had done. "How's everyone else in the family? Are Dylan and Hunter staying out of trouble?"

"Dylan seems to have his head on straight. Hunter—who knows? Last I heard, he was going on vacation to try helicopter skiing."

"What is that?"

"As far as I know, you get dropped out of a helicopter on an unreachable mountain peak, and you ski down."

"Sounds insane."

"That's Hunter."

"You'd think he'd get enough of an adrenaline rush from charging into burning buildings."

"You'd think." He moved away from the counter. "I have to get some sleep."

"Go ahead. I'll be quiet."

He paused in the doorway. "You know, Mom is going to kill you if she finds out you're in the city and didn't tell her."

"Then let's make sure she doesn't find out."

—➤➤◀◀—

As Kate walked down the hall of the building where San Francisco's Fire Investigative Unit was housed, she thought about her conversation with her brother the night before. If she didn't want her mom to know she was in town, speaking to Emma was a risk. But if she wanted to help Devin solve his case, she had to take the chance.

While Emma was an outgoing, blue-eyed blonde who tended to meddle in everyone's business with good-natured affection, she was also good at keeping a confidence. She'd keep their conversation private if Kate asked her to, and she intended to do just that.

After pausing at a reception desk, she was waved down another hall. She knocked on a glass door, seeing Emma sitting behind one of the two desks in the room. Thankfully, the other desk was empty. She wanted to have this conversation with Emma in private.

She pushed open the door, ready to greet her cousin with a big, happy grin when she saw Emma dab at her eyes and then force a smile onto her tense face.

"Hey, Em," she said, crossing the room as Emma got to her feet.

"Kate," Emma said. "What a surprise! How are you?"

"I'm good." She gave Emma a hug, followed up by a speculative look. "What's wrong?"

"Nothing," Emma said, blinking her watery blue eyes.

"You were crying."

"I had some dust in my eye. What brings you here?" Emma added, as she sat down behind her desk.

Kate took the chair in front of the desk. "Before we get into that, you have to tell me what's wrong, because clearly something is off. It's not Max, is it? Your husband is still treating you right?"

"Max is great. He adores me. I adore him. I've never been so happy."

"I might believe you if you didn't look like you were about to cry."

"I'm just having a moment."

"Why?"

Emma sighed. "You can't tell anyone in the family, Kate."

"I won't. I promise."

"I had a miscarriage two days ago. It was super early. I was barely pregnant. I shouldn't be this upset."

"I'm so sorry," she said, wanting to give her cousin another hug, but the desk was between them, and Emma seemed almost too fragile to take the sympathy.

"It's the second time in a year. I'm beginning to think my body is not made for having children."

"What does the doctor say?"

Emma shrugged. "Everything looks fine to her. She doesn't see why I can't have a healthy pregnancy, but so far I can't. I didn't even tell Max this time. He was so sad after the first miscarriage; I couldn't bring myself to tell him about this one."

"Em, you have to tell him. You can't carry the grief alone. He wouldn't want you to do that."

"I think it will be easier if I just don't say anything. Why should both of us be unhappy?"

"It won't be easier; it will be harder. You should tell your family, too—at least your mom or your sisters. You need support."

"They won't know what to say, and they'll just feel bad. Plus, with Ria and Sara nursing along pregnancies, I don't want to throw shade over their happy time."

She could understand where Emma was coming from, but she still thought the secrecy was a bad thing. "Then just talk to Max. He deserves to know. It was his child, too." She paused. "He's probably going to think something else is terribly wrong if you don't say anything, because you're not really hiding your emotions."

"I know. You're right. I will talk to him tonight. In the meantime, is there anything I can do for you? I thought you were living in DC."

"I am, but I came back for the wedding."

Emma raised an eyebrow. "Ten days early? What else is going on? Why do I have the feeling this is not just a personal call?"

"Because it isn't. I hate to bother you with this now, but it is important."

"Please, I could use a distraction. I feel stupid for getting so emotional at work. I usually manage to keep my tears out of the workplace. It's difficult enough being a woman in this job, without crying in front of anyone."

"I can totally relate, and I think I'm the only one who saw you wipe a tear from your eyes," she said, as they exchanged a commiserating look. "You shouldn't feel bad or guilty. You're human. Bad things happen and people cry. It's not a crime."

"I know, but crying doesn't get you anywhere. Anyway, talk. Tell me what's going on."

"I'm working on a case that involves a series of fires here in the city."

Emma's gaze narrowed. "Is this about the agent who was killed in a fire last year?"

"Yes. I'm working with Devin Scott, a former agent. He's convinced that his partner, Agent Samantha Parker, was not killed by the man who died beside her."

"Mr. Scott has already talked to my boss about all this, Kate. There's no evidence to support his theory."

"Are you sure? Devin said there was a fire at a Catholic high school on Monday. He believes it's the beginning of another string of fires."

"I know that he's been calling the department about that, but he hasn't brought us anything in the way of new evidence. And there have been several fires at schools in the city in the past few years that were the work of disgruntled students. It's very likely that the fire at St. Bernadette's falls into that category."

"Likely doesn't sound like certainty. Devin is not a crackpot, Emma. He's a former FBI agent who is trying to get justice for the death of his partner. He has a lot of information that he's put together over the past year and a half. I think you should at least hear him out."

"I'm sorry, Kate. I can't help you. My boss instructed me not to take his calls. They had some altercation last year, and until we have more than Mr. Scott's gut instinct, we're not talking to him."

"Emma, I've seen the case files. And I've looked at the pattern of fires. If Devin is right, then more fires are coming. I know you don't want that."

"I told you; I can't talk to him."

"What about me? If you wanted to have lunch with me, and we happened to run into Devin, would that be your fault?"

Emma stared back at her and then let out a breath. "You've always been able to find the angle, Kate."

"Is that a yes to lunch? I know you, Emma. You follow your gut, and so do I. So does Devin."

"We have limited resources, Kate. And arson is one of the most unsolvable crimes there is. We have to go with evidence."

"But this wasn't just arson; it was murder."

"And it was investigated," Emma said. "Not just by us but also by the FBI. They took over the case. You should be talking to your superiors."

"I have all the information that the FBI has on the case, and I'm going through Devin's files as well, but it appears to me that the case was closed a little too quickly. I think you should hear Devin out. You should talk to him about the most recent school fire, because if the arsonist is getting back into business, you're going to want to know."

Emma thought about her words. "If I talk to Devin, it has to be off the record."

"It will be. Where shall we meet?"

"Not anywhere near here."

"How about the Wild Garden on Union Street in the Marina?" she suggested.

"That sounds fine. None of the other investigators in this office would be caught dead in a vegetarian restaurant."

"Great. Is noon okay?"

"Let's make it one."

"Done." She felt a wave of relief that Emma had

agreed to talk to Devin. If she'd had to go back and say she couldn't even convince her cousin to help, she'd feel like a complete failure and as green and unseasoned as Devin thought she was. "Thanks, Em. I owe you one."

"Don't expect too much, Kate. I really don't think your guy is operating on anything more than guilt and grief."

"Hear him out. Then decide." As she got to her feet, she added, "And if you don't mind, I'd prefer if you didn't tell anyone in the family you saw me today."

Emma raised an eyebrow. "Why not?"

"I'm not supposed to be getting into town until next Wednesday, and I need to keep the family out of my business until then."

"Good luck. A lot of people in this town know you or one of our relatives. I'm not sure you can get out of this building without running into someone you know."

"I'm going to give it a shot. See you in a couple of hours."

"I'll be there, and just so you know, Kate, you're buying."

"Of course." She opened the door, then looked back at her cousin. "It's going to happen for you, Em—having a baby. I know it. And when it does, you'll make an amazing mother."

"Thanks, Kate. I really hope you're right."

"I usually am. No one ever seems to realize that, but it's true."

Emma laughed. "I often feel the same way."

Five

—➤➤◄◄◄—

"We have lunch with Emma," Kate said, as she walked into Devin's office thirty minutes later. "You can say thank-you." She sat down in the chair in front of his desk with a satisfied, smug smile. "It was not easy to get her to say yes. Apparently, you're on everyone's blacklist, but I convinced her you were worth a meet. I can be very persuasive."

"I wouldn't think your cousin would be the toughest target, but okay," he said dryly. He actually was a little impressed, but he wasn't going to tell her that, if only for the fun of seeing the angry, irritated blue fire fill her eyes. Kate definitely wore her emotions on her face. If she wanted to be a good agent, she'd have to learn how to put on a better mask.

"Emma might be my cousin, but she's putting her job on the line for this. She's been ordered not to talk to you. She said you got into an altercation with her boss."

He shrugged. "It was a discussion; that's all."

"I have a feeling he doesn't remember it that way. Anyway, lunch is at one o'clock at the Wild Garden down the street."

He groaned. "Vegetarian? Is she one of those?"

"Actually, no, Emma is not a vegetarian, but it's a good restaurant. It has excellent reviews, and I suspect you could use a few vegetables in your diet." She picked up the empty bag of chips on the top of his desk. "Breakfast of champions?"

He took the bag out of her hand and tossed it in the trash. "I've been working. I didn't have time to make breakfast."

"What have you been working on? PI stuff or the fires?"

"Both. I spoke to Brenda earlier."

"Did she have it out with her husband?"

"She did but not until she spoke to her lawyer. Because we gave her a heads-up, she was able to prevent Russell from selling his stake in the company to Lily Holbright. After she informed him of that fact, she threw him out of the house, and said she was filing for divorce."

Kate nodded approvingly. "Good. I'm glad she stayed strong. So are you done with that case now?"

"I am."

"What about other cases?"

"I've been working for a couple of law firms. They keep me busy, but I also have the ability to turn down jobs, which I did as soon as I heard about the fire at St. Bernadette's."

"Emma said you're going to need more than gut instinct to convince anyone the serial arsonist is back. They've had other school fires that were set by students."

"St. Bernadette's fits the pattern. Let's go in the back and look at the map again." He got to his feet. If he was going to convince Emma Callaway to help him, he needed to convince Kate first.

He led the way down the hall to the wall map. "The

green thumbtacks are school fires started at Catholic schools in the past five years. There have been five, not counting St. Bernadette's." He pointed out the tacks. "They form three-quarters of a circle."

"That's true," she murmured, crossing her arms in front of her chest as she studied the map.

"The blue thumbtacks represent the community or recreation center fires. There have been five of those as well. All of the fires took place within three miles of a school fire—basically within the same community. They form a V in the middle of the almost complete circle."

"I can see that. And the historical structures go in a straight line or relatively straight. Line to the bottom of the V. Nothing is exact, though."

"But close enough that you can see the pattern." He pointed to the one yellow thumbtack. "That's St. Bernadette's. Do you see where it falls? Do you see how it's following the arc of the circle?"

"I do," she said, tilting her head to the right as if to get a different angle. "Devin."

"Yes?" he asked, seeing a light in her eyes as she turned her gaze on him.

"You know what this is, right?"

"I have an idea. What do you think it is?" he asked.

"I think the arsonist is making a huge peace sign."

As her gaze met his, he felt in sync with someone for the first time in a very long time. "So do I."

"I didn't see anything about this pattern in the files Hal gave me." She paused, frowning. "There was a map, but it didn't look exactly like this." She turned back to the wall. "What's different about yours?"

"There were a few other fires on the Bureau's map. Sam and I were looking at some additional fires that I now don't believe were part of the pattern. They had similar characteristics, which led us to put them on the list. But during the past year, I've been able to eliminate a couple of them. So this map looks different than the one in the old files."

"Have you shown it to anyone but me?"

He sighed. "I sent a picture to Hal, but he wasn't convinced."

"What about the local fire department?"

"They don't agree that all of these fires are part of a pattern. There are at least three or four they would dispute."

She sent him a speculative look. "There was a fire about eight months ago that you thought was the work of the arsonist, right?"

He really hated to admit that he'd been wrong, but there was no way around it. "Yes, but a suspect was caught and confessed to the arson. His story was irrefutable." He paused and placed his finger on the map where there was a small *X*. "That fire was here. It didn't quite fit the pattern, but it was close enough to make me concerned."

"So you were wrong, and now no one will listen to you," she said bluntly.

"That about sums it up. But just because I was wrong then doesn't mean I'm wrong now."

"It doesn't mean you're right, either." She looked back at the map. "This pattern means something, but what?"

"I've been asking myself that question for a long time. What does the peace sign mean to the arsonist?"

"Maybe he's looking for peace."

"It's as good an answer as any. The most important part of this pattern is not necessarily answering the question of *why* but rather *where*. I haven't had a chance to show anyone in the fire department how St. Bernadette's fits into the pattern."

"We should show Emma." She grabbed her phone and took several photos of the map.

"I believe the next fire has to be within this area." He moved his finger around the uncompleted portion of the circle.

"How many miles does that cover?"

"About five miles. But San Francisco is a dense city with blocks of buildings that share common walls."

"So there are only about a thousand targets," she said with a sigh.

"For houses, yes; for community centers, no." He moved over to his computer that was open on the kitchen table. "I've made a list of potential targets."

She walked up next to him to peer over his shoulder. For a moment, he was distracted by her scent, by her closeness. In fact, his body had an instantly appreciative reaction to her hips as they came into contact with his.

"It looks like you've expanded beyond community centers," she said.

"What?" he asked, his brain taking a second to refocus on the computer screen.

"What is Delores Hall?"

"That's a senior citizen center," he said, clearing his throat and moving far enough away from her that they weren't touching. "Raymond Street Rec is an after-school program at Raymond Park. It's mostly outdoor activities, but there is a small one-room building on the property where the smaller kids do art projects. Payton Community Center runs a complete program of activities for toddlers to seniors. Bayside Neighborhood Club is a teen program run out of a Victorian house."

"That sounds like it fits two criteria—community

center and possibly a historic building."

"It's not on the register, but that could be just because no one tried to put it on there," he said.

She turned her head, giving him a smile. "I should have figured you already checked."

"I did. I like it as a possible target, though. I didn't put these in order but that's at the top of my list." He turned his attention back to the screen. "Bric-A-Brac offers art classes for kids. It's run out of a studio in the back of the owner's house." He moved on to the next one. "Keystone is another senior center. It's part of an assisted living program at Keystone Residences. It's a little out of the target range, but close enough to be included. Basically, I put anything on the list that had an outreach to the community—some type of classes for kids, seniors, at-risk teens, whatever."

"Oh, my God," Kate said suddenly, her body stiffening.

"What?"

"Ashbury Studios? Why would you put a music studio on the list?"

"They offer music and dance classes for kids after school. It's a free program for at-risk teens. That's what I just said. I included any business that reached out to the community and was within a five-mile radius of St. Bernadette's." He paused, feeling the tension rolling off her body. "What's wrong?"

"My cousin Sean owns the music studio, and his wife Jessica runs the dance program." She gave him a concerned look. "If they're a target, I need to warn them."

"Then you should warn them," he said evenly. It was actually refreshing to have Kate take his assessment at face value and to give his theory some respect. "But I wouldn't say that studio is at the top of the list."

"It doesn't matter. It's on the list. The least I can do is tell them to be extra vigilant on doors and windows, since the arsonist often seems to have an easy entry point. They probably have some kind of security system. They need to make sure that's working properly. Maybe I'll go by there after lunch."

He nodded. "Is your cousin Sean related to Emma?"

"Yes. He's her younger brother by a year or two."

"Then maybe we should show her this list."

Kate met his gaze. "Print it out. But don't be surprised if she questions whether the studio made the list because you wanted to get her attention."

"Since I didn't know there was a connection until thirty seconds ago, hopefully you can set her straight." He hit Print on his computer.

"Have you spoken to any of the other targets?" she asked.

"No. I have to be careful in my approach."

She raised an eyebrow. "You? Careful? Those two words don't seem to go together, especially in this situation."

He tipped his head. "They didn't always go together, but the police paid me a visit after I tried to warn the principal of a school that they might be a target. They told me to stop inciting fear and panic and said that I could be charged for harassment if I didn't cease and desist."

"You pissed someone off."

"More than one person I'm sure."

"Was St. Bernadette's on your target list for schools?" she asked curiously.

He leaned over, tapped a few keys and opened a new file on his computer. "Take a look for yourself."

"It's there," she said. "But you never went there?"

"No. Besides the fact that I didn't feel like getting

thrown into jail for a few hours, I've found that warning people is usually a waste of breath, time and energy. What I need to do is figure out the target, stake it out, and catch the arsonist."

"Well, that sounds simple," she said with an edge of sarcasm. "I'm surprised you haven't done it already."

"I had to wait for the arsonist to show up again. Obviously, he went underground after Sam's death. But he wasn't going to stay buried forever. The thrill, the release, the excitement—whatever emotion he needs to fill by setting a fire is always simmering beneath the surface." He took a breath and let it out. "I was wrong eight months ago, but my gut tells me I'm right this time. That's why I went out on a limb and contacted Hal. I knew he would probably laugh and hang up on me, but I had to take the chance. Not for me—for Sam. This has never been about me; it's always been about her."

Kate's blue gaze clung to his, and she looked at him in such a way that he felt like she could see right into his soul. For a split second he wanted to turn away; he'd always had a strong guard in place, but somehow Kate was getting past it.

"I believe you," she said slowly.

His heart flipped over in his chest. "That I'm not doing this out of ego? A desire to prove I'm the smartest; I'm the best?"

"Yes. Although, I don't doubt your ego is involved, because you are a man, after all. But mostly I believe that you're right about these fires, about the arsonist, about more blazes coming and the possibility of more people getting hurt. So let's stop him."

She might be green as grass, but he liked her fire, her determination, and the fact that she'd been so quickly able to understand what so many other people had not. Maybe that was because she was naïve, optimistic, idealistic, but whatever it was, he'd take it. It had been a long time since anyone had looked at him without disbelief, anger or disgust.

"Okay," he said with a nod.

"That's okay, *partner*." She emphasized the word *partner* with a smile. "And don't tell me I'm still on probation, because you need me."

He did need her; he hadn't realized how much until this second. Unfortunately, his need had to do with a little more than just work. Standing this close to her, he had to fight the almost irresistible impulse to lean over and kiss her smart mouth.

Luckily for him, Kate's phone buzzed, and she walked around the table to pull it out of her bag.

"It's a text from Emma. She got to the restaurant a little early. I'll tell her we're on our way."

He nodded, happy to get out of the apartment and away from at least a few bad ideas.

—⇢⇥⇤⇠—

As they walked down Union Street in San Francisco's Marina District Thursday afternoon, Kate felt on edge—not a dangerous kind of on edge, but a tingly kind of on edge. The way Devin had looked at her in his apartment had gotten her pulse pounding. She'd thought for a second there he was going to kiss her, an idea that seemed both ridiculous and appealing at the same time.

They were coworkers, colleagues, partners, and that was it. They were not friends and definitely not kissing friends.

But she couldn't deny there was an attraction.

She'd always been drawn to bad boys, especially

those with sharp minds, and passionate drive. Unfortunately, those bad boys usually ended up to be really bad boyfriends. They might have had passion for her, but love, respect, tenderness…they'd always come up short in those areas. While a fling would no doubt be really enjoyable, she was done flinging…she was a serious FBI agent now. She had to focus on her career and prove how good she was, because just saying it wasn't enough to make it true.

While Agent Roman probably didn't care all that much about her performance on this case, because he didn't believe there was a case, he would care if she screwed up, if she missed something, if she didn't perform to the highest level of her ability. And she would care even more. Not just because it was a case, but because it was a case that involved the death of an agent.

She understood how important it was to Devin to get justice for his partner, because she would feel exactly the same way. She might not have gone about it in the same manner, but she would have wanted to keep fighting.

At least…she thought she would have. She did wonder if she would have been able to stand as strong as Devin had in the face of so many doubters. Would all those disbelievers have shaken her faith in herself, in her instincts?

But this wasn't about her. And as Devin had said, it wasn't even about him. It was about an arsonist and the people who had died and the destruction still to come. That's all she needed to think about.

Glancing over at Devin, she wondered what was on his mind. He hadn't said a word since they'd left his building. Maybe he was just focusing on their upcoming meeting. She really hoped it would be productive.

As they stopped at a traffic light, she said, "This is a

charming street, one of my favorites in San Francisco."

"It's not bad," he admitted.

"Your office is in an old Victorian house—how much more charming could you get?"

He tipped his head. "I got lucky. A friend of mine owns the place. He had to move to New York and was looking for a tenant. He gave me a deal. As you know, this area is pricey."

She nodded. The clothing boutiques, art galleries, and restaurants on Union Street were definitely upscale. "You are lucky. Rents are high and apartments are scarce around here." She took off her sweater as a wave of heat ran through her. "I can't believe it's this warm in April. Spring has definitely arrived. I hope the good weather lasts for my sister's wedding."

"Where is she getting married?"

"At a chapel in the Presidio with the reception in a nearby hall, which will be packed."

"With all those Callaways," he said.

"And friends. Lots and lots of friends." As they neared the restaurant, she added, "Speaking of Callaways, there's Emma."

Emma sat at an outdoor café table and got to her feet as they arrived. She looked a lot better than she had earlier that morning, no signs of tears or drama. She also looked official in her SFFD uniform, reminding Kate that this was very much a business lunch.

After introducing Emma and Devin, Kate sat down between them, leaving Devin and Emma to face each other. So far, they'd both been polite but also restrained.

"Have you two met before?" Kate asked.

"No," Emma said. "As you know, Mr. Scott is not a popular person in my office."

"You can call me Devin," he said. "And I'm very

aware of my unpopularity. I'm just trying to help your office catch a homicidal arsonist."

"My office believes we already did that," Emma returned.

"Then how do you explain the fire at St. Bernadette's on Monday?"

"Student vandals."

Devin rolled his eyes. "That's easy."

"It's also true that most fires at schools are started by juveniles. Kids like to mess with matches."

"Is that how you want to play this conversation?" Devin challenged. "I thought you were interested in actually having a discussion."

Emma frowned at his answer. "If I wasn't interested, I wouldn't be here."

"Okay," Kate said loudly. "I don't think we've gotten off on the right foot. We all have the same goal. We all want to stop anyone else from getting hurt. We can agree on that, can't we?"

Devin folded his arms across his chest but gave a nod. Emma did the same.

"Good. Let's talk about the fire at St. Bernadette's. Was there anything found at the scene, any evidence that wasn't reported in the news?"

"St. Bernadette's was not my case," Emma said. "But I did look at the file before I came here. The fire was started with gasoline-soaked rags in a Dumpster that was moved about twenty-five feet from its original position."

"What was the original location?" Devin asked quickly.

"By the cafeteria. The Dumpster was pushed against the wall underneath the counseling office. A brick was thrown through the window and a lit rag followed. The fire alarms went off and the fire was extinguished fairly quickly. Damage was limited to the counseling office and the Dumpster."

"Was there anything found at the scene?" Devin asked.

"Nothing of significance," Emma replied.

"What about a St. Christopher's medal?"

"Why would you ask?"

"A St. Christopher's medal was found at three other fire scenes."

"Have you looked at the photos from the scene?" Kate asked.

"Not in any detail," Emma said. "I didn't see mention of a St. Christopher's medal in the report."

"Would you look at the photos again?" Kate asked. "If there is a medal there, it should be noted as being relevant to the pattern of the other fires." She paused. "Was the Dumpster full? Would it have been too heavy for one person to move?"

"It wasn't full. There had been a garbage pickup earlier that day. And I think it was on wheels," Emma said. "It probably wouldn't have been difficult to move."

"What does the school have to say?" Devin asked.

"Interviews were conducted with the janitorial service, who were the last people at the school. The fire was started after midnight. There were no witnesses. There's an apartment building next to the school, but none of the neighbors saw anything."

"So there's not much to go on," Kate said.

"There's never much to go on when it comes to arson. It's the one crime where the evidence is destroyed in the process of the crime," Emma said.

"How do you do it? How do you not lose your mind with so many unsolved crimes?" she asked, genuinely curious.

"I try to focus on the ones I can solve." Emma looked at Devin. "The department is not trying to stand in your way, but the case was closed, and we have limited resources. We have to work on active investigations."

"The case is active again. St. Bernadette's was the beginning of a new trio of fires," he said.

"Have you read through the files on the other fires that Devin is referring to?" Kate asked.

"Not completely. I've seen some of them, but not all. I know there's a lack of agreement as to which fires fit the pattern Devin has come up with."

"It's pretty compelling," Kate said. "I took a picture of the map he's created. I'll text it to both of you, so we can talk about it."

Before they could discuss the map, the waiter appeared. They took a moment to order drinks and lunch and then went back to their phones.

"As you can see there's a distinct pattern to the fires," Devin said. "The circle is unfinished, and I believe that's where the arsonist will strike again. Since the second fire has always been set at a community or social recreation center, I've made up a list of potential targets."

"Send me that, too," Emma said, her brows drawing together as she studied the phone. "This looks like something, but what is it?"

"A peace sign," Kate put in.

"Whoa, you're right. That's odd."

"It also shows premeditation. The locations of the fires are being carefully chosen and executed to the pattern." Kate paused. "The arsonist isn't done."

"If the arsonist didn't die in the fire along with your partner, then how do you explain the man's presence at the scene?" Emma asked Devin. "It's my understanding that he was not the owner, nor a tenant, nor anyone who had any link to that house. So how did he get caught up in the fire?"

"I don't know yet," Devin said. "We talked to his coworkers, his friends, his neighbors, but no one could tell us why he was there. In fact, no one could tell us much of anything. Rick Baines was a twenty-six-year-old loner. He went to community college for a couple of years but never finished. He worked at a gym and lived in an apartment with four other guys who said they weren't friends; Rick had just answered an ad a few weeks earlier and moved in."

"He also wanted to be a firefighter. He'd applied and was rejected a few weeks before your partner was killed. Put that with everything else you just told me, and Rick Baines looks like the arsonist," Emma said.

Devin sighed. "Except he wasn't. That's exactly what Sam was trying to tell me. She said the profile was wrong. It wasn't what we thought. I don't know how or why Rick Baines was in that house, but I know he's not the one—or he's not the *only* one—who set that fire."

Kate looked at Devin in surprise. "You didn't say that before. You didn't say you thought Baines had a partner or that more than one person set the fire."

"I don't have evidence, just a gut instinct. Because as Emma pointed out, there has to be a reason why Baines was in that house with Sam. He's linked to the arsonist, but I don't know how."

"Or," Emma began, "it's possible that the fire at St. Bernadette's is a copycat crime. Not that I'm saying I don't still think it was vandals, but arsonists can sometimes have a mutual admiration society. They're fascinated with fire. They like each other's work. Sometimes they show up at fires to see what someone else did."

"That's creepy," Kate said. "You're telling me that

arsonists have fans or groupies?"

Emma nodded. "That's exactly what I'm saying. Some of them listen to scanners. They follow the police and fire trucks to the scene. I know there were some individuals who showed up at some of the fires Devin has been tracking, but none of them were proven to be guilty."

"They weren't proven to be innocent, either," Devin said.

"Well, whether St. Bernadette's is the work of Sam's killer or the work of a copycat, we still need to stop them from striking again. And we need to work together," Kate put in.

"Is the FBI officially involved?" Emma asked.

"I've been given limited participation," Kate said. "But I plan to speak with my boss to see if I can expand that. We're going to need your help, too."

Emma stared back at them for a long minute. "I'll think about how best to make that happen."

Kate was relieved by her answer. "Thank you." She gave Devin a smile. "I told you we could count on Emma."

He didn't look completely convinced, but he nodded. "I'm happy you brought us together."

"I told you I'd be helpful," she reminded him.

"Yes, you have—several times now," he said dryly. "It helps to have family connections."

She made a face at him. "It's not just my connections that will help you. It's this, too." She tapped her head. "I have a smart brain."

"And a smart mouth. I hope you don't let the Bureau drive that out of you." He put his napkin on the table and stood up. "I'll be back in a moment."

As Devin left, Emma gave her a speculative smile.

"Let's get to the real question now, Kate."

"What's that?" she asked, sure she already knew.

"What's going on with you and the hot ex-FBI agent turned PI? The look he just gave you made my toes curl."

"Don't be silly. He didn't look at me in any particular way. In fact, he was annoyed if anything. He thinks I'm too unseasoned to help him. That's why I've been reminding him of how helpful I am."

Emma gave her a knowing smile. "You can tell yourself there's nothing going on, Kate, but I could feel the vibe between you. You like him. And why wouldn't you? He's not bad on the eyes. He might want to shave a little more often, maybe get a little more sleep now and then, but he's hot."

"He's attractive, yes. And when he gives me a rare smile, I find myself imagining how fun it would be to make out with him, but I can't. We're working together. I'm a professional. I don't do stupid things—at least not if I can help it. And good looks aside, Devin can also be annoying, cocky, opinionated, and it's not like I need more men like that in my life."

Emma laughed. "You remind me of myself when I first met Max. We were working on an arson-homicide case, too. He was the police detective and I was the fire investigator. We both wanted to solve the crime, and we were pretty territorial about our roles. He rubbed me the wrong way a lot of the time, but I think that was mostly because I really wanted him to rub me the right way," she said with a wicked sparkle in her eye.

"You are bad."

"So are you, Kate," Emma said with a laugh. "Or you used to be. I remember when you brought that guy with all the tattoos and piercings to Grandma's birthday party. I thought my dad and your dad and Grandpa were going to take him in the back and beat the crap out of him."

"He wasn't that bad. He was seventeen and upset about his parents' divorce. His rebellion was just grief. He was a lost soul."

"And you wanted to save him, to fix him." Emma paused. "Is that what you're doing with Devin?"

"No. No," she added for emphasis. "I was assigned to come and work with Devin. I didn't seek him out. It's a job. And when it's over, it's over."

"When will it be over? Are you going to stay in San Francisco past the wedding?"

"Right now, my boss just asked me to give Devin my help until next Wednesday when I'm taking time off for the wedding. I guess we'll see what happens before then." She paused, turning more serious. "I was skeptical at first. My boss told me he thought Devin was on a wild-goose chase, but after talking to Devin, after looking at the map, I think he might be right, Emma. And if there's a chance he is…"

"I know. I agree."

"Do you think your boss will agree?"

"He'll need more persuasion. I'm going to do some digging on my own, and if I can pull it all together in a way that makes sense, I'll bring my boss in. But doing it prematurely isn't going to help anyone. Devin probably has one shot left. Actually, he probably has no shots left. He's gotten into some loud and messy conflicts with several people in the fire department. He's kind of like a bull in a china shop."

"I think some of his initial anger and frustration has passed. He's still intense, but he's working the case in a smarter way now."

"I hope so."

Kate sat back as Devin returned to the table.

"Did I miss anything?" he asked.

"Just girl talk," Emma told him.

He sighed as he looked over at Kate. "How did I fare?"

"Probably not as bad as you think."

"Okay, not the best compliment, but not the worst by a long shot. I'll take it."

He gave her that smile that she'd told Emma about, the one that made her want to grab his face with both hands and plant a hot kiss on his lips.

"Everything okay?" Devin asked, his look turning quizzical.

"Yes, I just need some water," she said, reaching for her glass. "It really is hot today."

"For some people," Emma murmured.

She shot her cousin a dark, pointed look, but thankfully Emma had no chance to say anything more provocative. Lunch had arrived—not a moment too soon.

Six

Lunch was actually entertaining, Devin thought, as he reached for the bill while Emma and Kate talked about some family member who had dyed her hair purple. He'd expected another tense conversation with a member of the fire department, but while Emma had given him somewhat of the party line, she'd also been open-minded enough not to dismiss his ideas out of hand.

He probably had Kate to thank for that. She'd smoothed the way, and her confidence in his theories had persuaded Emma to take another look at the evidence.

So he might have been a little wrong about Kate's ability to help him. So far she'd made herself useful.

He'd thought Hal was giving him lip service by sending him the newest agent he had, but Kate's connections were proving valuable.

Her personality was a nice change, too. Kate was bold and blunt, smart and funny, beautiful and sexy…He cleared his throat, reminding himself she was his partner, and a temporary one at that. And he was probably reacting to her in such a strong way because he'd been so isolated the past year and a half. He hadn't realized how small and narrow his life had gotten since Sam's death.

He'd almost forgotten how to relax, how to just be in the moment, but Kate's arrival had changed that. She was pulling him back into the world.

As Kate threw back her head and laughed at something Emma said, he couldn't help but smile. Kate had a lot of life in her, and she wasn't good at hiding her feelings. When she was happy, she showed it. When she was pissed off, she showed that, too. At some point, her job would turn her into an unemotional, cold agent. At least, that's what had happened to him.

Turning his attention back to the bill, he signed the receipt and returned the card to his wallet.

"I'm happy to pay my share," Emma said.

"It's on me. And it's not a bribe," he added quickly. "I'm just buying lunch for Kate's cousin."

A gleam of approval ran through Emma's eyes. "I like the way you think. You know, you're not as bad as I've heard."

"And you're not as bad as I thought you would be," he said.

She laughed. "You are direct."

"So are you. So is Kate. It must be a Callaway trait."

"It is," Kate said. "When you're one of many siblings, many cousins, you learn the importance of speaking up for yourself, or you get run over."

"Which helps both of us now," Emma added. "It's easy to get run over in the fields we're in. There are a lot of men who think they know far more than they do."

"I agree," Kate said. "Present company excluded."

He smiled at that. "Thanks for throwing me that crumb. You two must be hell on your brothers."

"They're hell on us," Kate corrected.

"She's right. And any man who comes into the family

has to be able to hold his own," Emma said. "My brothers were very tough on my boyfriends."

"What about you?" he asked Kate. "Did your brothers scare anyone off?"

"Only one, and the fact that he got scared off just told me how wrong he was for me," Kate replied. "So they did me a favor."

"I doubt you saw it that way at the time."

She met his gaze. "No, I didn't. I was furious. I took Dylan's precious car to the beach and dumped sand all over the inside."

"Ouch," he said with a wince. "You messed with your brother's car?"

"I was sixteen," she said defensively. "He deserved it."

"But his car? A man's car is sacred, especially when he's young."

"Oh, whatever," Kate said with an uncaring wave of her hand. "It was a fifteen-year-old car with dents and stains on the upholstery. It wasn't a Corvette."

"Still…"

She shrugged. "He shouldn't have screwed with my relationship. Dylan is my oldest brother, and sometimes he thinks he's like a second dad to the rest of us. But we have a father, and we don't need another one."

"Burke is the same way." Emma looked at Devin. "Burke is my oldest brother. I'm one of eight."

"And I thought Kate's family was big."

"My family is more of a yours, mine, and ours scenario," Emma explained. "My mom had my sister Nicole and me. She divorced my dad and married Jack Callaway, who was a widower with four boys. We were all really small when it happened, so it wasn't that difficult to merge the families. Then my mom and Jack sealed the deal with the birth of twins."

"More twins?" He looked back at Kate. "They obviously run in the family."

"Yeah, and somehow they come at the end, which my mom always says is a good thing, because if she'd had twins first, she might not have had so many other children," Kate said. "Oh, and when she says that, she is definitely talking about me being the handful, not Mia. She was the perfect child."

"Not perfect, but quieter," Emma put in.

"True. My sister was sick a lot when she was really young. She had severe asthma and other respiratory problems. If she caught a cold, she'd end up in the hospital. Eventually, she got better, and her immune system got stronger. But for a lot of years she was pretty frail. We all watched over her, worried about her. She kind of hated that. Now, she's as strong and independent as the rest of us."

"Is she the first to get married?"

Kate nodded. "Yes, she is. The youngest goes first, which takes the heat off my older siblings, especially since Mia is bringing a stepchild into the family. My mom is thrilled to have a grandchild."

"The first of many, I'm sure," Emma said.

"Not like your family," Kate said. "There's a baby boom going on."

As Kate and Emma talked more about the pregnant women in the family, he couldn't help but think how normal their conversation was. He couldn't remember the last time he'd talked about anything that didn't have to do with fire or historic buildings or arsonists.

But it wasn't just the hunt for Sam's killer that had kept him from those kinds of conversations; he didn't have the extended family Kate had. And his friends were scattered around the country. His job had been his life for almost a decade.

He hadn't been wrong when he'd told Kate the Bureau would change her. She might think she could juggle everything, but he doubted she could. He certainly hadn't been able to. Then again, maybe she could do it. Maybe she could keep her job and not lose herself.

Emma pushed back her chair. "I need to get back to work. Thanks for lunch, Devin. I will look into everything we talked about, and I'll be in touch."

"I appreciate your help," he said.

"Well, I haven't helped yet, so save your thanks."

"Just hearing me out was a welcome change."

She nodded, then gave Kate a quick hug.

"Remember, Em, don't tell anyone in the family I'm in town yet," Kate said.

"I told you I wouldn't," Emma said. "But you won't be able to fly under the radar for long."

"I just need a couple of days so I can concentrate on this case and not get roped into pre-wedding plans."

"Got it."

As Emma left the table, Kate glanced over at him with an enquiring look in her eyes. "Well, what do you think about Emma?"

"I'm guardedly optimistic."

She raised an eyebrow. "That excited, huh?"

"For me, that's a big change. It's not in my nature to react to anything but reality," he added. "Even Emma said she hasn't done anything to help us yet, except come to lunch."

"She will help us. Emma is very passionate about her job. And she will fight for what's right. It's something I've always admired about her."

"I can see why the two of you get along so well. You

have similar interests."

"We do, but we also both get along with everyone. When you're in a big family, you learn to accept everyone for who they are. So, what's next?"

He'd been thinking about that. "I'd like to go by St. Bernadette's."

"You haven't done that already?"

"I have," he admitted. "But I just did a drive-by. I didn't go into the school. Now that the fire department has cleared the scene and school is back in session, I'd like to talk to the staff in the counseling office since that seemed to be part of the target."

"Good idea. And you'll probably get a little further with an FBI agent at your side."

"Probably," he admitted.

She gave him a teasing smile. "Should I say it again?"

He didn't have to ask her what she meant. "Please don't." He tossed his napkin on the table and stood up. "Let's get out of here."

"Okay, partner, whatever you say."

When they got to the high school, Devin showed Kate the still-blackened wall where the fire had leapt out of the Dumpster. But a new Dumpster had already replaced the old one and was in its original position by the cafeteria. The broken window in the counseling office had also already been replaced.

"It's almost like it never happened," she murmured.

"I suspect there's a little more damage inside from what Emma told us."

She looked around the quad of the high school. There

were only a few students wandering around. It was after three and the kids who weren't on the baseball or soccer fields or in the gym were probably on their way home. "I haven't been here in a long time," she murmured. "Not since my senior year of high school. I dated a kid who went here. He took me to his prom. That seems like a million years ago."

"What high school did you go to?"

"St. Ignatius."

He nodded. "I should have figured. Catholic family."

"Very Catholic. One of my uncles is a priest. And I have a great-aunt who is a nun." She gave him a thoughtful look. "What about you? What's your religion?"

"I was baptized Catholic, but I haven't been to church in a long time."

"There's one right over there," she said, tipping her head toward the chapel that adjoined the high school. "We could take a few minutes if you want to go to confession."

"I have nothing to confess."

"Nothing, not one little thing?" she teased.

"My confessions don't need to be made in what looks like a closet. I can have my own personal conversations."

She nodded, not surprised Devin wasn't into organized religion. "Sometimes I wonder how you lasted so long in the FBI," she said.

He raised an eyebrow. "What does that have to do with the confessional?"

She realized she'd made the jump in her own head. "It doesn't. I was just thinking that you don't like structure and ritual, whether it's in the church or the government. So how did you last in such a rigid organization as the FBI?"

"To be honest, I don't know. I guess when I was younger, I was more willing to follow without question, to jump when I was told to jump, to play the game I'd volunteered to play."

"To be your dad. That was part of it, right?"

"Definitely." He dug his hands into the pockets of his jeans. "I wanted to see what had taken my father away from me all those years. Maybe I wanted the job to be worth it, not just for me but for him, for what it had done to our family."

She was taken aback by Devin's words, by his self-awareness, by how much he'd shared with her in such an unexpected way.

He looked just as rattled by his admission. Clearing his throat, he said, "Let's go inside and see if we can talk to someone in the counseling department."

As she followed Devin into the school, she wanted to tell him that the job was worth it, but what did she know? She only had one year under her belt, and she had to admit that she hadn't spent much time with family and friends in that year. But it didn't have to be an all-or-nothing job—did it?

She was still pondering that question when they entered the main hall.

The counseling office was to the right. The door was open, and inside a man was replacing damaged drywall. There were tarps thrown across the filing cabinets and the desk and there were obvious signs of fire and smoke damage. The scene made the arson cases she'd been reading about feel more real. Glancing at the bookshelves, she saw the charred remnants of college guides, reminding her that the last time she'd been in an office like this was when she was deciding what college to go to, what career to pursue.

"I feel like I'm back in high school again," she said. "All that angst about how was I going to get to where I am now. If only I could go back and tell my younger self..."

"Tell her what?" Devin asked curiously.

"To relax, trust her instincts, follow her own path, and don't worry about anyone else's plan for her life, including her parents'."

"They didn't want you to go into the FBI?"

"They weren't thrilled with the idea. They thought it would be too dangerous."

"It can be."

"No risk, no reward, right?"

"That's right."

"Did you ever consider a different field, Devin? Or was it always about following your dad?"

"There was a time when I thought I could play pro baseball, but beyond that crazy dream, it was all about becoming a special agent."

"Pro baseball, huh? Were you good enough?"

"I was good, but probably not good enough."

"Excuse me, can I help you?"

Kate turned to the middle-aged woman who'd come up behind them.

"Are you the counselor?" she asked.

"Yes. I'm Marion Baker."

"I'm Special Agent Kate Callaway from the FBI," she said, flashing her badge for Mrs. Baker. "And this is Devin Scott, a private investigator."

"The FBI?" Mrs. Baker echoed, a worried look entering her eyes. "I don't understand. I thought this was just the work of some students."

"It could be," Kate said. "But it's an ongoing investigation. Do you have any idea who might have set the fire? Who would have targeted this office? Has anyone made any threats against you? Have you spoken to any unhappy students?"

"I talk to unhappy students every day," she said with a sigh. "High school is very stressful these days. The pressure put on teenagers trying to get into college is unbelievable. I've been a counselor here for fifteen years, and I don't think I've ever seen the atmosphere so tense. We have students with perfect 4.0's and they're afraid they won't get into the college they want, and their fear is not unjustified."

Kate realized that Marion had quickly gone off track. "I know that it's more difficult now," she said, cutting off her rant. "But have you run into any students who are particularly unhappy?"

"In what way?"

"Depressed, angry, frustrated," Devin put in. "Anyone who's ranted on social media about the school or who has talked about being bullied?"

"Well, I don't think anyone fits that criteria. We've had a few students report bullying incidents, but we were able to work those out."

Kate wondered if that were true, if the problem had really ended, or if the school had just thought they'd done their part. "Has there been anyone who has tried to see you, but perhaps you were busy and they couldn't get in?" she asked.

Marion's eyes widened with alarm. "You think the fire was a threat against me?"

"We don't think anything," she replied. "We're just asking questions."

"I get along very well with the students. I always make myself available to them. If someone needs help, they can count on me. I don't know that I believe this office was targeted, or if whoever threw the brick just picked a random window."

"The Dumpster was also moved under your window," Devin reminded her.

"That's true. Okay, now I'm worried again."

"We didn't come to worry you," Kate said gently. "As I said, we're just trying to think of every possible scenario. What you just said about everything being random could be true." She paused as her gaze drifted back to the bookshelf of college guides. "I know when I was a junior and senior, I haunted my counselor's office to ask questions about how to be an FBI agent. Have you had any students recently express an interest in firefighting or fire investigation as a career?"

Marion thought for a moment, then shook her head. "In the past, yes, but not this year. I don't believe anyone has asked about that. Several years ago, I worked really hard to set up a shadow program at the local firehouse, because I had a student back then who was desperate to learn more about the job and wanted to see the actual work involved. I had a lot of red tape to cut through, but I finally got it approved. That's how hard I work for my students. Rick was over the moon when I told him he could go there."

Kate stiffened at the name. The man who had died in the fire with Samantha Parker had also been named Rick. It was a common name. It had to be a coincidence.

She looked at Devin. He stared back at her, his face pale, his eyes bright. Then he swung his gaze to Marion.

"What was Rick's last name?" he asked.

She thought for a moment. "Let me think. It was several years ago now. And I've talked to a lot of students."

Kate's tension increased as the seconds ticked off.

Then Devin cut through the silence with a question. "It wasn't Rick Baines, was it?"

Seven

"Baines—yes. That was it. Richard Baines. He had dark red hair, pale skin and a lot of freckles on his face. He was a quiet student, very introverted. I remember thinking that I'd never seen him as animated as he was when he talked about being a firefighter." Marion paused, a frown crossing her lips. "Why are you asking about him?"

"Rick Baines didn't graduate from this high school," Devin said in a tense voice. "He went to Northern Marin High School. Maybe we're talking about a different kid."

"No. Now that you mention it, I remember that Rick did transfer schools. It was right after he did his shadow at the firehouse. I always wondered if he went into that career."

"Do you remember why he transferred schools?"

"I don't remember specifically, but I know he had a troubled family life. Parents were in and out. His aunt took care of him for a while."

Kate couldn't believe it. Marion Baker was definitely talking about the man labeled in her FBI file as an arsonist and a murderer. Given his high school fascination with fire, was it possible that Rick Baines had been the arsonist who killed Sam? Who got caught up in his own fire? But then who had set the fire here at the school?

"Can you tell me what's going on?" Marion asked. "Are you thinking that Rick came back and set this fire after so many years?"

"No," Devin said. "He did not set this fire, because he died eighteen months ago in another fire."

Marion put a hand to her mouth. "I had no idea. How awful. And in a fire? I can't believe it."

"Yes, he died in a suspicious fire. An FBI agent was killed along with him."

"That's why you're involved." Marion looked at Kate. "How does this fire link to that one?"

"We're still figuring that out," she replied. "Is there anything else you can tell us about Rick?"

"I don't think so."

"Would you be willing to speak to some of the other teachers, the principal, see if anyone remembers Rick and would be willing to talk to us about him?" Kate asked.

"I could do that. The principal, Mrs. Barclay, only came to the school last year, so she didn't know Rick, but some of the other teachers might remember him."

Kate pulled out her card and handed it to her. "This is my number. I'm especially interested in anyone who might have kept in contact with Rick over the years."

"I'll let you know if I find out anything."

"We'd also like to get a class list, the names of students who were in Rick's grade."

"I don't know if I can give you that," Marion said hesitantly.

"What about a yearbook from the years that Rick went to school here?" Devin asked. "Do you have any of those lying around?"

"We have copies of yearbooks from the last twenty

years in the library," she said. "It's already closed for the day, but if you come back in the morning, Mrs. Valens can help you. She comes in at ten."

"We'll come back then," Kate said. "Thank you."

"Whatever I can do to help, I'm happy to do."

Devin added his thanks, then they walked out of the school. They didn't speak until they got into Devin's car.

"What do you think?" she asked. "It's a big and crazy coincidence that Rick Baines went to school here."

"I'll say," Devin agreed, his gaze on the school. "I was not expecting to hear that." He looked over at her. "Out of all the possible scenarios or connections I imagined, that wasn't one of them. I never looked past Northern Marin High School. I knew he'd come from a broken home and had been in and out of foster care and had lived with relatives, but I didn't pay that much attention to the school records. How could I have missed that?"

"Because you were focused on where he graduated and where he went to college and where he was living and working at the time of the fires, which all happened in his twenties. High school wasn't that important."

"Maybe it was."

"Well, we know he didn't set this fire," she said, forcing him to come back to the present and forget about what he hadn't done before. "But this does back up your theory that Rick might have had a connection to the real arsonist. And if the arsonist decided to strike St. Bernadette's, then it makes sense that the school ties the two of them together. Hopefully, the yearbook will be helpful. I'm sure I can get the class records as well."

"The photos might mean more than just the data," Devin said.

"I agree. Maybe we'll get lucky and spot Rick and his

best friends all tagged in a photo together."

"That would be lucky and probably doubtful."

"Well, I'm going to stay optimistic until I see what's there." She pulled out her phone. "I'll also call Emma and let her know what we've discovered." A few minutes later, her call was routed to Emma's voicemail. She left a message asking Emma to call, saying she had new information, but nothing further. She didn't want to get into details until she could get Emma on the phone and talk things out.

As Devin drove away from the school, she said, "We need to refocus on Baines. You probably know every last thing about him, but I need to get a better handle on him. It's interesting that he stood out in Marion Baker's mind because he'd been obsessed with being a firefighter."

"Yeah, that's great," he said heavily.

She could tell he was still brooding about the past. "Snap out of it, Devin. Maybe you made a mistake, maybe you didn't, but there's nothing to do about it now."

"That's a hell of a pep talk."

"I wasn't trying to cheer you up, just get your attention. We have to move forward."

"And do what?"

She thought for a moment. "Rick worked at a local gym. I assume you've been there."

"Several times after the fire, but not in the past year. The manager was helpful, but he didn't know anything personal about Rick. The staff also had the same story: nice guy, keeps to himself, does his job, don't know anything more about him."

"Did you talk to any gym members?"

"No, and after the FBI closed the case, the manager stopped talking to me."

"I'm beginning to see a pattern. A lot of doors shut in

your face."

"Yes, they did."

"Well, let's open them back up. Let's go to the gym. Maybe we can find someone who has remembered something or might be more willing to talk now."

"It's a long shot, Kate."

"High odds don't scare me."

"Then we'll go to the gym."

———•➤➤◄◄•———

When they arrived at the fitness center, Devin let Kate take the lead. She'd done a good job with Marion Baker, and her FBI credentials carried more weight than his PI license. Plus, his impatience and desire to get to the truth as fast as possible often turned people off. Kate was warmer, more nurturing. Although, Kate hadn't been very kind to him with her 'snap out of it' order. He'd gotten no sympathy, just a kick in the ass.

But he'd needed that kick in the ass, so he could hardly complain.

Kate was right. He didn't have time to stew about what he hadn't seen before. He had to look at what was right in front of him now, and follow any new lead he could get. He wasn't expecting much from this trip, but maybe he would be surprised.

Kate showed her badge to the receptionist, and a few minutes later they were escorted into the manager's office. The manager was not the same balding, middle-aged man Devin had spoken to before. This was a younger guy, early thirties, bleach-blond hair, and a great tan.

"I'm Pete Stanley. How can I help you?" he asked, as they sat down in front of his desk.

"We want to talk to you about a former employee—

Rick Baines," Kate said. "He was killed in a fire eighteen months ago."

"Yeah, I was around then. I was working the desk those days. How I can help you? Is there some new evidence? Was someone else involved in Rick's death? Is that why you're back?"

"We think someone else might have been involved," Kate said. "We're trying to retrace Rick's movements in the days before his death."

"Wow. You know I never thought he could kill someone. After we all heard the news, it shook me. I couldn't believe the guy I worked with was a murderer, but you're saying maybe he wasn't?"

"Were you close to Rick?" Kate asked, ignoring Rick's question.

"I wouldn't say close. I knew him well enough to have a beer with him, but there were always a lot of other people around. We didn't spend time together after work or anything."

"Did Rick ever talk about high school friends?" Devin interjected.

Pete thought for a moment. "There was a guy who used to come to the gym who told me after the fire that he'd gone to high school with Rick. We were talking about how we couldn't believe he'd done what everyone said he did."

"What was his name?"

"Alan Jenkins."

"Do you have his contact information?" Kate asked.

"He hasn't been here in about a year." Pete got on his computer and typed in Alan's name. "Wait, I still have it." He printed out a piece of paper and handed it to Kate. "This is the address and phone number he gave us, and you didn't get that from me, all right? I want to help, but the owner would probably not appreciate me giving out personal information."

"I understand," Kate said. "This is really helpful."

"Well, I'm always happy to help the FBI," Pete said, giving Kate an appreciative look.

"I have one more question," Kate said, smiling back at Pete. "Did Rick have a girlfriend?"

"I don't think so."

"Was he close with any of the female staff members? And are any of those members working today?"

"He did a lot of spin classes on his off-time with Casey Hughes. She'll be in tonight if you want to come back. Hey, you can take her class, too, if you're interested. She's one of the best in the city. On the house, of course."

"That's very nice of you," Kate said. "We would like to talk to her. I'm not sure we'll spin, but we'll come back."

"Great. I'll let the girls at the front desk know." He got up to usher them out of the office. "If you need a club, keep us in mind. We have a full program of classes. You look like you work out, Agent Callaway."

"Sometimes," Kate said. "Probably not as much as I should."

"I used to train people. I'd be happy to show you how to get the best out of your body whenever you want to come back."

"That's so nice of you," Kate said.

"I'm a nice guy. Ask anyone."

"I'm sure you are."

As Kate and Pete exchanged a smile, Devin felt a wave of unexpected irritation run through him. Kate could not seriously be buying this guy's charm, could she? He was either trying to sell her a membership or get a day, which took nerve since they'd come to talk to him about a murder investigation.

"He was cooperative," Kate said as they left the gym.

Devin gave her a disbelieving look. "He wanted to sell you a membership, Kate—among other things."

"Well, I wasn't going to buy one."

"Really? Because you looked like you were buying everything he was selling."

She frowned. "You sound jealous."

"Don't be stupid."

"And now you sound defensive."

"I'm just annoyed. We went there to get information not for you to get a date."

"We got information. Pete gave us the name and contact information for someone who might have gone to high school with Baines. And he told us that Casey might know something about Rick. We have two new leads to follow."

"Why didn't he give up those names before?" he challenged, not sure why he was feeling so worked up, but he couldn't seem to bring himself down. "I didn't interview him personally, but I know the fire investigative unit talked to every staff member."

"He wasn't the manager before. Maybe he wasn't asked that exact question. Or perhaps now he isn't rattled by a swarm of feds and arson investigators and has had time to think. Breaks in cold cases often come because a potential witness suddenly remembers or feels more willing to talk."

"You don't have to educate me about cold cases or witness testimony," he said, flipping open the locks to the car. "I've interviewed thousands of people, which I'm guessing is thousands more than you."

She got into her seat as he slid behind the wheel. "You're really annoying, Devin."

"I'm the annoying one?"

"Yes, you. Whatever the hell is your problem right now, you need to get over it."

Her blue eyes spit fire at him, and he was both angry and in awe of the fact that he couldn't intimidate her at all.

"Say whatever you need to say," she continued. "Do whatever you need to do so we can go back to the case and concentrate on what's important. All right?"

"Okay. If that's what you want." He leaned over, slid one hand around the back of her head and pulled her into the hot, hard kiss he'd been wanting to give her since she first walked into his office.

She tensed, her lips parting under his in surprise.

He took advantage of the moment, changing up the kiss to one that was more persuasive, more compelling, and damn if she didn't kiss him right back.

Now he was the one who was taken off guard.

The kiss wasn't his anymore. It wasn't hers, either. It was theirs.

It was hot and sexy and more than a little dangerous.

They came to the same conclusion at the same time, breaking apart, staring at each other in disbelief. Yet, the desire to kiss again was still there.

"Devin," Kate got out, but couldn't seem to find more words.

He didn't know what to say, either.

"What the hell was that?" she asked finally.

"You said to do what I needed to do."

"And that's what you needed to do?"

"That guy was all over you," he said, knowing that was about the lamest explanation he could have come up with.

"So you decided to get all over me?"

"You kissed me back, Kate."

"I was startled."

"And attracted." He had to go on offense, because his defense was really weak.

She sat back in her seat. "Maybe," she admitted.

His heart sped up at her response. That one word made him want to reach for her again, but he couldn't do that. He *shouldn't* do that.

Forcing himself to look away from her soft pink lips and sparkling blue eyes took about every last ounce of willpower he had. He started the car and pulled out of the parking space.

They drove back to his apartment in silence. He parked in the garage and they walked up the stairs in more silence.

He opened the front door and led them down the hall, past his office, past his bedroom, and into the den.

Kate walked over to the map and stared at it, but he didn't think her mind was on the pattern of fires.

He went into the kitchen and grabbed two bottled waters out of the refrigerator and took one over to her.

"Thanks," she said, uttering the first word she'd spoken since *maybe*.

He took a long drink of water, finishing almost half the bottle in one swallow. Kate did the same.

"Okay," she said, facing him. "So that can't happen again."

"Agreed."

"We're working together. We have a case to solve."

He couldn't believe he was the one who needed the reminder, but for a few minutes, he'd completely forgotten about the obsession that had driven every waking moment of his life for the past year and a half. That realization was mind-boggling. He'd never let a woman distract him from work, not before he left the FBI and not after...until now.

He sat down at the table and opened his computer, because he needed something to look at besides Kate.

"I think we should call Alan Jenkins. I have his information here," she said.

"Go for it."

She punched in the number and put her phone on speaker. A second later, a woman answered.

"Is Alan Jenkins there?" Kate asked.

"No. This isn't his number anymore," the woman said abruptly. "He moved out a year ago."

Before Kate could say another word, the phone went to dial tone.

"So much for our lead," she said. "I guess that number was a landline. I wonder if we can find his cell."

"You have more resources than I do. Use them."

"I will, but if we don't get any more definitive information, I think we should go back to the gym at seven and take that spin class. Maybe Casey didn't just know Rick but also Alan."

"We don't need to take the class. We'll just talk to her afterwards."

"Oh, I am definitely taking the class," Kate said. "I just need to stop at my brother's place on the way and grab some clothes. But I could use a workout. You probably could, too."

Now there was a hint of cockiness back in her eyes. "I probably could," he admitted, thinking that the best way to get rid of all the tension in his body was a hard workout.

"Did you really think I was falling for Pete's lines earlier?" she challenged.

"You looked like you were enjoying his conversation."

"It was an interview. I was working the witness. He

liked me. I used it."

"So you didn't like him at all?"

She shrugged. "I don't know him. He's attractive. He probably doesn't have as many problems as you do."

"I don't have problems," he denied.

"Are you kidding? You are carrying a ton of baggage, Devin. I have no idea what's in all your bags, but I know they're full, and they're weighing you down."

Her comment was a little too close to the mark, reminding him that Kate wasn't just beautiful; she was also extremely insightful. "Let's get to work."

"I never stopped. You were the one who—"

"I don't want to talk about it anymore." Talking about kissing her only made him want to do it again. "Let's not speak for a while. Think you can manage that?"

"I can if you can."

"I definitely can."

"You say that, but you keep talking."

He let out a sigh, letting her have the last word. Her triumphant smile should have pissed him off, but damn if it didn't make him like her more. He did need a workout. He just hoped he could make it until seven, before he found another way to quiet her smart mouth.

Eight

-->=>⋘<--

Casey Hughes ran an aggressively difficult spin class, Kate thought three hours later, as she gasped for breath on a one-minute sprint. Sweat was running in rivers between her breasts, her thighs ached with exertion, and her heart rate was probably higher than it had ever been, but she wasn't going to quit, not with the incredibly fit Devin by her side. He didn't seem to be nearly as winded as she was.

How on earth had she gotten so out of shape? She tried to run at least three times a week, but it had been a few weeks, she reminded herself. She'd spent more time on airplanes and sitting at desks in the last several months. She needed to change that up, or she would lose the fitness she'd always prided herself on.

When the music and the class finally came to an end, she was filled with euphoric relief, but she stumbled a little as she got off the bike, her legs not quite recovered from the punishment she'd put them through.

"Easy," Devin said, putting a steadying hand on her shoulder.

And just like that, all the sexual tension she'd been

trying to burn off came right back.

Why him? Why now?

They were pointless questions to ask, because attraction never came on demand, and it was almost always the wrong person at the wrong time.

"Are you all right?" Devin asked, wiping his face with a towel. "That was a workout."

"I'm fine. Thanks." She stepped away and used her own towel to mop up her sweat. She'd put her hair up in a high ponytail and was thrilled when the air conditioning in the gym finally began to register against the heat in her body. "Casey is almost done talking to everyone," she said, her eyes on the teacher. "Let's hope she can tell us something about Alan Jenkins."

She'd been able to find both an address in San Diego and a cell phone number for Alan Jenkins, but he hadn't answered her call. Hopefully, he would call her back.

While it was somewhat interesting that Jenkins had left town after the fire, it could mean absolutely nothing at all. The thread that tied Jenkins to Baines was about as tenuous as it could be. They needed someone—hopefully Casey—to give them something else to go on. Otherwise, they could be chasing a non-existent lead.

Devin led the way to the front of the studio and gave a warm smile to the attractive brunette with the pretty green eyes and killer body.

"Great class," Devin said.

"I'm glad you liked it. You're new," Casey said. "I haven't seen you around here before."

"First time. This is my friend Kate."

"Hi," Kate said. "Thanks for the workout."

"You're welcome. You two kept up pretty well for newcomers. I hope you'll come back."

"Definitely," Devin said. "Would it be possible for us

to talk to you for a few minutes?"

"Sure? What about?"

"We spoke to Pete earlier. He said that you were friends with Rick Baines."

Kate immediately noted the change that came over Casey's face when Devin mentioned Baines.

"This isn't about those fires again, is it?" she asked. "Are you cops?"

"No, I'm with the FBI," Kate said. "And Devin is a private investigator."

"I told the FBI everything I knew, which wasn't much of anything," Casey said. "I worked with Rick, and I thought he was a nice guy, but I guess he wasn't."

"We actually don't think Baines set the fire," Devin said. "We think he was a victim."

"Really? That's not what everyone said before."

"Things have changed. How close were you and Rick?"

"We weren't close. We were just gym friends. Occasionally, we'd have a drink together. He was kind of a lonely guy. He told me he had a rough childhood. His parents were in and out of rehab. He had to live with relatives. He said working out was one thing that always made him happy."

"Did you know Alan Jenkins?" Devin asked.

Casey nodded. "Sure. He was here three to four times a week. But he dropped his membership a long time ago."

"Three weeks after Baines died," Kate said.

"Is that supposed to mean something?" Casey asked.

"We don't know," she said. "Did Alan and Rick spend time together? Pete told us earlier that he thought they were high school friends."

"Now that you mention it, I think they did go to high school together. They were friends, but they could get into it, too. Alan left a sweaty towel on a machine one day, and Rick got after him about it. They had a shouting match in the middle of the gym. I think that was right before Rick died. But I do remember that after we all heard the news, Alan was very upset."

"Do you know why Alan moved to San Diego?" Devin asked.

"No idea. Sorry." She paused. "So you think someone else killed Rick and that woman? Are you suggesting that it was Alan?"

"Would Alan be capable of committing such a crime?"

"I can't imagine that he would be, but then I didn't think Rick could do it, either."

"Thanks for your time," Devin said. "And thanks for the class. It was great."

"I'm glad you enjoyed it. I'm sorry I can't help you more."

As they walked out of the studio into the main gym, Kate said, "The class was better than the information we gathered."

"Casey didn't have much to give us," he agreed. "Hopefully, we can confirm Alan Jenkins went to St. Bernadette's when we get the yearbooks tomorrow."

"But Jenkins doesn't live here anymore, so he couldn't have set Monday's fire at the school."

"He's still a connection. We have to find a way to reach him."

"We've called him. Not much else we can do at this point," he said.

"Then I think I'll take a shower. Maybe the hot water will give me some new ideas," she said, as they walked toward the locker room.

"Ever the optimist."

"Investigating is always one step forward, two steps back—you know that, Devin."

"In my case, it's usually one step forward, a hundred steps back," he said cynically.

She gave him a playful punch in the arm. "As long as there's still that one step in a positive direction..."

Her words teased a reluctant smile out of him.

"Take your shower and come up with a brilliant new plan," he said. "Maybe then I'll be as optimistic as you are."

A half an hour later, she was warm, dry, and clear-headed. Unfortunately, she had no brilliant plan in her head, just a lot of swirling thoughts. She stuffed her sweaty clothes into a duffel bag, then went out to the lobby.

Devin was waiting for her. "How do you feel about sushi?" he asked.

"We have a long-term, committed relationship."

He smiled. "Good to know. There's a great place not far from here."

"Excellent. I think we've earned ourselves some calories."

As they drove toward the sushi place, she checked her phone. "Nothing from Emma. I don't know why she hasn't called me back."

"She could have been ordered to stay out of it."

"I hope not. I'm going to assume she's just super busy." She saw the gleam in his eyes and beat him to the punch. "And, yes, I know I'm being optimistic. It's who I am, Devin. You're going to have to deal with it—for at least the next few days. Then you can be spared my happy thoughts."

"I guess I can last that long," he said dryly. "Just don't try to make me hopeful."

"I don't believe in knocking my head against a brick wall—too painful."

"I think you like to knock your head against a brick wall. The harder the better—the sweeter the victory."

Okay, he might be partially right, but she wasn't going to tell him that. "Just drive."

"I don't have to; we're here."

He pulled into a parking lot, and a few minutes later, they entered the restaurant.

Kaz Sushi was a trendy Japanese restaurant, and even at nine o'clock on a Thursday night, it was still crowded with diners. After perusing the menu, they ordered several platters to share and a couple of glasses of water. She drank half of hers in one long sip.

"Still hydrating?" he teased.

"That class was not for amateurs."

"I thought you were a runner."

"I've been busy lately. And you can't seriously tell me you didn't feel a little challenged by the workout."

"It was intense, but I enjoyed it. Working out has been the only thing keeping me sane."

"All evidence to the contrary," she joked.

"Hey, I was worse right after the fire."

"I believe that." She set down her water glass. "Have you ever thought about quitting, Devin? It's been a long time. I know since Monday's fire, you've gotten amped up again, but what about before? What about all the long months in between?"

"They were hell, but I never thought about quitting. I haven't found Sam's killer, and until I do, I'll keep working the case."

"Even when there's nothing to work? What about your life, Devin? What about your dreams?"

"My only dream is to solve this puzzle."

"What about friends? Do you have any? Do you ever do anything fun? Do you go to ballgames? Do you drink? Pick up women? Any of the above?"

"Are you done?"

"That depends on if you're going to answer any of my questions."

"Why do you care what I do with my life?"

"I don't care, but I'm curious. You seem...isolated."

"Work can do that. Aren't you just as isolated? The job takes everything from you."

"I still make time for friends, for myself." She frowned, thinking that wasn't completely true, but she was living far from her friends and forging a new life for herself. "And I'm working for me, for my career, my goals. The devotion and loyalty you have for Sam is admirable and amazing. But I can't imagine that she holds you responsible for her death."

"You don't know that."

"I've worked with partners and so have you. We all do our best, but sometimes bad things still happen. I might have only been on the job a year, but I've already seen that." She took a breath. "I would hate for you to wake up one day and suddenly realize a decade had passed, and you were still stuck in the same place."

"This won't take a decade."

"It might."

"Hey, you're supposed to be the optimistic one," he reminded her. "Don't go dark on me now."

"Fine, let's talk about something else."

"Thank God."

She smiled at his heartfelt relief. "Most men like to

talk about themselves. They brag and boast for hours on end, and then at the last minute, right before you're about to leave, they say something like: how was your day?"

"I can't believe you let anyone get away with that."

"Sometimes it's hard to get a word in edgewise."

"You seem up to the task," he said with a smile. "Have you dated anyone at the Bureau?"

She immediately shook her head. "No, I don't need to add that complication into my life."

"Not even at Quantico? I saw more than a few relationships start there."

"I wouldn't call them relationships. And, no, I didn't get involved with anyone there. I was more concerned with passing all the tests and becoming an agent. There's no way I could have gone back to my family if I flunked out."

"What do you like about the job so far?"

"Everything."

He rested his forearms on the table as he gave her a thoughtful look. "Not everything. Be more specific."

"I don't know. I've been moved around a lot the past year."

He nodded. "There's always a process to get agents with the right skillsets for the right jobs. What have you worked on?"

"I've done a couple of fraud investigations, a counterfeit operation sting, and most recently I was part of a task force trailing a possible domestic terrorist group in Colorado. They were all interesting."

"But?"

"I didn't say *but...*"

He held her gaze. "Kate."

"But," she admitted, "I really want to work kidnappings. I want to find people who are lost. I want to help put their families back together. Unfortunately, for some reason that's one of the jobs I haven't been given a shot at yet."

"That's on purpose. The Bureau knows your background. They want to test your mettle before they put you on a case that will have more of an emotional impact."

"I think I've proven my mettle."

"They have to think so, too. You're young. You have a long way to go. But you'll go at the Bureau's pace, not yours."

"I know. I'm really not complaining. I love the job. And I tell myself that whatever I'm working on is important."

"Does that help?"

"Most of the time," she said, acknowledging the gleam in his eyes. "I can't help it. I'm a little impatient. I always have been. When I want something, I want it that second."

He smiled. "Something we have in common."

The way he looked at her reminded her of the moment just before he'd kissed her earlier that day.

She'd had the reckless urge to lean across the table and kiss him again.

Fortunately, the waiter arrived with their food, and with the platters of sushi between them, Kate concentrated on filling her stomach and not the other hunger filling her soul.

"Do you want to come back to my apartment?" Devin asked as they finished dinner. "To look at the files again?"

She wondered why he'd felt the need to clarify, but she wasn't going to ask. She also thought ending the night and going to her brother's house was a better idea. "I think I'll grab a cab and go back to my brother's apartment. It's been a long day. We both need to rest and regroup."

"All right. I'll drive you."

"It's out of your way."

"Who cares?" he asked. "I'm sure it's not that far. I can pick you up in the morning on the way to St. Bernadette's."

"That's a good plan."

Devin paid the check, and they walked out to his car. "So which brother are you staying with? One of the firefighters?"

"No, I'm staying with Ian. He's a scientist. And don't ask me any specifics. He's very cagey about what he does."

"Sounds intriguing. I can't believe you haven't dug into it."

"I've thought about it, but I try to stay out of my siblings' business, because then they stay out of mine."

"Got it."

"You can turn right at the next street," she said, directing him to Ian's apartment.

"Whatever he's doing, he must make some good cash," Devin commented as he double-parked in front of the building. "This is nice."

"That's why I decided to stay here." She opened her door. "I'll see you tomorrow."

"I'll come by a little before ten."

"I'll be ready. I think we'll get a new lead tomorrow."

"There's that optimism again."

"Good-night, Devin."

"Good-night, Kate," he murmured, his gaze holding hers for a long second. Then she got out of the car and shut it firmly behind her before she could decide that going home with Devin would have actually been the better idea.

Nine

~~➤➤◄◄◄~~

Devin woke up early and went for a run before breakfast. His legs ached from the spin class the night before, but it felt good to get outside. His usual route took him through the Marina and along the waterfront to the base of the Golden Gate Bridge. It was a popular trail, especially on the weekends, but on Friday morning before eight it was fairly empty.

As he ran, his thoughts drifted back to Kate, to all her questions about his life. He hadn't answered any of them, not because he thought she was prying, but because he didn't have any answers.

It had been a long time since anyone had questioned what he was doing with his life. He barely kept in contact with what little family he had left, and his friends were scattered. There were a few guys in the city who he knew. He occasionally picked up a game of basketball at the gym or went out to a club for a drink and some conversation. But most of the time, he just had his head down, buried in a case that would probably haunt him until he died.

Which was why he had to solve it.

And it had to happen now—during this trio of fires. If he missed this opportunity, who knew when another one would come his way?

The second fire would most likely happen within the next few days, which reminded him that after they went to St. Bernadette's, they needed to focus on potential targets and decide if they could rule any out, and if not, how they could cover all the bases that needed to be covered.

He wished he had a team, five people he could send to stake out every possibility, but it was just him and Kate. Their partnership of two was going to have to be enough.

He had to admit she had proved to be incredibly helpful so far, more than he'd imagined when she'd first entered his office. But still, she was only one person.

Maybe Emma would get involved and bring some of her department with her. That was probably his only hope for getting more help.

When he reached the bridge, he slowed his pace down to a walk. For several long minutes he looked up at the bridge and out beyond it—at the Pacific Ocean. It was the first time he'd looked beyond the bridge, beyond the immediate goal in a long time, and that was because of Kate and all her damn questions about how isolated his life had become.

He didn't like that she was getting into his head. He hadn't dreamed about anything but fire in the last year until last night when he'd dreamed about her, when his brain had relived the kiss between them in excruciating detail.

That kiss couldn't have been that good, could it?

It was just because it had been a while, that was all.

But was it?

He'd never been good at lying to himself.

He hadn't kissed Kate just because she was there, and she was pretty. He'd kissed her because he couldn't stop himself.

But it wouldn't happen again. She'd said so. And while he hadn't exactly agreed, he knew she was right. He couldn't let his desire for Kate distract him from his goals.

With that thought in mind, he turned and ran even faster back the way he'd come. But no matter how fast he ran, he couldn't outrun his brain, and Kate stayed on his mind through a colder-than-normal shower, a quick breakfast, and a drive across town to pick her up.

Kate was waiting outside the apartment building when he pulled up. She wore black slacks and a short-sleeved silky cream-colored top.

"Good morning," she said, as she got into the car.

"You know you don't have to dress official for me."

"I'm not dressing for you, but I'm officially on the job, so I thought I should look the part, especially if I'm going to be flashing my badge around town. Did you have any brainstorms last night?"

He could hardly tell her all of his brainstorms had to do with getting her into bed. *Dammit*. He shook his head. He couldn't remember when he'd been this distracted. "No," he said shortly. "Nothing."

"I was thinking we should get back into the potential target sites today. As much as I don't want to alert my family to my presence here in the city, we should go by Ashbury Studios so I can let Sean and Jessica know they should beef up their security. And what about the other places? Shall we try to warn them? I know you didn't have much luck before when you tried to contact schools, but I feel like we should do something."

"Since I have you on the team, we might get better reception," he said. "Let's see if we can narrow down the list after we go by St. Bernadette's."

"Good idea. I was also making a list of suspects this morning, and it seems to be getting longer instead of shorter. But that could be a good thing. Better to have more prospects than none. It gives us new leads to chase, new paths to take."

"You woke up with a lot of energy."

"Mental energy," she said with a laugh. "My legs are in pain from last night's spin class. What about you?"

"I felt fine. I went for a run this morning."

"Really? So you are Superman."

"Probably only in my own head," he said dryly.

"You spend too much time in your head, Devin."

He had, until about three days ago when Kate had shown up in his office. "Did you see your brother last night? Has he asked you any questions about what you're doing here?"

"He was out. A woman came by to visit him though, one of his neighbors. She was very pretty but kind of nervous. She was really surprised to see me there. I quickly explained I was Ian's sister, but I'm not sure she believed me. It was kind of odd really."

"It doesn't sound that odd. A beautiful neighbor stops by to visit your single brother—what's so strange about that?"

"I don't know. It was just sisterly instinct. I've answered the door for a lot of girls looking for one of my brothers. And there was just something a little off about this one. Oh, and she told me not to mention she'd stopped by, that she'd just see Ian later. She really didn't want me to tell him she was there."

"Maybe she got embarrassed."

"Maybe." Kate didn't sound convinced.

He looked over at her. "What are you thinking?"

"That I'd like to check her out, maybe run her name through a database."

"That's against Bureau rules, Kate."

"I wasn't thinking of using the Bureau. I happen to know a private investigator who seems to have some skills."

"You want to hire me?"

"God, no. I don't have money for that. I want you to do me a favor."

He laughed. "You're always direct. I do like that about you."

"I don't know how else to be. I hate games. A guy I used to date was very passive-aggressive. He'd agree with me on everything, then he just wouldn't do it. I wish he would have just said he didn't want to do something instead of stringing me along."

"You won't have that problem with me—not that we're dating," he added quickly.

"We certainly wouldn't do that," she agreed.

He was happy to see St. Bernadette's on the next block. They were veering back into dangerous territory.

Since school was in session, they first stopped in the office where the principal told them that the counselor had already reported the details of their conversation. She escorted them to the library and asked the librarian to get them the yearbooks from the years when Rick Baines attended school there. She went on to say that she couldn't provide contact information, even if she had it, which she didn't, since it had been twelve years since Baines had attended the school.

A few moments later, the librarian handed them the yearbooks in question. "You're welcome to take them with you, but we hope you'll bring them back."

"We will," Devin promised, happy that they could

take the books out of the library.

As they left the school, Kate said, "There's a café not too far from here. In fact, we can walk. Want to get some coffee while we go through these?"

"Sounds good." He fell into step with her as they walked down a residential street, then into a more commercial area with shops and restaurants.

The Bird's View Café was on the third-floor rooftop deck of a building, offering a view of the city from the outdoor tables.

"This is cool," he said, as they took their coffees out to the deck. "I didn't know it was here."

"We used to come here in high school when we were cramming for tests. I wasn't sure it was still open." Kate tilted her head as she looked at him. "It occurs to me that I don't know very much about you, Devin. Where did you grow up? Was it here in San Francisco?"

"No, I grew up in Sacramento."

"Does your mom still live there?"

"She lives in Sonoma now with her husband and her daughter."

"She remarried after your dad died?"

"She remarried before he died. My mom left my dad when I was about ten. She said she got tired of waiting for him to come home from work."

"I'm sorry." Kate's eyes filled with compassion. "I didn't know that."

"It was a long time ago."

"Who did you live with after the divorce?

"Technically, my parents shared custody, but I mostly lived with my mom. Then she fell in love and got remarried and was happier for me to spend more time with my dad. When she had my half-sister, she really had no room in her house for me, so whenever my father was in town, I was with him. But then he died, and I was back with her and her second family." He let out a breath, irritated with himself for telling Kate so much, because he'd only ignited more questions.

"How old is your sister now?" she asked.

"Jordan is twenty. She's a junior at Sonoma State."

"Do you see her? Do you see your mom?"

"Not very often."

"When was the last time?"

"I don't know—Christmas a couple of years ago."

"You haven't seen them since you moved here, since you've been living like an hour away from them?"

"I'm not part of their lives."

"That's ridiculous. Your mom is always going to be your mom. She loves you. And I'm betting your sister does, too."

He shrugged. "It's all fine. We don't hate each other. We just don't see each other."

Her lips tightened. "If that's the case, it's not all fine."

"Hey, you've been in the city three days and haven't told your parents you're home."

"That's different. I'm working a job, and I will see them next week."

"Hand me a yearbook."

Her grip tightened on the books. "A couple more questions."

"Why? I just told you my life story."

"That was a headline, not a story, and I like to know who I'm working with."

"There's nothing more to tell. There's no big drama. I had parents; they divorced. I bounced around. We all moved on."

"No wonder you're so guarded. You locked down your emotions a long time ago, didn't you?"

"Kate, don't try to psychoanalyze me. You're nowhere near qualified."

"I have eyes and instinct, and I can see a man who has closed himself off. I thought it was just because of Sam—your guilt, your grief—but now I think the walls went up long before her death."

"You should put up some walls," he advised.

"Why would I want to do that?"

"Because you're too vulnerable. It wouldn't be hard to hurt you."

She stared back at him with those questioning blue eyes, and he realized just how true his statement had been. "Are you warning me about you, Devin?"

"I'm warning you about life. You're open. You have a big heart. You like people. You believe in hope and truth and justice, and you have no idea how many times you're going to be disappointed in your life."

"I've been disappointed before," she said quietly. "But just because one person fails you doesn't mean everyone will. I choose to believe in the good in people. I'd rather live my life that way, than..."

"Like me?" he finished.

"Maybe you're too afraid of getting hurt, Devin. You block everything out. The bad stuff stays on the other side of the wall, but so does the good stuff. Do you ever let anyone in?"

"I've let people in."

"And..."

"Nothing."

She tilted her head and gave him a pointed look. "Really? That's all you're going to give me?"

"I've given you way too much already. We're on a case, Kate. Let's get back to work."

"You can be so frustrating."

"Right back at you. Now give me a yearbook."

"Fine. Which year do you want? Freshman or sophomore?"

"Whatever is on top."

"That would be Rick's freshman year." She slid the book across the table.

He flipped through the pages to the freshman class photos. Sure enough, a younger version of Rick Baines stared back at him. His hair was long and stringy, his eyes kind of dull, his expression rather bored. "Baines definitely went to school at St. Bernadette's."

"I've got him, too," Kate said, turning around her yearbook to show him the class photo from a year later.

"He cut his hair between freshman and sophomore year," he commented. "Otherwise, he looks pretty much the same." He moved slowly through the list of names in the class. "I've got Alan Jenkins, blond, good-looking, and much happier than Baines."

"I see him as well. He looks like a jock. Who else are we looking for?"

"Let's see if we can find any photos with Baines or Jenkins connected to each other and/or other students. We need to create some links even if we don't know whether they go anywhere."

"Okay."

They moved through their books quietly for the next few minutes. It quickly became clear that while Baines didn't seek the camera, Jenkins did. He was on the football team and the homecoming court and involved in student government. He was photographed with numerous pretty girls at many school events. But there was never a photo of him and Baines together...until the spring of freshman year.

"Baines was on the baseball team with Jenkins," he

said. As he stared at the page full of shots from baseball season, he lost his focus for a minute. He wasn't seeing those kids anymore, but himself.

Baseball had been his escape from divorce and death. When he'd been swinging a bat or chasing down a ball at shortstop, he hadn't had time to think about anything but winning. And those games, those sometimes long, endless games, had been the only time where he'd felt normal, happy... until he looked up in the stands and realized no one was there for him.

He shook his head, silently damning Kate for bringing up all the old memories with her probing questions. The last thing he wanted to do right now was think about his past.

"Baines must have quit after freshman year. He's not on the team in my book," Kate said.

"Probably wasn't good enough." Devin flipped to the next page. He paused, almost surprised to see a group photo of Baines and Jenkins and two girls. They were sitting at a lunch table. The girls were tagged as Kristina Strem and Lindsay Blake.

"Do you have something?" Kate asked.

He turned the book so she could see the photo. "It's the only candid I've found."

Her eyes lit up. "This is great. We have two more names, two more links to Baines. We just have to find them."

He couldn't help but smile at the fire in her eyes. "Sounds like a plan."

"Why aren't you more excited? This could be a break."

"I'll celebrate when we get to the end of this whole thing."

"See, that's one of your problems, Devin. You don't

let yourself enjoy the good moments. Not everything has to be a homerun. Sometimes you get a single, or the pitcher hits you in the arm and you walk your way on base. But once you're on base, anything can happen."

He grinned. "You're seriously giving me a baseball metaphor?"

"Yes. I'm trying to speak your language. And my dad talks a lot in baseball metaphors. He also played in high school and college. I can't tell you how many times he said, 'Kate, you can't steal second with one foot on the base.'"

"That's what he said to you?"

"To me and to every other one of my siblings. He wanted me to understand that there's little reward without some risk."

"So you get some of your fearless instincts from your dad."

"Definitely. He was a firefighter. He liked impossible challenges; he still does. Right now he's trying to convince my mom to go on some crazy-ass, two-thousand mile bike ride across two states."

"They bike?"

"No, they don't bike, except to ride around town or the bay. But he saw this trip and he's convinced they should start training for it. He's a little bored in retirement. My mom told him no way, but I have a feeling he's going to wear her down." She paused. "Getting back to you—"

"Let's not get back to me. Let's get back to the apartment and use our resources to track down two former students from St. Bernadette's."

"Okay, fine, but I'm going to buy you a cookie on the way out to celebrate."

"Knock yourself out."

Ten

Kate didn't just buy Devin a huge oatmeal raisin cookie at the Bird's View Café; she also grabbed some ready-made sandwiches and salads to have for lunch later. She had a feeling they were going to be buried in research for the next few hours.

She knew Devin thought she jumped a little too fast into optimism, and maybe she did, but she felt good about the new leads. Since she'd arrived, she'd been able to help Devin cover new ground, and she really hoped that new ground was leading them in the right direction.

Devin pulled into his garage, and then they walked back out to the street to go into the building. Before they could hit the stairs, a woman called Devin's name.

"Shit," he muttered.

"You know her?" she asked as a dark-haired woman wearing a short dress and high heels approached them.

"Devin. I've been calling you for days," she said. Her gaze turned on Kate, her eyes filling with anger. "Who's this? Is she the reason you haven't been calling me back?"

"No," he said evenly. "This is Agent Kate Callaway from the FBI."

"Oh," the woman said, taken aback. "I thought...I'm sorry." She looked at Kate. "I'm Valerie Parker. Has there been a break in Sam's case?"

Kate immediately surmised that with the same last name, Val was Sam's sister or some kind of relative. Before she could answer the question, Devin jumped in.

"There was a new fire on Monday," he said. "I asked the Bureau for help, and they sent Kate."

"A new fire?" she echoed in surprise. "Where?"

"St. Bernadette's Catholic High School."

"Another school," Val murmured. "Are you sure this one is tied into the others, because last time—"

"I think it's tied in," he said, cutting her off. "So we're a little busy right now, Val. Can we talk another time?"

"This isn't about us, Devin. It's about my mother. She is losing it. Over the past few months, she's gotten more and more depressed. She doesn't even get up or get dressed some days. And you know what she asks me every single time I see her? 'Have you heard from Devin? Is there any news?'"

Devin took a quick breath, and Kate could see that Val's words had stabbed him like a knife. She suddenly saw something she hadn't seen before. Devin wasn't just fighting this battle for himself; he was fighting it for Sam's family.

"I'm working as hard as I can," Devin said evenly.

"She's counting on you to get justice."

"I know that."

"And I know you're busy, but could you go by and visit her? I think it would really help. If she sees you, talks to you, she'll feel better again. She'll know that you'll keep going until you catch Sam's killer. I wouldn't ask you to take the time if I wasn't really worried about her."

"I'll try to get over there in the next few days."

"How about this afternoon?"

"Val—"

"My father is out of town on business. He's been traveling a lot lately. My mother escapes into her pills and her sleep, and my dad stays on the road. It's hard to watch my family disintegrate, Devin. I know I haven't been the best daughter, certainly not as good as Sam was, but I'm trying to help them, and I'm at my wits' end. It's just been going on so long. It seems like we'll never get to the truth, and I think that's why my mother is getting worse. She's giving up. She needs to see that you haven't given up."

Devin slowly nodded, his jaw tight. "I'll go over there this afternoon."

Relief flooded Val's eyes. "Thank you." Val looked back at Kate. "Sorry to interrupt."

Kate shrugged and offered a compassionate smile. "It's fine."

"Devin, I'll see you soon." With that parting reminder, Val walked briskly across the street and disappeared around the corner.

Devin headed up the stairs and Kate quickly followed him into the apartment and down the hall.

She set the food down on the table by their computers and said, "So, do you want to tell me about Sam's family?"

"Not really," he said, taking a seat.

She gazed at his hard, guarded expression and knew she was going to piss him off, but she couldn't let him keep her at a distance, not when the subject matter had to do with the case.

"You said Sam was your partner, nothing more, but that's not really true, is it?"

"It's true," he said, meeting her gaze. "Sam and I were not having sex. We were not romantically involved. I don't know how else to say it."

"Then it was Val. You were involved with her sister. When she first came up to us, she said, 'this isn't about me or about us.' That implies there was an *us*—as in you and her."

Devin dug into the bag she'd brought from the café. "Is this sandwich up for grabs?"

"Yes. I'm having the salad, and you still have to answer the question."

As Devin unwrapped his turkey and cranberry on ciabatta bread, he said, "Val and I hooked up a couple of times. It wasn't a relationship."

"Did she know that?"

Devin shot her a dark look. "She knew exactly what was going on."

"Sometimes men think women are on the same page, but they're not."

"We both knew what was going on, and we both knew it was a bad idea. Val and I were not a good match."

"Why not?"

He shrugged. "We didn't have anything in common, except maybe a tendency to blow up our lives every so often."

"How long did it last?"

"A few weeks."

She frowned. "If it was that short, how did you get to be almost like a son to Val's mother?"

He chewed and swallowed, then said, "Sam and I met at Quantico. We were in the same class, and we were instant friends. Over the years, she'd take me home with her on holidays, and her family treated me like one of their own. It was a lot more fun to be with them than to be with my mother and her second family and all her second husband's relatives. I never felt like I fit in there."

"So you knew Val a long time, too."

"I'd see her occasionally on those holidays, but she wasn't always around. She was younger than Sam. First she was away at college, then she was living in Dallas for work. She had a boyfriend for a couple of years, who always came with her to Christmas. I never thought of her as anything more than Sam's little sister. But when Sam and I came to the city to work on the arson fires, I ran into her one night in a bar. We had too much to drink and one thing led to another."

"What did Sam think about it?"

He shook his head. "She was pissed. She told me I was crazy and that she couldn't imagine two people who were worse for each other. She didn't like that I'd gotten involved with her sister, and thought it was going to complicate all our lives. She was right. It was a disaster."

"Did you break up before or after Sam died?"

"A few days before. Like I said, it wasn't a relationship. We hooked up like three or four times."

Kate gave him a long, speculative look.

"What?" he asked.

"There's something you're not telling me."

"I can't think of anything. I answered your questions."

"But I haven't asked you the right question yet, have I?"

He took another bite of his sandwich and gave her what appeared to be an uncaring shrug, but she could see the tension in his body.

"Val has something to do with Sam's death," she guessed.

He set down his sandwich and got up to get a drink out of the refrigerator.

When he sat back down again, she said, "You weren't

with Sam the day she died. You said you had to meet someone, and that's why you didn't pick up her call and that's why you were late getting her message. You were meeting Val, weren't you?"

He stared back at her with pain in his eyes. "Yes. She'd been calling me all day, saying she just wanted to talk to me, and I should hear her out. So I went to meet her. She was upset about a lot of things besides just me. When I finally got out of the bar, I listened to Sam's message. Unfortunately, by the time I got to the house, it was engulfed in flames. The fire department was already on their way inside."

"I'm sorry," she whispered, seeing the guilty agony in every tight line of his face. "That's why you blame yourself. It wasn't just the case; it was the personal stuff, too."

"I let Sam down. I didn't have her back. I was distracted. It was the first time I ever let my personal life get in the way of a case. And I wasn't the one who paid the price; that was Sam. She was probably my closest friend." He cleared his throat. "Are you satisfied?"

She didn't like the question, because it made her feel like she'd pushed too hard, but maybe she'd needed to do that.

Devin could have lied. He could have avoided her questions, but he hadn't. Was there a chance he'd needed to make the admission to someone else besides himself?

"I'm glad you told me," she said. "It helps me to understand."

"I don't need your understanding; I need you to help me find a killer. And whether I was involved with Sam's sister has nothing to do with that."

"You're right. Your relationship with Val has nothing to do with the case now. But I also wonder if it has as much to do with what happened to Sam as you think it did. Were you on the verge of some groundbreaking moment when you went to meet Val?"

He frowned. "No."

"So you didn't leave Sam in the lurch. You didn't know something big was coming?"

"Don't try to make me feel better."

"I'm just getting to the truth. What were you doing that day besides meeting Val?"

He drew in a breath as if he wasn't sure he wanted to keep talking, but in the end he said, "I went to meet with the fire investigator. We were going over the evidence again—or lack of evidence. Sam was focusing on the persons of interest. We were supposed to meet up that night to compare notes."

"So you were working independently that day."

He shrugged. "I guess. It doesn't matter."

She thought it mattered a lot more than he was saying but decided she'd pushed enough on that part of the conversation. "Tell me more about Sam. Not who she was as an agent, but as a person."

"Why? Who Sam was is not important to what we're doing now. We should be focusing on potential fire targets."

"We'll get there. But you're eating, and so am I." She grabbed the salad and a plastic fork to make her statement true. "Tell me about Sam's family if talking about her is too difficult."

He sighed. "Fine. Sam was the center of her family. She was very smart, excelled at everything. Her mother adored her. Her father respected her. Val was always in her shadow. Sam didn't put her there, but Val couldn't escape it. Val was always rebelling. Whatever Sam did, Val would do the opposite. That's why she often found herself in trouble."

"What did Sam's parents do?"

"Her mother was a stay-at-home mom. She volunteered at school and city fundraisers. Now she doesn't do much of anything. Her dad is a salesman for a software company. He's gregarious and bigger than life. Sam was a mix of her quiet mom and her outgoing dad. She was friendly but introverted. She liked analysis more than she liked people. She preferred to profile than to interview or take action. That's why we were a good team."

"Did Sam enjoy being near her family for this assignment?"

"She did. We had several dinners over there in the weeks before she died." He paused. "When I had to call her mom and tell her what had happened." He shook his head. "Worst call of my life."

She couldn't even imagine. She impulsively reached across the table and put her hand over his. "You went through hell. I'm so sorry, Devin."

He squeezed her fingers. "Thanks." He drew in a breath and let it out. "The hell got worse when the Bureau closed the case, and I was reassigned. I spent three days on that new assignment and then said to hell with it. I quit that day, and I've been here ever since—working and waiting. Now, the wait is almost over."

She nodded. "We're going to find the bastard who killed Sam. I believe that."

"I believe it, too," he said, surprising her with the admission.

"So you can be optimistic," she said, trying for a lighter tone.

The tension eased from his face. "On that one point, I've never lost the faith. It's been shaken badly at times, but it's never disappeared." He let go of her hand. "After you finish eating, we'll take a look at targets."

"And suspects. We need to review the list again. Knowing now that Rick went to St. Bernadette's and had at least a few acquaintances there, maybe we can connect some new dots. But before we do all that, Devin..."

"What?" he asked warily.

"We should go see Sam's mom."

"We?" he asked with an arch of his eyebrow. "I don't think that's a *we* job."

"Do you really want to go alone? Sit with Val and her depressed mom all by yourself?"

"Okay, you have a point. But let's push that back awhile and do some work first."

—➤➤◄◄◄—

After lunch, Devin opened his computer and pulled up the file on people he had listed as persons of interest.

"Do you want me to go down the list?" he asked.

Kate nodded, her computer open in front of her. "I'll follow along."

"Let's start with Ron Dillingsworth. Thirty-four years old, thinning brown hair and brown eyes. He has authored a series of books about firefighters. He was photographed at three of the fire scenes, but he claims that he goes to the scenes for research for his books."

"He published the first book five years ago, two months after the first school fire in your pattern of fires," Kate finished. She looked up at him. "You sat in on his interview after the fire. What was your personal take on him?"

"I couldn't catch him in a lie, but he didn't seem to be telling the entire truth. He had alibis for several of the fires, although no real alibi for the fire that killed Sam. He alleged that he was at home alone. A neighbor verified that she'd seen him enter his apartment that evening, but whether or not he left after that sighting was unknown."

"Sometimes when people are lying, they're not lying about the actual case," she said. "Maybe he had other secrets."

"Like what?"

"Perhaps he doesn't write the books himself? He could have a ghostwriter and not want anyone to know. Or maybe he was cheating on his girlfriend, and one of his alibis had to do with that. It says he was dating a model at the time of the fire but they've since broken up."

"It's possible."

"We could talk to him again. It's been a year and a half. Maybe I could get a different read on him."

"After his interview, his lawyer started intercepting all of his calls. Dillingsworth has also gotten to be very popular in the last year. His most recent book hit high on the *New York Times* Bestseller List. He has become an author celebrity."

"He has to have a life. There must be some way we can catch him off guard. Let's think about that. Go on to the next one," she said.

"Bennett Rogers. He's a forty-six-year-old real-estate developer. He owned two of the historic properties that were torched and both had insurance policies that paid off. He's since built new homes on those sites." He paused. "He doesn't work for the rest of the fires, though."

"And he's a lot older than Baines, so he wouldn't have been connected to him through high school. I'm going to pull up the background on each of these people while we're talking. It goes into more detail than your general notes." She paused for a moment. "Okay,

Dillingsworth grew up in San Francisco, and he attended Catholic school through the sixth grade. He went to St. Mary's." She looked at Devin. "There weren't any fires at St. Mary's, were there?"

"The second one," Devin said. "But he had an airtight alibi for that fire. He's at the bottom of my list." He moved on to the next name. "Eileen Raffin is an interior designer and a member of the San Francisco Historic Preservation Commission. She approved the certification for three of the structures that burned down. She works at the architectural firm of Connors and Holt."

"Mrs. Raffin seemed forthcoming in her interview. She's a fifty-seven-year-old woman with a good job and long ties to the community. What bothered you about her?" Kate asked.

"It wasn't Eileen that bothered me as much as her friend and the owner of the firm she works for—Gerilyn Connors."

Kate glanced back at her computer. "Gerilyn is a forty-two-year-old architect. She drew up the plans for the remodel additions on two of the houses that were targeted."

"And one of those houses was the one that Sam was killed in," he said.

Kate met his gaze. "Four of the five historic structure fires are connected to Gerilyn and Eileen in some way. That's a lot. But your real interest isn't even Gerilyn; it's Gerilyn's ex-husband."

"Yes," he agreed. "Brad Connors is an ex-firefighter with an alcohol and substance abuse problem. He got kicked off the job for drinking at work. He had several domestic violence complaints against him that Gerilyn later dropped after they got divorced, but it's possible he went after projects she was involved in for revenge against her."

Kate nodded, liking that theory. "He burns down what she builds up. That makes sense. Although, it's easier to come up with motives for the historic structures; the schools and the community centers are tougher."

"It is. I cannot find a link between Brad and the other fires. And I do not believe any of these fires are random. Each site is selected for a specific reason."

"I agree. Okay, so last on the list is Marty Price."

Devin consulted his notes again. "Marty is twenty-three-year-old wanna-be firefighter who tried out three times to get into the fire academy without success. He was spotted in the crowd at four of the fires. He lives near St. Bernadette's, but he did not go to Catholic school. He went to public elementary school and high school. In his interview, he stated that he goes to fires to watch the firefighters at work and that all of the fires he was seen at are near his apartment, which they were. So he lives in the right area."

"He's also the right age to know Baines," she said. "Even if they didn't go to school together, they could have known each other."

"I have looked at that angle, but I haven't found anything that ties them together."

"What about the gym? It's the kind of place where people meet, but no one would really put them together there."

"Why don't you call your good buddy Pete and see if Marty Price had a membership there?" Devin suggested. "I'm sure he'd tell you."

"That's a good idea," she said, ignoring his not-so-subtle dig about Pete's interest in her. She looked back at her computer. "Marty works at a coffee house. That's another place he could have met Baines. Maybe we should do some more digging into him." She let out a breath as she considered all the suspects. "Out of all these people, I'm most interested in the writer Dillingsworth, the ex-husband firefighter, and Marty Price. What about you?"

"They seem the most likely candidates, but there's a part of me that doesn't think it's any of these people, that I've missed something big along the way."

She was surprised that Devin was so honest in his assessment of his work. She'd thought he was impossibly cocky when they first met, but as she got to know him, she realized that he had very high expectations for himself as well as everyone around him. "If you missed something, it wasn't big," she told him. "It was something small, something hidden, something that appeared insignificant in context but wasn't."

"That doesn't narrow it down much, Kate."

"I know." She paused as her phone buzzed. "It's Emma—finally. I'll put her on speaker."

"So sorry, Kate," Emma said immediately. "I got caught up in a warehouse fire, and I've been swamped since we had lunch yesterday."

It was strange to hear about another fire, Kate thought. They'd been so focused on school and community center fires that she hadn't paid any attention to other fires in the city. "Was the warehouse fire arson?"

"It looks like it was an unhappy employee, and I don't believe it's tied to the fires you're tracking."

"It doesn't sound like it. I'm with Devin, by the way. You're on speaker."

"Hi, Devin."

"Emma."

"So what have you learned?" Emma asked.

"Rick Baines—the man believed to be the arsonist—

was a student at St. Bernadette's before he transferred his junior year to Northern Marin High School," Kate said.

"Really?" Emma asked. "I don't recall seeing that in the files."

"It wasn't in there," Devin said. "I didn't look back beyond Northern Marin High School."

"How did you get this information?" Emma asked.

"We talked to the counselor at the school," Kate replied. "We also looked in the yearbook. We've been researching Baines since we found out he was a student there. While he obviously didn't set the fire on Monday, it fits the pattern, which makes it likely that this arsonist might have known Baines or at least been familiar with his work."

"That makes sense," Emma said.

"We went through the St. Bernadette yearbook from that time period and located a couple of people who appeared to be friends with Baines. One of them went to the gym where Baines worked. The other two are women. We have not had a chance to track down yet."

"Give me their names. I'll see if I can get any info on them," Emma said.

"Kristina Strem and Lindsay Blake," she said. "The man from the gym is Alan Jenkins. He apparently moved to southern California over a year ago. We've left messages for him, but he hasn't returned calls."

"Okay, I'll do some digging myself."

"Did you have a chance to study the photos from the fire on Monday?" Devin asked.

"I did look at them again. You were right. There was a St. Christopher's medal found near the Dumpster. I spoke to my boss. He's not declaring anything officially open again, but he said I can talk to you."

"I'm glad we don't have to meet in secret," Kate said.

"I'm going to look at everything again this weekend, and I'd like to bring Max in, if you don't mind."

"Of course not. We'll take all the help we can get."

"Let's stay in touch."

"We will," Kate promised as she ended the call. "The St. Christopher's medal solidifies your theory, Devin."

"For the fire investigators. It was already rock solid in my mind."

"I know."

"What does Max do?" Devin asked.

"He's a homicide detective. He's Emma's husband. I'm sure he'll do whatever he can to help."

"Happy to have more members on the team."

"It's actually starting to feel like a team." As Devin glanced at his watch, she realized how late it was getting. "We should go see Mrs. Parker. It's almost four."

"You really don't have to come, Kate."

She hesitated, knowing she was probably intruding, but there was something about the way he'd said it that told her he wanted her to be her usual pushy self. "I'm coming," she said. "My presence might reassure them, let them know the FBI is involved again."

"Or you might get their hopes up. We both know your help comes with an expiration date."

"Well, for the next few days I'm officially yours."

"Officially mine?" he teased.

"I didn't mean it like that."

"Too late to take it back. You can come with me, but I have to warn you if there's anything that's going to drive the hope out of your soul, it will probably be visiting Sam's mother."

"I'll take the risk. Maybe we'll turn things around. We won't let her bring us down; we'll bring her up."

Eleven

—➤➤◆◆◆—

Kate's optimism definitely took a hit when she and Devin walked into the Parkers' home, a small three-bedroom house on Potrero Hill, tucked in the middle of a street of attached homes.

Valerie had met them at the door with a relieved smile, but inside the house, the air was dark, cold, and tense. Every curtain, every blind was drawn to block out the light.

While the house wasn't dirty, there was a thickness to the air as if grief permeated every room, every corner. She wondered if she'd made the best choice coming with Devin. He was already operating on too much emotion, too much pain; she was supposed to be the cool, objective one, but meeting Sam's mother was only going to make Samantha Parker and her death more real.

Val flipped the lights on in the living room. "My mom won't let me open the curtains. She says the light hurts her eyes. She has a lot of headaches these days. Lying in a dark, cold room seems to be the only thing that makes her feel marginally better."

"Is she feeling well enough to see us?" Devin asked.

"I'm sure she'll see you. You're her lifeline to Sam." Val paused, giving Devin a pointed look. "Mine, too."

Devin drew in a quick breath, his jaw tightening. "I'm no one's lifeline. I'm just trying to find answers."

"I wish you wouldn't shut me out. We could help each other. It doesn't have to be this way."

"Val, stop. I just came to see your mom."

"I know you blame me, but it's not my fault." Val turned to Kate. "Did he tell you that we were together, that it's my fault he was late getting to Sam? Did he tell you that he can't look at me without hating me?"

Kate couldn't begin to understand whatever was going on between Devin and Val, but she could see the pain in the woman's eyes.

"Don't bring her into this," Devin said. "And I don't hate you. It wasn't your fault. I've told you that dozens of times."

"You say it, but you don't mean it—not really."

Devin sighed. "I don't know what else to tell you. Just get your mom."

Val frowned but did as he asked.

"Sorry," Devin muttered. "I have told Val it's not her fault a thousand times."

"Probably as many times as everyone in your life has told you, but guilt isn't something that gets talked away."

"That's true."

"Maybe Val cared more for you than you cared for her."

"It's not about that. She's been involved with two different men since Sam died. She broke up with the latest one last week; that's why she's suddenly looking at me again. She doesn't like to be alone. She never did, but now it's worse, because before she had a sister to call when her life got too quiet, too empty. I'm fairly sure she used her mom to get me to come over here—not just for her mom, but also for her. Look at this house. It's like a mausoleum."

"It is depressing." She walked across the room and paused in front of the fireplace. On the mantel were several framed photographs, one a family shot of the Parkers, obviously taken in happier times. Like Val, Samantha had dark brown hair and eyes, but she was more serious in expression than Val. She had a penetrating gaze that was sharp and intelligent. Her face matched that of her dad while her mom seemed to look more like Val, with rounder, softer features. "Good-looking family," she commented as Devin joined her.

"I used to tease Sam about that picture. I told her she looked suspicious, as if she thought the cameraman was there for some other reason than to take a family photograph."

She smiled, happy to hear more nostalgic fondness than pain in Devin's voice. "She does have a wary look about her."

"She was always wary. She was always looking for a hidden agenda, a dark secret. She would try to take people at face value, but she just couldn't do it."

"Suspicion can make a good analyst, but it can also weigh you down."

"It weighed her down," Devin agreed. "I used to tell her to take some time off, go on vacation, not take her work so seriously, but she never listened. When she was on a case, she was a bulldog. She wouldn't eat, wouldn't sleep. I think she had a little obsessive-compulsive in her. But that determination usually got her to the truth. I remember one of the training exercises at the academy. We were supposed to figure out where two kidnappers had hidden three hostages they'd taken during a bank robbery. There were six of us on the team, and five of us went in one direction and Sam went in the other. She was convinced there was a connection between one of the hostages and one of the kidnappers."

"I'm betting she was right."

"Yes, she was. She was always looking for the angle."

"You do that, too, Devin."

"Maybe I learned something from her."

"Maybe she learned something from you. I have a feeling your partnership wasn't one-sided. I've only been working with you a few days, and I already know that you bring a lot to the table."

"I'm surprised you'd say that. I haven't accomplished much the last year and a half."

"You've done a lot, but you're following someone who goes underground for periods of time. You've had to wait, but you've kept the pressure on, and you're still on the case. If you weren't, no one would know that Monday's fire was important and connected to those in the past."

"Well, we still have to catch the person. We're a long way from doing that."

"Maybe not. Maybe we're closer than we think."

He smiled. "And here I thought this house would suck the life out of you."

"It is hard to be here, but in some ways it makes me more determined. It reminds me that there's a real person whose life was lost."

He put his arm around her shoulders and gave her a hug. "Thanks, Kate."

"You're welcome," she said, wishing his hug hadn't ended so fast. As she turned her gaze back on the pictures, she saw one of the family with Devin at a baseball game.

"Hey, you made the mantel."

"I told them to take that down, but since Sam is in it, it stays."

"And why shouldn't it? Your friendship with Sam was important to not just the both of you but also the family." She moved on to the next picture of a group of friends: Sam and Val with some other young men and women. "Did Sam have a boyfriend?" she asked curiously.

"She had some off-and-on relationships. She dated a police officer here in the city. When we came back for the arson cases, they reconnected for a while. He was really distraught when she died."

Her gut tightened at that piece of unexpected information. "Sam was dating a cop here in the city?"

"Yes." Devin's gaze narrowed. "Why do you say it like it means something?"

"You said that you didn't know where she'd gotten the information to change her profile ideas. Maybe it was from him. Was he helping you with the case?"

"No, he wasn't involved in that at all. He worked narcotics."

"But he still had access to police records. What was his name?"

"Rob Hamilton. He wasn't involved in the case, Kate. We were working with police and fire arson investigators. Hamilton wasn't talking to Sam about her work. He wanted to sleep with her. That was his interest."

"It just seems a little odd that I never saw that information in any of the files."

"Because it wasn't relevant."

"You don't think there's any way that Rob could have given Sam the clue that led her to that house?"

Devin stared back at her, his jaw firm, his eyes

annoyed but reflective. "I can't be a hundred percent sure, but he told me he hadn't talked to Sam for a few days before her death, and he was wrecked after she was killed. I saw him at the fire, at the funeral and at Sam's parents' house. He knew I wanted to find her killer, that I wasn't convinced Baines was it, or that he was working alone. If he'd known something he would have told me. But all he talked about was Sam—how he'd wanted to get back together with her, but Sam was hesitant to start something up with him again. Her heart was still in her job and she wanted the freedom to go where she needed to go, and that's why they'd broken up in the first place. He'd wanted her to put him first, but she couldn't. He was broken up about it. He said he wished he'd spent more time enjoying their relationship instead of wanting more."

"That's sad." She paused, thinking that Sam was sounding a little like her. Would a man expect her to put him first over her job? Probably. It never seemed to be as big a question when it was the man with the big job and not the woman. She turned to Devin. "Would you ever change your life for a woman? If her work was important, would you want her to continue doing it?"

"Why are we talking about me?"

"Because I'm curious. If you loved a woman, and her job took her to another city, and it was something she loved to do, would you go with her?"

He let out a sigh. "I'd go now. I might not have gone before, because I had bigger career goals. Now, not so much."

"That might change once you find Sam's killer."

He shrugged. "Who knows? But why do I feel like we're not really talking about me or Sam? This is about the guy who broke up with you when you left for Quantico."

"Maybe a little. I guess I was just wondering when love trumps career."

"It obviously hasn't been a strong enough factor for either of us to consider."

"But you threw away your career for Sam."

"Not out of romantic love—out of friendship and loyalty."

"But you still did it."

"If something or someone matters enough to you, you won't hesitate; you'll know what to do," Devin said.

As Devin finished speaking, Val came into the room with a thin, dark-haired woman wearing black leggings and an oversized sweater. Her hair was streaked with gray, her face pale, her eyes dull, but a small spark appeared in her gaze when she saw Devin. She crossed the room and took his hands in hers.

"Devin," she said. "It's so good to see you. Is there news?"

"Not yet," he said. "But the Bureau sent someone to help me. This is Special Agent Kate Callaway."

"Mrs. Parker," Kate said, as the woman turned her head to look at her. "I'm very sorry for your loss."

"I don't want any more apologies or condolences. I want answers. I want my daughter's killer to be in jail. It's about time they sent someone to help." She turned back to Devin. "Val told me there was another fire earlier this week. Is it connected?"

"I believe so," he replied.

"You knew he would strike again. You kept telling me we had to be patient. You were right. So what's going to happen next?"

"We're going to catch him," Devin said.

"How?" Val asked.

"We have a couple of new leads," Devin said. "I

know that I'm getting your hopes up, and I just want to warn you it's not going to be easy. Whoever is doing this is very good at staying hidden."

"Samantha always said that you were very good, Devin," Mrs. Parker said with a sad smile. "She said you were the best agent she'd ever worked with."

Kate saw Devin tense at the words, another reminder that he'd let down someone who'd really believed in him.

"I'm going to do my best," he said.

"Do you want something to drink? I could make us some coffee or tea," Val offered. "We could chat for a while. You'd like that, wouldn't you, Mom?"

Mrs. Parker immediately shook her head. "I'm feeling tired. I think I'll go back to bed. You all have your tea and talk. I just don't feel up to it."

"Mom, you've been in bed all day," Val protested. "It would be good for you to stay up for a while."

"I'm sorry, Val." Mrs. Parker looked back at Devin. "Thank you for fighting for Samantha. I know you're doing your best. Please let us know if there's any news."

"I will," he promised.

"Do you see how bad she is?" Valerie asked, as her mother left the room. "It gets worse every day. It's been a year and a half. Is she ever going to get better? Is she ever going to wake up and look around and see she still has one daughter left?"

"I hope so," Devin said. "I know it's rough on you, Val."

"It has been rough, and it won't get better until you find Sam's killer. I feel like that's the only way Mom will be able to move on. She's just in horrible limbo right now."

"I understand. I'm trying to give her that closure."

"I wish you'd never told her that you had doubts

about the man who died with Sam. Maybe Mom could have let go of this a long time ago. Maybe I could have, too."

"I can't take back what happened."

"I know, but you can make it right. We've all been waiting too long."

"I don't think you have to tell Devin that," Kate couldn't help pointing out, irritated that Val was making Devin out to be the bad guy.

Valerie shot her an annoyed look. "And I don't think I need your opinion, Agent Callaway. When did you get on the case? Two days ago? We've been living this nightmare for over a year."

"We're going to take off," Devin said before she could respond. "I'll be in touch, Val."

"You better," Val said, not bothering to walk them to the door.

When they got in the car, Devin said, "I don't need you to defend me, Kate. It wasn't your place to get in the middle of a conversation between Val and me."

"You're mad at me because I spoke up for you?" she asked in surprise. "She was acting like you've done nothing to solve this case."

"She's angry and sad."

"So are you. But if you need to yell at someone, then you can yell at me. I can handle it."

He ran a hand through his hair as he let out a breath. "I'm sorry. I don't want to take it out on you. I'm just…pissed. I need to hit something."

"I said you could yell at me, not hit me."

His tension eased at her words. "I would never hit you or any other woman. I have a better idea. Are you game?"

"For hitting something—always. Do I need to change

into workout clothes?"

His gaze ran down her body. "You're fine."

As his eyes met hers again, she saw a flicker of desire, and she couldn't help but respond. "Most men think I'm better than *fine*," she said, giving in to a reckless impulse.

"I bet they do, but I haven't seen the whole show."

"And you're not going to see the whole show," she said, immediately regretting her teasing words. "Forget I said that."

"Too late."

"So where are we going?"

"You'll see."

She'd thought they were going to a gym, but twenty minutes later, Devin pulled into a parking lot behind a large warehouse building south of Market. It wasn't until they got out of the car that she saw the sign for the batting cages.

"We're going to hit baseballs?" she asked, as they walked toward the front door.

"It's a good way to release stress." He opened the door and waved her inside.

She stepped into the large, cavernous building. It was late afternoon, and the sound of bats hitting baseballs echoed through the air. Along with a dozen batting cages, there was a huge arcade area with video games, air hockey, and Ping-Pong, all of which were being enjoyed by kids ranging from elementary school age on up to high school.

The air from a nearby snack bar was filled with the aroma of buttery, salty popcorn and cheeseburgers and onions on the grill.

Devin walked up to the counter, and within a few minutes, they had bats, helmets, and a cage to use.

"You want to go first?" he asked as they got into the cage.

"How fast is the ball going to come?"

He showed her the controller. "There are different pitches. You can practice on fastballs, curves, sliders, breaking balls and change-ups. I'd start with a fastball at the slowest speed."

"Which would be what?" she asked, putting the helmet on her head.

"Slowest they go is fifty. You up for it?"

"I'll give it a shot. Worst I can do is strike out, right?"

"It's a batting cage, so you won't actually strike out. Your money will just run out."

"Good point."

"Have you ever hit a baseball before?"

"A few."

"Do you want me to give you some tips?"

"My dad always used to tell me to keep my eye on the ball."

"That would be a good place to start. Ready?"

She stepped into the batter's box while Devin went over to put tokens into the machine. She took a few warm-up swings, then said, "Ready."

The first ball came much faster than she expected. She swung and missed completely.

"Remember the part about keeping your eye on the ball," Devin said.

She shot him a dark look, seeing the humor in his eyes. "I remember." But she'd barely finished speaking when the next baseball took her by surprise. She jumped back.

"I told you; eye on the ball, not me," Devin said.

She focused on the next pitch, determined to show Devin she could handle a baseball. All those years of shagging balls for her brothers and taking swings with her dad came back to her. It had been a decade since she'd swung a bat, but she knew what to do.

She connected with the next pitch in the sweet spot of the bat, and her ball went flying over the pitching machine into the farthest part of the net. She gave Devin a triumphant smile. "Not bad for a girl."

"Not bad," he agreed with a nod. "Let's see if you can make it two in a row."

She waited for the next pitch and hit a line drive. Now that she was back in her rhythm, muscle memory kicked in. She hit the next six balls and then her time was up.

She felt excited and happy and far more relaxed than she'd been when they arrived. "That was great," she said, giving Devin a grin.

He smiled back at her. "You're a natural. You were hustling me a little, weren't you?"

"I truly haven't swung a bat in years, but I did play softball when I was younger."

"I should have figured."

"Three older brothers and a dad who loved the game," she reminded him. "Your turn."

She took off her helmet as Devin stepped into the box. "What speed are you going for?"

"Fastest they've got."

"You do like to push yourself, don't you?"

"If you can't beat the best, what's the point?"

She shrugged and put a token into the machine.

Devin didn't need a few warm-up swings. He was on point with the first pitch, and one ball after another soared high and away. Watching Devin's body in motion made her very aware of his masculinity. He was athletic and powerful, determined and focused, and her heart beat a little faster the longer she watched him.

It was fun to see him away from the job, testing himself in sport instead of work, letting out his inner baseball player, the kid who'd dreamed of the big leagues. He probably would have made it if he'd really wanted it. He had obvious talent, but more than that, he had tremendous desire and will when he wanted something.

She couldn't help wondering if he'd ever wanted a woman with that same level of passion and will. It didn't seem like it. He hadn't mentioned anyone that he'd been serious about and definitely no long-term relationships, but that probably had more to do with the wall he'd built around his heart than anything else.

If someone could tear down that wall, unleash all that passion…that could be something else. Her whole body tingled with the thought of that *someone* being her.

Which was crazy, she reminded herself.

They were partners, coworkers. They couldn't be more. *Could they?*

That question lingered for only a minute before a dozen answers—all negative—filled her head. And all those answers had to do with what she wanted, and that was a career. This wasn't the right time for her to meet someone, to fall in love, to want to commit.

But who said she had to commit to anything? Maybe Devin was the perfect person to enjoy some non-committed fun.

Only problem was she had a hard time divorcing her heart from her body. It was probably her best-kept secret. Most people thought she had no problem doing that, but she did. Which was why she didn't get involved with people who could in any possible way touch her heart.

When Devin's pitches ran out, he set down the bat and gave her a questioning look. "Well?"

"Not bad."

"That's all you've got? Most people would say I'm better than not bad." He repeated her earlier teasing words with a slight variation.

"Well, I haven't seen the whole show."

He laughed. "Unlike you, I'm not against that happening, Kate."

"I don't mix business with pleasure. And even if I did, you and I would not be a good match."

"Why is that?"

She had to think for a moment, because two seconds ago she'd been pondering how magnificent they could be together. "Let's see. You're moody, intense, and cynical, and I'm a happy person who likes to have a positive outlook on life."

"There is that," he said with a nod. "But sometimes opposites attract. And we do have some things in common."

"Like what?"

"Passion. Determination. Fearlessness."

Her heart skipped a beat—not just at the word *passion* but at the look in his eyes.

She cleared her throat. "Let's try some curve balls."

"I thought I just threw you one."

She saw the teasing light in his eyes and liked seeing this lighter side of Devin. "Let's see how you do when the ball surprises you." She put another token in the machine and urged him back to the plate.

Devin handled the curve balls as well as he'd done the fastballs, and she got more turned-on by every swing, especially when his T-shirt crept up, revealing his muscled abs.

"Your turn," Devin said.

As much as she was happy not to have to look at him anymore, she wasn't sure she wanted his gaze on her now. "Let's switch it up. How are you at Ping-Pong?"

"As good as I am at baseball."

"Of course you are. Are there any sports you're not good at?"

"I can't think of any."

"Your humility is amazing."

"You asked. I answered." He took off his helmet. "But I can let my play speak for itself."

"We'll see."

Over the next hour, Devin unfortunately backed up all of his cockiness with a winning streak at the Ping-Pong table and two out of three wins at air-hockey. But when they got to skee ball, Kate found her strength. She beat Devin three games in a row making him mutter to himself.

"Looks like I win," she told him.

"One more game."

"We've already played three."

"I can do better."

That was Devin, she was beginning to realize. He didn't accept anything that felt like failure within himself. He went back after the victory time and time again.

She shook her head. "You remind me of someone."

"Who?"

"Did you ever see that movie *Tin Cup*?"

"It was about golf, wasn't it?"

"Yes. The protagonist can't stand the fact that he didn't put the ball in the hole in one stroke, and he refuses to leave the course until he does it, even though he ends up losing the tournament because he can't move past that one hole."

He stared back at her. "And I'm that guy?"

"You do need to win."

"I like to win; I don't have to win."

"Really? Don't you?"

"This isn't about skee ball or Ping-Pong, is it? You think I'm wrong about Baines, but I'm not. It's not about winning. It's about being right. And I'm right."

"In this case, that's kind of the same as winning."

"I thought you were on my side."

She didn't like the disappointment in his eyes. It surprised her a little that he cared so much what she thought. "I am on your side, Devin."

He walked across the cage and looked into her eyes. "I hope so. Because I believe that Sam's killer is still out there. Guilt keeps me up at night, anger makes my heart hurt, but it's what I know in my gut that keeps me looking for the truth. I was trained to be skeptical, to look beyond the obvious, to read between the lines and see past the shadows. I know what I have to do. Whether you want to do it with me is up to you. You don't have to believe. You can still walk away."

There was nothing but pure honesty in his eyes, and she was persuaded not just by his words but also by his will.

A lot of people talked the talk, but she'd never met anyone who was really willing to walk the walk, to put everything he or she believed in on the line for their beliefs. To look all the naysayers in the eye and say you're wrong took a lot of strength. Devin was one of a kind, and she couldn't help but admire him.

"Kate? What's it going to be?" Devin questioned.

"I'm not walking away. I believe in your instincts. And to put it in baseball terms, I respect your willingness to leave everything on the field."

A small smile played across his lips. "I don't know any other way to play. But this isn't a game, and I know that, Kate. You don't have to worry that I don't understand what's at stake."

"Good, because if we do get close to discovering Sam's real killer, that could put us in danger, and I'd like to know that the man at my side is keeping his eye on that ball, too."

"You've got it. I think we should seal the deal with a hot dog. What do you say?"

She grinned. "A hot dog sounds perfect. Actually, I'm going to get mine with chili and onions."

He smiled back at her. "If you think onions are going to scare me away…"

"Scare you away?" she echoed. "I don't know what you're talking about."

"Yes, you do."

"Let's just eat."

"I thought you were fearless."

"When it's warranted, I am. This isn't that time."

Twelve

---⟶≫⫷⟵---

Kate was right, Devin thought, as they made their way to the snack bar. This wasn't the time to be messing around, but he had enjoyed seeing the guilty sparkle in her eyes when he'd brought up the heat between them.

Too bad they were both smart enough not to act on it.

After they collected their hot dogs and french fries, they sat down at a table near the arcade.

"So tell me about your baseball career," Kate said as she wiped some chili off her lips.

"It wasn't a career. I played on competitive teams growing up, in high school and two years of college. I got some draft offers after my sophomore year, but they weren't offering much money, so I said no. Then I hurt my shoulder and ended up sitting out my junior year. The time off brought some clarity. I decided to hang up my cleats and go after a real career."

Having seen his intensity, she was a little surprised he'd given up on that dream, but it was nice to know that Devin could take a step back and look at a situation with a more critical eye. He didn't always let emotion influence his judgment.

"It worked out for the best," Devin added.

"No regrets?"

"Not about baseball. I'll always love the game, but it wasn't going to be my career." He paused. "Tell me about your baseball career. You didn't get that swing in two seconds tonight."

"I played softball until I was twelve, but it was never my thing. It was way too slow. Every game seemed to take forever. I dabbled a little in soccer and volleyball, and they had more action, but while I liked being on a team, I discovered that I liked controlling the outcome even more. That's why running appealed to me so much; it was just me against the trail. I was in charge of my own fate. In team sports, you're only as good as your weakest link. In running, I didn't have to rely on anyone else to win. I'm sure you can relate to that."

"I can relate, but I have to admit that having been on my own the last year and a half, I've missed having a partner, someone to bounce ideas off of."

"Well, I'm here now. So what are we going to do next? You said the second fire usually occurs within four to seven days after the first fire. It's Friday, and the fire was Monday. We're in the target zone. Which reminds me, I do want to go by Ashbury Studios and warn my cousin and his wife. They've worked really hard to build that studio up."

"I thought you didn't want to see your family."

"Well, I doubt Sean and Jessica will go running to my mother, but even if they did, this is more important."

"That's fine, but I don't think the studio is the next target. My money is on the Bayside Neighborhood Club. It's a teen center in an old house. The manager of the club lives on the third floor of the house, but other than her, the house is empty after ten o'clock at night." He paused. "I might drive by some of the targets later tonight, between the hours of midnight and three, see if anyone is around any of the sites."

"That seems a little random."

"It's better than nothing. I'll focus in on the three sites without alarm systems." He pulled out his phone as he got a text. "The boss is checking up on you," he said.

"What do you mean? I talked to Agent Roman earlier today."

"He just wants to know if you're able to help me."

"I hope you're going to tell him that I'm doing nothing but helping you," she said pointedly. "I even tried to teach you how to win at skee ball."

"I don't recall any teaching, only boasting."

"Because I finally found something I could beat you at."

He sent a text back to Roman, then said, "Are you ready to get out of here?"

"Hold on. What did you tell my boss?"

"That he couldn't have sent me anyone greener."

Disappointment ran through her. "Seriously? We're back to that?"

He opened his phone and showed her the text. "No, I said you've been more helpful than anyone else at the Bureau."

She skimmed the text. "Okay, good. But since the Bureau set the bar for helping you really low, I'm not sure that's much of a compliment."

"Just take it."

"Fine, I'll take it. Let's stop at Ashbury Studios on the way back to your place."

"Whatever you want."

"If you still need to burn off some energy, we could probably crash Jessica's ballroom dance class," she suggested. "I think she teaches it around this time on Friday nights."

"I don't think so. I have no ability to dance."

"I don't believe you. You're very light on your feet."

"Only when I'm hitting baseballs."

"It could be fun. I would even let you lead."

"As tempting as that offer is, I still say no."

"We'll see."

"Hey, you're not going to change my mind," he added, as he followed her out of the batting cages.

She gave him a mischievous smile. "I bet I could if I really tried."

"Then don't try," he said a little desperately.

She liked that she could rattle him, too. "Like I said, we'll see."

Kate hadn't been at Ashbury Studios since she'd joined the FBI. The entire first floor of the converted warehouse had been turned into small to medium-sized music and recording rooms, with one main studio for more important artists and bigger bands. Her cousin Sean, who was an excellent musician and singer, and apparently also a good businessman, had opened the studio with a partner a few years earlier.

The upper floor offered a variety of dance studios for fitness, ballet, yoga, hip-hop, salsa and ballroom dancing, all overseen by Sean's wife Jessica.

After entering through the side door, they headed down a hall lined with photographs. Kate paused in front of one. "This is Sean's band," she told Devin. "He's been performing since he was fifteen. He's really good. I hope he's here tonight. I'd love for you to meet him. He and

Jessica have an interesting love story."

"How so?" Devin asked curiously, as they continued down the hall.

"It's a long and complicated tale, but these are the highlights. Jessica used to dance in Vegas. She met and married a single dad, whose son Kyle was about four or five years old. Then her husband died tragically, and she was left to raise her stepson Kyle."

"When does Sean come in?"

"Pretty soon. Jessica had her hands full raising Kyle on her own. Then things got worse. Kyle was kidnapped from a birthday party."

Devin arched an eyebrow. "Okay, getting more interesting. I'm guessing this is a happy story by your tone."

"It is, but it took awhile to get there. At the same time that Kyle was kidnapped in Angel's Bay—"

"Wait—your sister lives in Angel's Bay."

"Right, but Mia wasn't there then. This was before that. At the same time Kyle was kidnapped, my cousin Nicole's son Brandon was also kidnapped. Brandon is autistic, so it was even more terrifying, because he was torn away from everything and everyone he knew."

"There's a link between Kyle and Brandon, isn't there?" Devin asked, his quick mind putting together the pieces of her story.

"Yes. They turned out to be identical twins. It quickly became clear that they had been separated at birth and adopted individually. My cousin Nicole had no idea that her son was a twin. She and her husband Ryan went racing down to Angel's Bay, and Sean went there to help with the search. That's where he met Jessica. Eventually, the boys were found, and Nicole, Ryan and Jessica decided that they needed to stay together, so Jessica moved to San Francisco with Kyle, and she and Sean fell in love."

Devin smiled as they reached the main lobby. "That is quite a story. Do they all live together?"

"They live near each other but not together. The boys adore each other, and Kyle, who is not autistic, is so great with Brandon. He really brings him into the world. He instinctively knows what Brandon needs."

"The twin thing strikes again."

"It does," she said with a laugh. "Anyway, let's go upstairs."

They walked up to the second floor and into the main dance studio where Jessica was fiddling with her stereo system while two couples chatted before class.

Jessica was a leggy brunette with dark brown eyes and a warm smile. Wearing heels, a spaghetti-strapped top and flowing skirt, she looked like she was ready to dance.

"Kate," she said with surprise in her eyes. "How nice to see you. Did you come for the class?"

She knew Devin didn't want to dance, but she'd gone to the batting cages with him; maybe he could do something she wanted to do. She'd always wanted to take a dance class from Jessica, and they had a little time before the stakeout he wanted to do later. "Yes," she said.

"Hold on," Devin said. "I told you I don't know how to dance."

"This is a beginner class," Jessica said. "And the start of a new session. No one knows how to dance. I'm Jessica Callaway." She extended her hand to Devin.

"Devin Scott. And we didn't come here to dance. Kate, tell her why we're here."

She sighed. "He's right I did have another more pressing reason."

"What's that?" Jessica asked.

She looked around. The other couples were talking to each other and not paying any attention to them. "There have been a series of arson fires in the city, and property owners in this area are being asked to be extra vigilant. Make sure all doors and windows are locked at night. When I saw the studios on the list, I wanted to come by personally and warn you."

"That sounds ominous. Should we be worried?" Jessica asked.

"Just careful."

"I didn't realize you were working in San Francisco, Kate."

"I'm just helping out on this case before Mia's wedding. I also came by because I wanted to see you," she said, trying to lighten the concern in Jessica's eyes.

"Well, I'm happy to see you, too, and glad you're watching out for us. I'll let Sean know what you said." Jessica looked at Devin. "Are you also in the FBI?"

"I was. I'm an investigator now."

"And I think he could be a really good ballroom dancer," Kate put in. Now that she'd gotten work out of the way, she wanted to dance.

Jessica smiled. "There's definitely room in the class. I think you would have fun. I'll let you two decide." She left them alone while she walked over to the other students.

Kate could see that Devin was going to be hard to win over, so she put her hand on his arm and gave him her best smile. "What do you say, we just try it out? If you're not having fun, we can leave." She squeezed her hand on his arm. "It's a little break before we spend half the night driving around the city."

"You're not playing fair," he said grumpily.

"What's not fair?"

He pointedly looked at where she was touching him. "I thought we had a hands-off policy."

"That's a no-kissing policy. Dancing is completely acceptable. And by the way, I can be just as determined as you when I want something."

He gazed into her eyes for a long moment. "Fine, I'll dance. But I will lead."

"I wouldn't expect anything else."

Jessica called them over, and they joined the other couples as a male dancer came into the studio. It was a clear he was also a professional. Jessica and her partner gave them a short demonstration, and then it was their turn to dance.

As Devin put one hand on her hip and grasped her other hand with his, pulling her close against his chest, she suddenly realized the danger of her impulsive decision to dance.

Jessica walked them through the first few stumbling steps. Kate felt even more awkward than Devin, who actually seemed to be picking up the moves more quickly than she was.

"You just have to relax and let me take you where you're supposed to go," Devin told her.

"Maybe this wasn't such a good idea."

"What happened to *I can be just as determined as you*?"

"Nothing, but I can see I don't have a talent for this."

"Your problem is you don't want to give up control," he told her.

He was probably right about that. She was worrying so much about getting the steps perfect and not dancing too close to him and not looking stupid that she was messing the whole thing up. So she took a deep breath, and let herself hear the music, and feel his moves.

Once she stopped fighting him, she started to do better.

Jessica came over to them a few times and interrupted just long enough to show them how they could improve a step, then left them alone to continue on with the dance.

By the time the class was over, Kate felt both exhilarated and tired.

Devin twirled her around in one last move that was completely made up, but since he was giving her his sexy smile, she went along with it, ending up in his arms.

"That was more fun than I thought it would be," he said.

"I know. It surprised me, too."

They were so close together, their faces just inches apart, she could feel his breath on her face and she wanted very much to close the gap between them and feel his lips on her mouth. Devin's gaze darkened, and his arms tightened around her body.

"Just kiss me already," she breathed.

Desire flickered in his eyes. But before he could move, she heard a guy call her name.

"Kate?"

Startled, she pulled abruptly away from Devin to see her cousin Sean making his way across the dance floor.

"Hey, nice to see you," he added, giving her a hug.

"You, too. I didn't think you were here tonight."

"Just got back from dinner. We have a band recording later. They like the late night start."

"This is Devin Scott," she said, introducing the two men.

Sean shook Devin's hand. "Nice to meet you. Jessica told me you're following an arsonist and that we might be a target?"

"Yes. I just got on the case a few days ago," she said. "But Devin has been investigating a series of fires over the past several years. We've isolated some potential targets."

"And this studio is one of them?" he asked in surprise.

"Actually, it's very low on the list," Devin interjected. "But the arsonist has been known to target organizations that provide services to the community for at-risk kids and senior citizens."

"Why the hell would anyone want to go after those groups?" Sean asked, bewilderment in his blue eyes.

"Still trying to figure that out," Devin replied.

"We actually have extra security for the next three nights," Sean said. "The recording artist coming in later is well-known, and he brings along his own team."

"Who is it?" Kate asked.

Sean smiled. "I can't tell you that. He values his privacy."

"So it's a *he*."

Sean shook his head in amazement. "You're just like Emma. So curious."

"I consider any resemblance to Emma to be a compliment."

"Speaking of Emma, why didn't my sister warn me about the possibility of arson?"

"She was just made aware of these potential new targets," Kate told him.

"Well, glad to hear she's not asleep on the job."

"You know that would never happen." Kate paused as Jessica came over. "Thanks for the class. That was fun."

"It looked fun," Jessica said with a twinkle in her eyes. "You two make good partners."

"When she lets me lead," Devin said with a grin.

"You stumbled a few times, too," she reminded him.

"That's when you stepped on my feet."

"Well, you'll both get better if you come back next week," Jessica put in.

Jessica's words reminded Kate that she wouldn't be coming back next week, because that was Mia's rehearsal dinner, and the following week she'd probably be back in DC getting assigned to another case.

"Sorry, I forgot next week is the wedding," Jessica said. "So maybe another time?"

"We'll see," she said. "Thanks again for letting us crash the class."

"There's always room for two more, especially family."

"Nice to meet you both," Devin added, as they said their goodbyes and headed back to the car.

As she got into the car and Devin started the engine, she glanced down at her watch. It was nine thirty, which meant they had a few hours to kill until they started to stake out the other targets, and she had a really terrible idea on how to fill that time.

She should go home, she told herself. She should ask Devin to drop her at Ian's place and then have him pick her up after midnight. She could take a quick nap. She could talk to Ian. She could do a lot of things besides get closer to Devin.

On the other hand, maybe fighting all the tension wasn't the greatest idea, either.

If they just gave into it, like the dance, maybe it would be better all the way around.

Yeah, that was a great rationalization.

With a sigh, she looked out the window as Devin stopped at a light. Ashbury Studios was in the once famous neighborhood known as Haight-Ashbury. It had been the center of the hippie movement in the sixties and had always had an eclectic and edgy atmosphere.

To her right was a clothing shop next to a tattoo parlor. Across the street was a more upscale home goods retailer next to a pot shop selling legalized marijuana and other herbal supplements.

As Devin drove through the intersection, she looked up the hilly street and saw an old bookstore with lights shining in the windows. And those lights almost brought her heart to a crashing stop.

"Stop," she said abruptly.

Devin slammed on the brakes, throwing her forward. "What?"

"Go around the block and come back down the street we just went through."

"Why?" he asked.

"Because I saw something in the window of a bookstore."

"What?"

"Just drive around the block."

He did as she asked, and as they came down the hill, she asked him to stop in front of the bookstore.

"Damn," he muttered, gazing at the front window in amazement.

"So I'm not crazy. That peace sign looks exactly like the map in your apartment, doesn't it?"

"With just part of the circle and one of the lines missing," he agreed.

"Weird coincidence?"

His jaw tightened. "I have no idea, but we need to find out."

Thirteen

—➤➤◆◀◀◀—

Devin thought about that peace sign all the way back to his apartment. It was quite a departure from what he'd been thinking about before, which was whether or not to answer Kate's very tempting demand to *kiss her already*.

The large lit peace sign in the window of the bookstore had definitely provided an unexpected distraction. Was it just a reminder to get back to work? Or was it a clue?

They'd been in Haight-Ashbury, the place where peace-loving hippies and flower children had gathered in the sixties to share love and protest war. It wasn't unusual to find a peace sign in that neighborhood. There were probably dozens of them within a few blocks.

But there was something about that particular sign that made his nerves tingle. He'd always trusted his gut, and his gut was telling him to pay attention.

Kate was quiet, her gaze on the streets, as if she were seeking another clue or trying to find a way to connect that bookstore to the fires.

"We need to find out who owns the store, the building and the land," he said, breaking through the silence.

She turned her head. "That would be a good place to start. The peace sign caught my eye from across the street. Perhaps it inspired our arsonist. They could live in the area, or they could have visited that bookstore."

"Or we just found a peace sign in the middle of a neighborhood that is probably full of them."

"That's looking at the glass half-full."

"Just being realistic."

She frowned. "It feels like fate, like we were meant to see that sign. It was a good thing we went to warn Sean and Jessica. And even that we danced. We might not have seen the sign if we'd left the studio in the daylight. It jumped out at me in the dark night."

He wanted to be as optimistic as she was, but he just couldn't quite get there—not yet anyway. He was, however, willing to invest some time and energy into researching the owner of the bookstore.

When they got back to his apartment, Kate immediately jumped on her computer, and he did the same.

Within five minutes, they both had the information they'd been looking for. "You want to go first?" he asked, as she gave him an expectant look. "And don't boast because you beat me. You have access to FBI resources; I don't."

She gave him a smile. "I didn't have to use the resources, just the county records. Haviland Real Estate owns the building. They own a dozen commercial buildings all over town."

He nodded, her information matching his. "The bookstore owner is Mitch Conroy. He's a sixty-four-year-old retired English professor from Stanford. He and his wife Beth opened the bookstore six years ago. They also own a house in the Richmond neighborhood." He thought for a moment, something niggling at his brain. "Do you have the bookstore website open?"

"I do. Why?"

"Do they do signings? Has Dillingsworth signed his books there?"

"Oh, my God, Devin, you're brilliant. Ron Dillingsworth signed at the store four months ago when his new book, *Captured by Fire,* was released. We just tied Dillingsworth to the peace sign."

He was feeling the same excitement he saw in her eyes, but he still didn't know what the connection meant. "It could mean nothing, Kate. It's a bookstore. He's a writer. Is it really that strong of a connection?"

"It's better than nothing. We need to talk to him. I know you said he puts all questions through his lawyer now, but he obviously does book signings."

"I'll check his website." He brought up Dillingsworth's website and clicked on the page for appearances. "He's signing copies of his book at a fundraiser tomorrow night at Market Lane Books, which is downtown. The bookstore, which has been around since before the 1906 earthquake, needs funds for a massive remodel." He looked over his computer screen at Kate, now sharing some of her excitement. "You're not going to believe this—the fundraiser was organized by Gerilyn Connors, whose architectural firm is in charge of the remodel of the building. They want to preserve its historic integrity."

Kate gave him a big smile. "Can you be more optimistic now?"

"I'm getting there."

"Get there faster. We just found a new link between Dillingsworth and Gerilyn Connors. We didn't have that before. And think about it—Dillingsworth writes about firefighters and Brad Connors was a firefighter. Maybe Dillingsworth used Brad for research."

"It's possible. I never put those two together."

"They weren't asked if they knew each other?"

"No," he said, thinking Dillingsworth should have been asked that question. Or at least asked about which firefighters, if any, he had spoken to while researching his book. As he looked at the familiar website, he realized something else. "This signing was put on his schedule recently, because I've been here before, and I did not see this appearance. Even without the peace sign at the Haight-Ashbury bookstore, the fact that Dillingsworth was going to be participating in an event hosted by Gerilyn Connors would have gotten my attention."

"Looks like we're going to a book signing tomorrow."

"Absolutely. I just wonder how I missed this connection."

"You didn't miss it. It just showed up."

"Maybe," he said, still wondering if he'd overlooked some clue.

"No maybe about it," she said firmly. "Now we have to figure out if the connection between these two men means anything. We haven't tied them to Rick Baines. Unless, Dillingsworth or Connors ever went to the gym?"

He could definitely answer that question. "They did not. That was determined a long time ago."

"Okay, so they don't go to the gym. They didn't obviously know Baines. Maybe it's a level down connection. Jenkins or one of the girls, or someone else who knew Baines..."

He sighed. "That narrows it down."

"We'll take them one at a time." Kate sat back in her chair. "We're making headway, Devin. We're starting to find connections that weren't there before. Maybe they pan out; maybe they don't. But we have something new to look at. That's a positive development."

Her smile was so warm, her eyes so caring as she tried quite obviously to pump him up that he felt a somewhat overwhelming rush of affection for her. It was different from the physical attraction that permeated every breath between them. It was deeper. It felt both good and unsettling. It was one to thing to want to sleep with her; it was another to actually like her.

She tilted her head. "You're staring at me."

He was staring. Sometimes he thought he could look at her forever and not get bored. "Your face changes a lot," he muttered.

She raised an eyebrow. "That doesn't exactly sound like a compliment."

"It's like watching a movie. I can always tell when the good part is coming because you light up like a Christmas tree."

"Okay, so definitely not a compliment to an FBI agent who is supposed to give a blank, neutral, non-readable expression. Special Agent Roman must have told me a hundred times: *You read them, they don't read you.*"

"Screw Hal and his advice. Sometimes charm and openness gets a suspect off guard. You sneak in because they think you like them. They think you care. That's your strength, Kate. It's only a weakness if you don't know how to use it. But if you channel your power in the right direction, you'll be able to get whatever you want from a person."

"I like that," she said.

"I like you," he told her, the words slipping out before he could stop them.

Her expression jumped with his words. "We're

getting off track."

"With you, that seems to be a common occurrence."

"Maybe it's time to get in the car and start driving around in the cold night air."

He laughed. "You think that will cool us off?"

"It's worth a shot. Despite your teasing, I know that you don't really want anything to happen between us."

The way his body felt right now...hard, hungry...he definitely wanted something to happen. "You're wrong about that."

"I don't mean about the sex; I mean everything else that comes with crossing that line."

"Nothing has to come with it, not if you don't want it to. Sometimes sex is just sex."

"I know it's supposed to be that simple, but it never seems to work out that way. We're working together. We're partners. We'll do better if we stay professional."

"Then we better get the hell out of this apartment."

She pushed back her chair and stood up. "I'm with you. But can we bring some snacks? I'm hungry again."

He laughed as he got up. "I'm going to grab a jacket, maybe an extra one for you, while you rummage through the kitchen. Whatever you can find, you can bring."

"Deal. And Devin," she said, as he started to move toward the bedroom.

"Yeah?"

"I like you, too."

She flushed a little at the end of her sentence and then bolted into the kitchen, leaving him with a heart that was beating way too fast. He couldn't remember the last time a woman had said such a simple phrase and had it mean so much. In the past few years, his relationships—or whatever you wanted to call them—had been about chemistry, desire, sex, not anything more.

He moved into his bedroom, trying not to imagine a naked Kate tangled up in his sheets, with her golden blonde hair draped over his pillows.

Just get the jackets and go, he told himself, wishing he had time for a cold shower, but the cold night air would have to do.

————

Had she really told Devin she liked him? Kate was still pondering the stupidity of that reckless comment as they drove slowly down the block in front of the Bayside Neighborhood Club. The street was quiet. Aside from a man walking his dog, there was no one out on the block. They pulled over in front of the house. All the lights were off. The owner was probably asleep as it was after eleven now.

There were lights on in the house next door, and some music wafting out of a window from three buildings away.

"What do you think?" she asked Devin, focusing on the job instead of on him.

"This neighborhood would be hard to get in and out of fast. There's no parking and I doubt the arsonist comes on foot." He put his foot on the gas and drove down the street. "Let's take a look at Raymond Park Rec. The location is more open, and the fact that the park sits between two blocks, and has access from multiple streets would be more appealing to someone trying to get in and out quickly."

"That makes sense. You're starting to think like an arsonist."

"I've tried putting myself in that person's shoes, but I'm missing the motivation. I just don't know what drives these fires."

She heard his frustration and could totally relate. "I don't think I'm going to make arson investigation my life's work. It's an easy crime to commit, and it's almost impossible to catch someone who can cause massive destruction with the strike of a match. The evidence goes up in smoke. I don't know how Emma does it without going crazy."

"I don't, either. When this case is done, I don't want to think about fire again."

She smiled at his heartfelt sincerity. "I really think you should consider going back to the Bureau when this is done."

"I burned too many bridges."

"I seriously doubt that. And if you bring home a win—which I'm confident you're going to do with my help—you'll be welcomed back with open arms."

"Why would I want to work for a company who closed the case on the death of a loyal agent, even with me standing right there telling them over and over again that they were wrong?"

She couldn't answer that. She could see why he'd lost his faith in the agency he'd been committed to for almost a decade. "Maybe going back will be a way for you to show the Bureau that they can't do what they did again. You could be a shining example of never giving up on a case when your gut tells you that the evidence is wrong."

"I'm usually an example of what not to do," he said dryly.

"Maybe it's just the way you go about it."

"I'm sure that's true." He turned a corner and tipped his head toward the grassy area ahead of them on the right. "That's Raymond Park, and the building next to the small parking lot is the rec center."

She straightened as he drove past the entrance to the lot, then made a U-turn and parked across the street. From their vantage point, they could see the empty lot and the one-room building. There was a streetlight in the parking lot and another at the far end of the park, but the rest of the area was shadowy.

A chill ran down Kate's spine as she looked around the park. There were a lot of trees, a lot of dark places, and if she were someone looking to start a fire somewhere, this was a good spot. "This looks like a better target than the other one. You can access the park from this street or the one on the other side of the building and maybe to the east, too. Wish we could be in three places at once."

"No kidding."

"So are we staking the park out?"

"For a while—see if we see anything. We could be completely off base. The arsonist could be at any number of locations or not even looking to set a fire tonight. They could be living their normal life."

"You're right. I can't make the mistake of thinking the arsonist is one-dimensional with only one goal on their to-do list. He could have a job, be married, have children. He could like dogs, play sports, make culinary masterpieces in the kitchen, run marathons or be a television junkie. He could be in bed asleep right now, having sex with someone he loves, or reading a novel while we're sitting in the cold next to a dark park wondering if he's going to make his move."

Devin shot her a look. "Do you think that was helpful?"

"Sorry. I was talking more to myself than you. Sometimes I talk too much."

"Sometimes?"

"I'm not that bad."

"You're chatty."

"I only seem that way because you're not very talkative."

"We've been doing nothing but talking, Kate. And I prefer action."

Judging by the look in his eyes, she knew what action he was talking about. "No flirting," she warned.

"How is that flirting?" he protested.

"You know. We're alone in a dark car. It's late. It's night. We need to stay focused."

"I'm focused. You're not?"

She could hear the tease in his voice, and she was actually a little surprised to hear it. When she'd first arrived, Devin had been all business all the time, but today she'd seen a more personal side to him; more humor, more joy. Maybe he was starting to come out of the dark funk he'd been living in. "Let's talk movies. What have you seen lately?"

"Nothing. I haven't been to a movie in two years."

"So not a movie person? Or just not lately?"

"I don't spend a lot of time in the theater. I'd rather be outside."

"Me, too," she said. "I get cabin fever when I'm indoors too long. I used to drive my mom crazy when I was little; I always wanted to have my sleepovers in a tent in the backyard."

"That sounds fun."

"Unfortunately, a lot of my friends didn't think so. My sleepovers became less popular when I got to middle school. But Mia was usually game to pitch a tent with me and tell ghost stories under a flashlight." She smiled to herself. "I can't believe she's getting married. My twin sister is going to have a husband. That will be weird."

"Why will it be weird?"

"We've always been so tightly connected. It's strange to think she'll have someone else to tell her secrets to."

"You will, too, at some point."

"I guess. But that's a long ways off, and Mia is getting married next week. Anyway, getting back to you. While you don't apparently like movies, I did notice that you have a lot of books in your house. And you also had an e-reader on your coffee table."

"Very observant."

"I am a highly trained special agent," she said with a laugh. "I also noticed when I walked by your bedroom earlier that you have an aversion to hangers."

"Is that a nice way of saying I'm a slob?"

"Not a slob, but clutter doesn't bother you, at least not in your personal life. In your professional life, you're one of the most organized agents I've ever worked with. Your files, your descriptions, your maps are the most detailed things I've seen."

"My job takes time. Who has time to hang up clothes? I'd like to see where you live, Kate. Are you a neat freak?"

"God, no. I definitely do not waste a lot of time on cleaning. And I share your aversion to hangers. I worked in a retail store at the mall when I was sixteen. I hated when they put me in the dressing room, and my entire job was turning clothes right side out, hanging them up and fastening the buttons and zipping the zips. I thought I might pull my hair out."

"How long did you last?"

"Two weeks. I quit after I got my first paycheck and also realized how little I was getting paid to do work I hated."

"What did you do next?"

"Lots of different stuff. I've made coffee, scooped ice cream, babysat, walked dogs, led nature hikes, and did some boring office stuff. Callaways are expected to work from a young age. Everyone has to pull their weight. My mom and dad are super hard workers."

"Did your mom work outside the house?"

"Yes, she's a nurse. She loves it. My dad is retired, but he doesn't really know the meaning of the word retired. He still does construction for my uncle, who employs a lot of the firefighters on their off days. I don't know why my dad wants to climb on ladders and hammer up drywall, but somehow he does. He does manage to get in some golf, though. And, of course, during baseball season, he makes a lot of ballgames. Now, he's thinking about going on this crazy long bike ride. He has a lot of ideas."

"Like his daughter," he said with a grin. "There's nothing wrong with keeping busy. He'd probably be bored otherwise."

"Probably. He has always had a lot of energy and of course he loves the adrenaline rush."

"You take after him."

"I do in some ways, but I have to say that between my two parents, it's my mom's voice that is in my head. She's the wise one, the person who always seems to have the right advice at the right time. She's very smart and analytical, but she also is nurturing. She likes to remind me that the most important things in life are love and family and taking time to be happy."

"You sound happy when you talk about your family," he commented, the odd note in his voice telling her he didn't think of his family in the same way.

"I love them. They can be frustrating and exhausting and just too much at times, but that never changes the love. It's always there."

"You're lucky."

"I am lucky. Maybe when this case is over, you should visit your mom and sister—reconnect with your family."

He shook his head. "Don't try to fix that relationship, Kate."

"I couldn't do that; only you could."

"There's nothing to fix."

"You just implied there was."

"We're all fine. No one is unhappy with the way things are."

"I don't think that's true."

"I grew up and out of needing a family a long time ago," he said sharply.

"Did you? Then why did you spend so many holidays with the Parkers? Why did they think of you as their son? Why are you on the mantel of their family home?" When he didn't respond right away, she said, "I think you adopted them, and they adopted you, which means you might like family more than you think."

"Well, I like *their* family. Sam's mom is a good cook, and I enjoy eating."

"That's not why you spent so much time there."

"They are nice people," he added. "But while they might think of me as a son, to me they were always Sam's parents. They were hers, not mine."

"Fine, whatever," she said with a sigh. "You're a tough guy; you don't need anyone."

"Finally, we're on the same page."

"You like to win too much, Devin."

"I think it's just the right amount. You're mad because you're trying to win right now by changing my mind, and I'm not going along with you."

He had a point. "I hate to see people sad and in pain when there's a solution—if they just wouldn't be too stubborn to see it."

"I'm fine, Kate—at least when it comes to family. That old wound scarred over a long time ago."

"Well, one day you'll have your own family. Maybe that will change things, or maybe not..." An odd look flashed through his eyes. "What? You don't want kids?"

"I don't know. I haven't thought much about it."

"You've never thought about marriage and family? It's not like you're getting any younger."

He frowned. "I'm not that old."

"Really? Because you like to tell me how old you are quite often."

"Only when it comes to being an agent, not the rest of life."

"I'm glad you're able to see the difference, because you do have a lot of living still to do, and I hope once we put Sam's killer away, you can start doing that again."

He tapped his fingers restlessly on the steering wheel. "Believe it or not, I want that, too. It's been a long year and a half. That's why it's so important that I catch this guy now, within the next few weeks. If he lights two more fires and then heads back underground, it could be another year before he comes up again."

"I know. I understand that the stakes are high. I wish we had an entire team of people to put at every potential target, but we don't, and I also understand that, too. There are a lot of cases the Bureau is working on that need manpower and resources, but we're both good, right? We can figure this out, and we will catch this guy."

"We have to. There's no other alternative."

Her gaze narrowed as she saw flashes of light on the other side of the park. "Devin, do you see that?"

He turned his head. "What?"

"Looks like a flashlight, moving through the trees."

"Stay here."

"No way," she said, reaching for her door handle. As she got out of the car, she smelled smoke. On the street on the other side of the building, she heard a car engine start up and saw headlights come on.

Devin swore. "That's him," he said jumping back into the car.

"Go after him," she said. "I'll call 9-1-1."

Devin slammed the door, raced down the street and around the corner.

When he disappeared from sight, she headed into the park. She'd gone only ten feet when an explosion lit up the air. She was knocked back on her ass by the force of the blast. She was a hundred yards away from the building that was now ablaze with fire. She stumbled to her feet and pulled out her phone to report the fire.

The operator told her the fire department was on the way. Several neighbors had also called it in. She asked if there was anyone inside the building. Kate said she didn't know, but the building had been completely dark before the blast, and there were no cars in the parking lot.

As she ended the call, she saw neighbors rushing out to the street from the nearby houses. As the crowd got bigger, she wondered about the arsonist. Was the person who'd set the fire the one Devin was chasing, or was he somewhere in this milling crowd, admiring his handiwork?

Devin smashed the gas pedal to the floor as he tried to catch up with the fast-moving sedan. This could be his guy, the one he'd been chasing for a year and a half. He could not lose him now.

The sedan was very aware of his tail, speeding through red lights and up and down the narrow, twisting, steep hills of San Francisco.

Devin spun around corners and weaved between slower-moving cars. At one point, he caught a glimpse of the license plate but only registered two letters before the car sped around a corner.

He couldn't get a good look at the driver, either. He registered some type of ball cap on the head of the dark figure behind the wheel, but that was it. He wished he could call in the cops, block some intersections, do something more than just follow, but right now that's all he could do.

Two-way streets turned into one-way streets, and as the SUV cut through an alley and onto another street, Devin found himself going in the wrong direction.

He swerved to avoid an oncoming car and ran up over the sidewalk, smashing into a parking meter. The car came to an abrupt stop, and the air bag deployed, punching him in the chest. His head hit the side of the door, and all he could see were stars exploding in the black night.

The car had vanished. The arsonist had gotten away—again.

Fourteen

As the fire department arrived at the park, Kate looked for some familiar faces, but none of her family members were on the call. With the focus on putting out the fire, there was no time to speak to any of the firefighters, so she walked around the perimeter of the park, looking for anyone who stood out in the crowd.

Most of the neighbors were in pajamas and bathrobes, and it appeared that they'd all come out of their homes. She was looking for someone who didn't belong, who might not have been woken up in the middle of the night and come running into the park to see what had happened.

Maybe one of the suspects on Devin's list: the author Dillingsworth, the wanna-be-firefighter, Price, the ex-firefighter and ex-husband Brad Connors. She'd mentally committed their images to her brain when she'd gone through the files, but no one in this crowd bore a resemblance to any of those men.

There were other suspects, too, that she didn't have an image in her head for: Baines's friend Alan Jenkins and the girls he'd gone to high school with.

And then there were any other number of people who might have never made the list who could be involved in this.

Frowning, she wondered why the hell she'd felt optimistic before. They really were still at the bottom of a very large mountain.

Working her way back to the line of firefighters, she saw Emma crossing the street. She was in uniform, so she'd obviously been on call tonight. Kate hurried over, wanting to catch her before she talked to the battalion chief.

"Kate," Emma said grimly. "Don't tell me this fire—"

"Was probably started by the arsonist Devin has been chasing," she finished. "We were staking out the park, because the recreation center was on Devin's list of potential targets. We were in a car on that street, and we saw a car take off on the other street," she said, using her hand to designate their positions. "Devin went after him. I was headed into the park when the building exploded."

"Is anyone hurt?"

"No, I don't believe anyone was inside. I was probably the closest to the blast." She shivered, remembering the heat of that explosion.

"Thank God you weren't any closer," Emma said.

"I don't know why it exploded."

"Probably accelerant inside the building. I looked up the building and programs on the way over here. They hold a lot of painting classes here. That means turpentine and other combustibles probably acted as fuel." She paused. "Did you get a look at the car? Did you talk to the police?"

"Yes. Unfortunately, I didn't have much information to give. I didn't see the person or the car. I've tried calling Devin, but he isn't answering. It's been almost an hour."

Her stomach twisted with worry at the reminder of how much time had passed.

"If he hasn't come back empty-handed, that's a good thing."

"I hope that's true. I was going to call you, but I didn't want to wake you in the middle of the night until I knew more."

"I'm on call tonight. I need to get over there and do my job."

"You'll keep me posted?"

"I will."

As Emma walked away, Kate's phone buzzed. It was Devin. *Thank God!* "Where are you?" she demanded.

"Westside Medical Center."

"What? Are you hurt? What happened? Did you catch him?"

"No, he got away from me. I got a partial plate. That's it."

She could hear the anger in his voice. "Why are you at the hospital?"

"I wrecked the car. I'm fine, though. What's happening where you are?"

"The fire is almost out. It was big, Devin. There was an explosion. Apparently, there were paint supplies inside the building."

"Are you all right, Kate? I shouldn't have left you there."

"I'm fine. I wasn't that close when the explosion occurred. I just talked to Emma. She's here. She's investigating, and she'll keep us apprised. I'm going to get a cab and come and get you."

"I can just meet you tomorrow, Kate. It's the middle of the night. Nothing else can be done now."

His voice was too fuzzy for her to agree to that. "I'll

be there as soon as I can. Just stay put, okay?"

"I'll be here." He paused and let out a long sigh. "I lost him, Kate. He was right there, and I couldn't catch him."

The despair in his voice made her heart go out to him. There were a million things she wanted to say, but she knew there was no way she could talk him out of the negative reaction he was having, and he was entitled to feel bad. She would, if their positions were reversed. And she wouldn't want someone telling her everything would be okay when there was no guarantee of that.

"We'll regroup and figure out our next move," she said. "We're going to get another chance. And maybe the partial license plate will help. It might match one of our suspects."

"That would be a miracle."

"Well, maybe you're due. We'll make a plan. The one thing I know for sure is that we're not done yet."

──❯❯❮❮──

It was almost four in the morning when Kate and Devin got back from the hospital. Devin hadn't said much on the ride home. He had some bruising on his face, but apparently they'd ruled out a concussion and internal injuries. He hadn't told her much about the accident beyond the fact that the chase had led him down the wrong way of a one-way street, and he'd smashed the car into a parking meter and lost the suspect.

She thought he was extremely lucky not to have lost his life. Car chases were always dangerous, especially when done in a car with no siren and no way to clear the path of other vehicles. But she knew that excuse wouldn't sit well with Devin, so she kept her thoughts to herself.

"Do you want something to drink or eat?" she asked, as they walked into his den.

"No, I'm fine."

"You're not even close to fine," she commented. "You're probably going to hurt tomorrow."

He shrugged. "Whatever. It is what it is. Let's see if we can do anything with the partial plate."

"Now?"

"We don't have time to waste."

"We have some time. The third fire has never happened less than three days after the second one, and I'm guessing that the car the suspect was driving is hidden away in some garage right now. You need to go to bed."

"No, I need to find the suspect," he said, glaring at her. "I need to work."

"You're in no condition to work. I'll do it if you go to bed. I can access resources you can't. So you can let me do my job, or you can stand here and argue with me for a couple more hours."

"You're really pissing me off right now."

"I don't care. Go to bed."

He gave her another irritated look, then said, "You wake me up as soon as you find something. If that plate comes close to matching any suspect we've talked about, I want to know."

"Got it."

"I mean it, Kate."

"And I said yes."

He walked out of the room and down the hall. She moved over to her computer and ran the partial plate through the Bureau's database. She really did hope they would get lucky and find a match to one of their suspects.

The partial plate unfortunately resulted in thousands of matches across the country, several hundred in

California alone. She turned her attention to the list of suspects and ran them through the DMV, almost holding her breath in the hopes that at least one of them had a license plate with the same three letters.

But there was no match—just hundreds of possible leads to check out, none of which could be done at this moment.

Stretching her arms over her head, she yawned. She was exhausted, but she was also wired from all the adrenaline.

Getting up from the table, she walked down the hall and into Devin's bedroom. The lights were out, but he hadn't closed the curtains and there was enough moonlight to see him sprawled on his stomach across the middle of the king-sized bed.

She turned to leave, but he called her name.

"I thought you were asleep," she said, as she moved into the room.

He rolled over and sat up in the bed, resting against the pillows and the headboard. "I can't sleep. I keep reliving every minute of the night, trying to remember if I saw anything that would be helpful. What did you find out?"

She shook her head. "Nothing. Sorry."

"Dammit."

"There are leads to check out, but no vehicles registered to anyone on our suspect list match the partial plate." She sat down next to him on the bed. "We'll start again tomorrow."

"We were right there, Kate. How did we miss him?"

"He came down the other street, probably with his lights off. Or he was there before we were and entered the building from the other side. He could have been in the building for awhile and just didn't have the lights on."

"We should have split up. We should have had you on one side and me on the other."

"That would have been a better plan," she agreed. "But it was a long shot we were even at the right location. And what about the other side of the park?"

"But we were at the right place, and he got away. I was behind the car, and I couldn't get close enough to see the person driving. I got nothing." He groaned and banged the back of his head against the headboard.

"Hey now, you've already bruised your head. Don't make it worse."

"It couldn't get worse."

"Yes, it could. You could have been killed tonight, Devin. But you weren't. You got the make of the car and a partial plate; that's not nothing."

"It's not enough, and you know it."

"I'm not willing to dismiss it that quickly. We just need to work the problem. We go back to investigating. It's what we're trained to do, and that's what we're going to do. But we can't do that when we're both exhausted." She paused, knowing she needed to say the words that had been running through her head for the past several hours. "This is my fault, Devin. This is on me. I was talking my ass off in the car. I distracted you. I distracted myself. It was unprofessional and worst of all, not smart. We were there for a reason, and I should have stayed razor-focused. This wouldn't have happened if you'd been by yourself. I was not helpful tonight. I was not a good partner, and I am really sorry."

"So you're finally admitting you weren't helpful. That's a first."

"I can admit when I'm wrong. And tonight I was wrong."

He stared back at her for a long minute, his gaze still

filled with angry shadows, but his tension was starting to ease. "It wasn't your fault," he said quietly. "It was mine."

"No, it wasn't. You got us to the right place. I should have had the foresight to think about splitting up."

"Why? I didn't. And I have more years than you on the job."

"But you're more emotionally invested than I am. I'm supposed to be the cool, objective party."

"I'm just as objective as you are."

"Well, I am going to make it up to you."

"How are you going to do that?"

"I won't stop working on this case until we find the person who killed Sam and who almost killed you. Even if Agent Roman pulls me off the assignment, I'll work it on the side, okay? I might have to take a few hours or a day off for Mia's wedding, but other than that, I will be doing everything I can to help you. Even if I'm sent back to DC, I'll be on the computer, I'll be on the phone with you. I'll recruit Emma and whatever other members of my family I can get to help you. You won't be alone." It felt so important to make him understand that this wasn't the end, and that she wasn't giving up on the truth or on him.

"Kate, are you done?"

"What? You don't believe me?"

"I believe you."

"Really?"

He nodded.

"Okay, good." She blew out a breath of relief. It wasn't really about screwing up the assignment that bothered her; it was about letting Devin down. She hadn't realized until just this second how badly she'd felt about it. But she'd come to respect him, to like him, to care about him, to want him to be free of the painful weight of the past year. She knew how much this case meant to him.

And while she wanted justice for Sam, mostly she wanted it for Devin.

"Your dedication to this assignment is really impressive, Kate. I couldn't have asked for a better partner. You've gone above and beyond the call of duty. Tonight was just another bad night."

"Tomorrow will be better," she said.

He gave her a reluctant smile. "You're relentless in your belief."

"That's how I get what I want. You do the same thing, Devin. Just sometimes from a more cynical place." She yawned at the end of her sentence. "I should probably go home."

"You could do that, or you could stay here," he said.

"Maybe that's a better idea," she agreed, thinking the last thing she wanted to do was go back out into the cold, dark night. "I'll lie down on the couch."

"Or you could lie down here."

His suggestion sent a tingle down her spine and definitely changed the tenor of their conversation.

"That's not a good idea, Devin," she said, as her brain was already coming up with an argument for why it was an excellent idea.

"It's the best one I've had all night."

She shook her head, fighting the temptation sweeping through her. "You need to rest. You're hurt. And I'm too wired to sleep. I'd probably toss and turn and keep you awake."

"I'm wired, too. My thoughts are running around in circles. Why didn't I do this? Why didn't I do that?"

"Just think about something else."

"I *am* thinking about something else—or I'm trying to."

"*That* is not going to solve anything."

He put his hand over hers, and she almost jumped off the bed at the heat of his touch.

"You've been so helpful to me, Kate, I'm thinking that maybe I should start trying to be helpful, too."

Another tingle shot through her body as his expression changed from somber to flirtatious and teasing. "Really? You want to help me?" she asked suspiciously. "Since when?"

"Actually since a lot longer than you might think."

"What did you have in mind?" She could barely get the words out because she had a feeling the answer was going to be more than a little tempting.

"I could help you relax."

"I don't think what you have in mind is going to be relaxing."

A small smile spread across his lips. "It will be— eventually. You'll sleep like a baby—after."

Her pulse sped up, and desire teased all of her hot spots. The look in his eyes, the promise in his voice, the warmth of his fingers as they played around hers—were all so damned irresistible.

It was reckless, foolish, stupid, unprofessional...

There were lots of reasons for *why not*, but all she could think of right now were all the reasons for *why*...

She wanted to make him feel better. She wanted to make herself feel better. She didn't want to think for a while. She just wanted to escape...

She didn't know who moved first, but suddenly the distance between them was gone, and the touch of their mouths felt like the answer to a million questions. The sparks between them had been simmering for days, and now there was no holding back. Their need for each other was released in one long, hot kiss.

Devin's lips were firm, demanding, and possessive.

This was no tender, tentative kiss of exploration for Devin. He was all in, and so was she.

She liked a man who knew what he wanted and went after it, and she especially liked a man who enjoyed kissing her as much as Devin did.

The deep groan in his throat between kisses, his hands threading through her hair to hold her head in place, made her pulse race even faster. Every time he lifted his head to breathe, she pulled him back to her.

She felt rushed and crushed by desire, by want.

Had it been a million years since she'd wanted someone as much as she wanted him? It certainly felt like it.

She grabbed his T-shirt and pulled it up and over his head, running her hands all over his warm, hard chest, loving the feel of his muscles and his power. He was all man, and she'd never felt more feminine in her life, a feeling that increased when Devin stripped off her top and her bra, his hands rushing to cup her full, suddenly heavy, and aching breasts.

Their mouths met again for a hungry kiss, and then Devin rolled her on to her back as he pulled the snap on her jeans and slid his hand into the heat between her legs.

Needing no more barriers between them, she wriggled out of her jeans and panties as Devin stripped off his boxers.

As he came back to her, she put a hand on his chest, forcing herself to take one second to think. "Wait."

"Second thoughts already?"

"Do you have anything?"

"Oh, yeah, of course." He pulled open the drawer next to the bed and pulled out a couple of condoms. "Got it covered."

"Not exactly, but you're close," she said with a grin.

"Let me help."

"You do like to be helpful, but first—it's my turn."

He pushed her back against the pillows and turned his beautiful, intense focus completely on her. She'd seen Devin be thorough, determined, competitive, and now she knew how good it could feel to have his concentration on her pleasure.

He kissed, stroked, licked and teased her body until she went out of her mind. She wanted to torture him, too, but he kept telling her tonight was all about her. And what woman didn't want to hear that?

So she let him have his way with her, and he took her places she'd never been before. When they came together in passion, it was unlike anything she'd ever experienced.

She didn't know how much time had passed, or when she'd drifted off to sleep, but at some point she became aware of the sun drifting through the windows, and a cooler air hitting the parts of her body that weren't completely draped around Devin.

She grabbed a blanket that had fallen by the wayside and pulled it over them.

Devin shifted and blinked his beautiful brown eyes open, giving her a sleepy but happy look.

"I thought it was a dream," he murmured, running his hand down the side of her face. "But you're here."

"I am here," she said, feeling a little awkward now that the night shadows had gone, and there was nowhere to hide from her impulsive actions. "I probably shouldn't be."

"There are no rules between us, Kate, so you didn't break any."

"Didn't I?" she asked with a little sigh, rolling onto her back as she stared at the ceiling.

Devin turned on to his side, propping his head on one

elbow as he looked at her. "So what? You feel guilty? Irresponsible? Unprofessional? Unsatisfied?"

"Definitely not unsatisfied," she said, seeing the gleam in his eyes. "But you already knew that."

"Still, good to have confirmed."

"I don't feel guilty or irresponsible or unprofessional; that's the problem. I feel good."

He grinned. "Good enough to take a shower with me?"

"Devin. You are way too—"

"Tempting? Irresistible? Hot?"

"What is it with the multiple choice questions?"

"You seem to have trouble putting words together, Kate."

He was right about that. She was still enjoying the delicious ache of her muscles and the memories of their night together. "Apparently, I don't wake up as fast and as sharp as you do."

"That's why a shower would do you good. I can help you wake up."

"You've helped me a lot already."

He laughed, and she felt a rush of warmth that she'd been the one to put the smile on his face, to make him forget for a while the darkness he'd been living in the past year and a half. "I'm glad to hear it."

"I'm surprised you want to spend time in the shower; I thought you'd want to get back to work right away," she said.

His smile dimmed. "That's true." Now, he was the one to flop over on his back and stare at the ceiling. "I just don't know what the hell to do next."

She rolled over to face him. "You know what to do."

"Work the problem?"

She nodded. "One step at a time."

"We're back at square one."

"I wouldn't go that far back. We have the partial plate, the make of the car. The police are interviewing witnesses around the fire scene. Emma is going to keep us in the loop. And tonight we have a book signing to go to where several suspects will probably be in attendance."

A light entered his eyes. "That's right. We have the fundraiser at the bookstore."

"There's a lot to do, Devin. We are not done by any stretch of the imagination."

He surprised her by putting his arm around her and pulling her down for a kiss. "You're right," he said. "Thanks for the pep talk."

"Any time."

"You made me feel better. Now it's my turn."

"It was your turn last time."

"So I get two turns." His hand ran down her bare back. "Are you complaining?"

"God, no," she said, already turned on. "Then we get back to work."

Fifteen

———⟫⟫⟪⟪⟪———

After another hour of mind-blowing fun in bed with Devin, Kate took a quick shower and then headed into the kitchen to make breakfast while Devin got dressed. Thinking about Devin made her smile.

Who would have thought the man who had tried so hard to get rid of her now had trouble keeping his hands off her?

She felt a little smug about that thought. But the truth was she had just as much trouble keeping her hands off him. It wasn't just the chemistry between them, either. There were already probably far too many emotions involved, at least on her part, but then she'd never been good at separating sex from feeling. She just didn't get naked with people she didn't care about.

But she needed to put a rein on her feelings when it came to Devin. They were ships passing in the night. There was no future plan. They didn't even live in the same city. Another week together and then who knew when they'd see each other? She couldn't let herself like him too much.

She just had a feeling she might have already crossed

that line.

So she'd step back. She could do that.

Devin would probably do the same. It wasn't like he wanted anything that required commitment.

They were on the same page.

She just wished that thought made her feel a little happier.

Turning her attention to the refrigerator, she was happy to see Devin had a fair amount of food. She grabbed eggs and vegetables and decided on a veggie scramble with turkey bacon and sourdough toast.

Devin walked into the kitchen as she was filling two plates with food.

He was barefoot, wearing jeans and a T-shirt, and his dark hair was still damp. He'd shaved, making the bruises around his left eye even more apparent. He looked so damn good she could eat him for breakfast.

The smile he gave her was personal, intimate, and he followed it up by stealing a quick kiss.

"Figured I better get that in before your walls go up," he said.

"You have more walls than I do."

He grinned and grabbed a piece of bacon off the plate. "Probably true. It smells good in here. Thanks for making breakfast."

"I was hungry." She handed him a full plate. "You had all the ingredients; I just put them together."

"Better than I could have. I'm impressed."

"Finally, I've impressed you. Stop the clock," she said wryly.

He grinned. "This isn't the first time you impressed me. Last night, you—"

"I don't want to talk about last night," she said, heading over to the kitchen table where she'd set out silverware, napkins and glasses of orange juice.

"That's unusual. Most women love to talk about last night."

"Not me. I'm good. I'm moving on."

Her words didn't seem to sit that well with him. His smile faded a little. "Good to know."

"You're moving on, too," she said quickly. "I mean, it's back to business, right?"

"Of course."

His agreement didn't sit that well with her now. "Devin, maybe we should talk."

"Nope. You had your chance," he said, taking a bite of his eggs. "These taste as good as they look."

"I'm glad."

They ate quietly for a few moments. When they'd finished, she said, "I was thinking I might run over to Emma's house this morning and see if she has any more information on last night's fire."

Devin nodded. "That's a good idea. Although, it's not really morning."

She looked at the clock. He was right. It was one o'clock in the afternoon. "I had no idea."

"Do you want me to go with you?"

"I can do it on my own. I know you want to work on researching the partial plate you got last night. I'll be back in an hour."

"Sure. I'd offer you my car, but it's totaled."

"I'll get a cab. What are you going to do for a car?"

"Call my insurance company and get a rental. I should probably do that now. One of us is going to need a vehicle. We're not going to catch the arsonist from a taxi."

She had a feeling they were going to need more than a car to catch the arsonist, but she didn't feel like pointing out what Devin already knew. She took her plate to the sink.

"I'll do the dishes," Devin said, following her into the kitchen.

"Okay."

He put a hand on her arm as she was about to walk past him. "Kate, last night was amazing. *You* were amazing. Just for the record."

She smiled happily. "I feel the same way. But...it can't happen again. There's nowhere for us to go with this, and we have other things to concentrate on."

He shrugged. "We'll see."

Her heart skipped a beat at his answer. She'd expected him to completely agree with her, not leave her with that tantalizing statement. "What does that mean?"

"It means, we'll see."

"It's not just up to you. I have a say in the matter."

"Well, if you ever want to say yes again, let me know, and then we'll see."

She rolled her eyes. "You're impossible." She yanked her arm away from him and walked across the room and grabbed her bag off the table.

"But you still like me," he said.

"How could I like someone as arrogant and annoying as you?"

He laughed. "Beats the hell out of me."

She turned and left the apartment, wondering exactly the same thing.

--=➤➤◄◄◄=--

Emma opened her door, wearing yoga pants, a tank top and a tired smile. "I had a feeling I'd be seeing you today, Kate. Come in."

"Did you get any sleep?" Kate asked, as she entered

Emma's apartment.

"A few hours. I was just making a salad for lunch. Do you want something to eat?"

"No, thanks, I just ate." She smiled at the tall, dark-haired man who was sitting at the kitchen table, a laptop in front of him. "Hi, Max."

Emma's husband got up and gave her a hug. "Kate, nice to see you. It's been awhile."

"Since Burke's wedding, I think."

"And now you're back for your sister's wedding. At least, all this love going around keeps the family in contact," he drawled.

"It does do that," she agreed.

"Have a seat," he said. "Emma has kept me up to date on what's going on. I've also been looking into Rick Baines for you. Emma suggested that there might be a connection between the recent fire at St. Bernadette's and some of Baines's former classmates."

She nodded. "We went through the yearbooks, found a couple of people who were in pictures with Mr. Baines, but unfortunately they have not been easy to locate. What did you find out?"

"Not a lot. I went through the old case files, read some of the initial interviews conducted both by the police department and the FBI. I decided to make a few calls and follow up on some of those witnesses, see if anyone remembers anything differently a year later."

She was surprised Max had taken things so far but she really shouldn't be. When family was involved, the Callaways went the extra step. Max might only be a Callaway by marriage, but he'd been around long enough to know the drill. "Who did you talk to?" she asked.

"Malcolm Homer. He was one of the four men who lived with Baines. He's since moved out of that apartment and lives in a studio. He said that he barely knew Baines. They'd occasionally talk while making coffee in the morning. The only friend he remembered Baines talking about was an old high school friend."

"Did he give a name?"

Max shook his head. "No, but he said that Baines had a new energy about him in the weeks before his death, that he said something about his old friend reminding him of his dream of becoming a firefighter, so he was looking into it again. He wanted to get out of the gym and get the job he'd always wanted."

Emma joined them at the table with her salad. "That's not news, Max. That's why everyone latched on to Rick Baines as the arsonist. He had recently applied for the fire academy and rejected firefighters are often part of an arson profile."

"That's true," Kate said. "But I'm more interested in who the high school friend was, because I think he could be the key."

"The roommate told me that Baines used to go to a bar called Rebel, Rebel in the Mission," Max said. "I haven't had a chance to check it out yet, but that might be a place for you to start."

Her pulse leapt. "That's great. Devin and I will go by there today. Thanks, Max. It's been rough trying to cover so much ground with just Devin and myself."

"Hey, I'm helping, too," Emma protested.

"I know. I'm thrilled to have both of you on the team. What can you tell me about how the fire started last night, Em?"

"The ignition was similar to the other fires—gasoline, rags—and this building had the added advantage of having a lot of those materials already inside," Emma replied.

"Was there anything found at the fire? A St. Christopher's medal perhaps?"

"No. But I'm going back there this afternoon to take another look." Emma paused. "I know the building was on Devin's target list. He was on the money."

"We were at the right building, wrong street. So close and yet not close enough. It's so frustrating."

"How is Devin feeling today?" Emma asked.

"He's angry with himself for losing the chase."

"What about his head injury? Your text messages were a little frightening."

"He just had some bruising. The airbag saved his life. He's going to be fine."

"I'm glad he didn't get more seriously hurt."

"Me, too. We're running the partial plate, but we haven't found anything close to a lead yet. The one thing we know for sure is that there's going to be another fire, and it's going to be bigger and more destructive."

Emma's lips tightened into a hard line. "Has Devin worked up a list of targets for the third fire?"

"He's doing that today. The last fire in every trio has occurred within a week of the preceding fire. We don't have a lot of time."

"Then we all better get back to work," Emma said. "I was thinking that Devin's partner, Agent Parker, obviously figured something out. How else would she have gotten to the house where she died? What was the clue she found that no one else has been able to find?"

"Devin has been asking those questions since she died," Kate replied. "He told me that she was on her own most of that day and whatever she'd discovered, she'd probably learned it right before she went to the house. She texted him the address and left him a voicemail that said they'd been wrong about the profile, but that was it. When he got to the house, it was too late."

Emma nodded, a gleam of compassionate understanding in her eyes. "No wonder he's so driven to find her killer. He feels responsible."

"He does. We all understand why. We've worked with partners. We know that the bond goes deep. We're supposed to be there to watch each other's back. And while I can see that Agent Parker went off on her own and didn't include Devin in whatever she was looking into, all Devin sees is an angry wave of guilt. The only way he's going to get free of it is to find the real killer." She let out a sigh. "But Sam will still be dead. Anger has been fueling Devin the past eighteen months. I worry about what will happen to him when he doesn't have an investigation to conduct."

"He's not your responsibility, Kate. You barely know him. Or have you gotten closer?" Emma asked.

There was a teasing light in Emma's eyes, but Kate didn't feel like talking about last night with anyone, not even her cousin. "I've gotten close enough to respect and admire his relentless devotion to find justice for his former partner."

"But you can't let this guy's mission become yours," Max put in. "I know what guilt feels like. Believe me, I've experienced guilt on a lot of levels over the years, but not all of it really belonged to me."

"I know you're both right. It's just difficult not to feel compassion when you can see how much pain someone is in."

"You don't sound like a hard-hearted FBI agent right now," Emma said with a smile.

"I'm still a work in progress," she admitted. "I know I have to get tougher."

"Don't get too tough," Max said. "Compassion and

understanding can be good investigative tools." He got to his feet. "On that note, I actually have to go to work. I have another case to look into."

"Thanks again for your help, Max."

"Hey, whatever I can do, I'm happy to do." He gave Emma a kiss. "See you later, babe."

"Bye," Emma said.

As Emma's gaze followed her husband out the door, Kate smiled. "You are still so in love, you can't take your eyes off him. It's very cute."

Emma smiled back at her. "He's hot. I like to look at him."

"Well, he's all yours."

"I told him, Kate, about the miscarriage."

"I'm glad you're not carrying that burden alone."

"It did feel better. He was a little rattled, but Max is good at bouncing back. And he helped me bounce back, too. We're not going to give up."

"I'm glad to hear it. You have lots of time, too."

"I know. I think watching everyone else in the family get pregnant got me a little too focused on babies. I'm happy with my job, and it wouldn't hurt me to work on my career for a while. When kids come along, I'll be further ahead in my job and it will be easier to take time off."

"That sounds very logical."

"And very much like Max. Those were pretty much his words," Emma said with a laugh. "But he's right. He usually is, dammit. Anyway, thanks for giving me the kick in the butt to talk to him about it."

"I'm surprised Nicole or Shayla didn't do that. Your sisters don't usually hold back."

"I haven't told them. I didn't want to bum anyone out. No one else needs to know."

"Okay, my lips are sealed." She pushed back her chair and stood up. "I should get going. There's a lot to do. We need to figure out the next target, and I need to get this case wrapped up before Mia arrives and the wedding festivities begin."

"That's a lot of ticking clocks."

"Too many. I don't want to let Devin down, but I also cannot let Mia down. When my boss sent me out here, he told me to give Devin five days of my time, but how can I walk away now?"

"I don't think you can, and not just because of the case. Because of him." Emma met her gaze. "Just be careful, Kate, and I'm not just talking about fire danger; I'm talking about your heart. You're involved with him. I can see it on your face."

"My heart is fine," she said, hoping that was true. "And I can handle our…involvement."

"I hope so."

She hoped so, too, but she didn't have time to worry about that now. She was more concerned that time was running out, and she did not want to have to choose between Devin and her family.

——»«——

Devin glanced at his watch, and then turned his attention back to his computer, annoyed that his thoughts kept drifting to Kate. It wasn't just that he wanted to know what she was finding out from Emma, but also because he couldn't stop thinking about her.

He couldn't remember the last time a woman had distracted him so much.

Kate was going to be hard to forget.

But he would have to forget her, because she would

move on, and so would he.

Just not quite yet.

The front door opened, and his pulse jumped as he heard her come down the hall.

"Hey," she said, entering the room. She gave him a smile as she set her bag on the table and sat down across from him. "How's it going?"

"It's going," he said with a shrug. "No hits on the partial plate. I've managed to get one of my friends at SFPD to check traffic cameras along the route of my chase yesterday. Hoping the car and complete plate were captured."

"That would be a break."

"Did you learn anything from your cousin?"

"She said the fire was started like all the rest of them. There was no St. Christopher's medal, but she's going back to the scene later today. She'd like us to text her a list of potential targets for the third fire. Have you been working on that?"

He nodded. "I have. We can go over them. Did she say anything else?"

"Not really. But Emma got her husband Max involved. I told you he's a police detective. He decided to re-interviewed a former roommate of Baines's, Malcolm Homer."

"I remember Homer. He had nothing of interest to say. None of the roommates did."

"Well, Max asked him specifically about any contacts Baines might have mentioned from high school, following up on the St. Bernadette's connection. I guess that wasn't a question anyone asked before."

Devin frowned. "Probably not. We definitely weren't thinking about friendships going that far back."

"Mr. Homer said that Baines had mentioned running

into a high school friend and that the friend had reminded him how much he'd wanted to be a firefighter. After they started talking again, Baines applied for the fire academy. Mr. Homer also said that Baines was in a good mood in the few weeks before he died, implying that this old friend had reinvigorated him in some way."

"I assume you didn't get a name of this friend."

"No. But Malcolm did say that Baines went to meet his friend at a bar called Rebel, Rebel in the Mission. I don't remember seeing that bar on the list of places visited during the initial investigation."

"First I've heard of it."

"I think we should go down there and show Baines's picture around and see if anyone remembers him and who he might have been with. I know there's a lot to do and maybe that's a wild-goose chase, but—"

"But it's worth a trip," he said with a nod. "Let's go now. We can look over the targets when we get back."

"I rented a car," she added. "So I can drive us."

"Great. I hadn't gotten around to that yet. You can expense it to the Bureau." He grinned. "Hal would love that."

"I'll figure it out later."

He felt better now that she was back, now that she was giving him ideas, and pepping him up with her positive attitude and energized smile.

He'd always been able to self-motivate, even through the long months when nothing had been going on. But lately, he'd been feeling the strain of fighting a solo battle, and it felt damn good to have her on his team, even if she was distracting him beyond belief. She still definitely brought more good than bad with her.

Rebel, Rebel was a hipster bar in the trendy part of town known as the Mission. During the day it was a bar and grill, serving lunch and early dinner. By nine at night the club turned into a music venue showing some of the hottest acts in town.

When they arrived, it was a little before four, and there were only about six patrons in the bar.

Devin was fine with the empty nature of the club. The young male bartender looked bored as he wiped down the counter.

"Hello," Kate said, giving the bartender a smile.

Devin couldn't help but notice how the man straightened and brightened as he took in just how pretty his new customer was.

"What can I get you?" the bartender asked.

"I'll take a beer. Devin?"

"Make that two." He slid onto the barstool next to her, giving her a subtle nod to take the lead. She had the bartender's attention, and there was no doubt in his mind that Kate could work this guy better than he could, so he was going to let her.

As the man set down two beer glasses, Kate said, "I was wondering if you might answer a few questions."

The bartender tensed. "About?"

"A customer. How long have you worked here?"

"Going on three years. Are you a cop?"

Kate pulled out her badge. "FBI."

"Whoa. I did not expect that," the bartender said. "I was almost going to card you."

"I'm definitely of age. The man's name was Rick Baines. He was killed in a fire eighteen months ago. We heard he used to come in here with some of his friends." She pulled out her phone and opened up a photo of Rick.

"Do you recognize him?"

"Sure," the bartender said, barely glancing at the picture. "I knew Rick."

"Did you know any of his friends?" Kate asked.

"Some of them. Alan Jenkins was a regular. He and Rick came in here a few times. But I heard Alan moved away." The bartender paused, his gazed narrowing. "I thought Rick torched some building and died in the fire. Are you saying Alan was involved? Because Alan told me he had no idea that Rick would do something like that."

Devin thought it was interesting that Alan and the bartender had actually spoken about the fire. "Did Alan come in here after the fire?" he asked.

"Yeah. He was messed up about Rick's death. He couldn't stop talking about it. He said it was ironic that Rick had died in a fire when he'd wanted so badly to be a firefighter."

"Did anyone else come in here with Alan and Rick?" Devin asked.

"I don't know. There definitely were other people around. There were a couple of good-looking women at their table one night. I never got their names."

"Anyone else stand out in your mind?"

A light entered the bartender's eyes. "There was another woman. She was serious looking, like a businesswoman or a cop. She met Rick the day of the fire."

Devin's gut tightened as a really bad feeling swept over him. "What did she look like?"

"Brown hair pulled back. Brown eyes. She walked in, said something to Rick and then they walked out. I remember wondering if Rick was in some kind of trouble, because she had a law enforcement vibe."

Devin reached into his pocket, his heart pounding

against his chest as impossible thoughts ran through his brain. He took out his phone and opened his photos. He pulled up the one of Sam that he looked at every time he felt guilty, every time he vowed to get her justice.

He slowly turned the phone so the bartender could see it, and through tight lips, he got out three important words. "Was this her?"

"Devin," Kate murmured, but his attention was on the bartender.

"Yeah, that's her," the guy said. "Who is she?"

Devin turned the phone so Kate could see the photo.

She sucked in a quick breath.

"She's an FBI agent," Devin said. "And she died in the fire with Baines."

Sixteen

—➤➤◆◆◄—

"I'm sorry," the bartender said, looking a little pale. "I guess I remember someone else was killed in the fire, but I didn't know who it was."

"Why didn't you tell the police any of this?" Kate asked.

"No one came here. No one asked me. I didn't know I knew anything," the bartender said nervously. "Why are you asking me all these questions now?"

"We're trying to find the person who killed Rick and this agent," Devin said, putting the phone back in his pocket.

"You mean Rick didn't set the fire?"

"We're trying to figure that out," Kate said.

"Do you remember anything else?" Devin pressed. "Something that maybe didn't seem significant at the time but now might be important?"

"I don't think so. Sorry."

Kate slid her card across the bar. "You've been very helpful. If you think of anything else, or if anyone comes into this bar who you saw with Rick, please call me, and see if you can get their names, phone numbers."

"Sure, of course, but I don't think I've seen any of his crowd in a long time."

Devin took a swig of his beer as the bartender moved down the counter to help another customer. He was still rattled by the information they'd received.

Sam had met with Baines here—before they'd gone to the house—before they died. Why hadn't she told him about Baines? About the meeting?

"Are you ready to go?" Kate asked.

He nodded, following her out of the bar. "Sam never mentioned Rick Baines to me," he said, as he got into the car. "She never said she had a meeting here or anywhere else."

"I figured she didn't, or you would have come here before."

"I can't believe Baines's roommate didn't tell me Rick liked to come to this bar. He'd obviously been here a few times."

"The roommate didn't know it was important."

"But I asked each one of those roommates where Baines spent his time outside of work. I was never given the name of this bar."

She gave him a helpless shrug. "I don't know what to say, Devin. Witnesses can be unreliable."

"You should say I screwed up."

"You didn't. I know you went back and re-interviewed the roommates a month after the fire. You can't force someone to tell you something."

"I should have gone back again, but I thought they were a dead end."

"The only reason Max went back to them this week was because we found the link between Baines and St. Bernadette's, Devin. And Max was curious to hear about Rick Baines from someone who knew him. He was trying to get a handle on the case. And before you say we should have immediately gone to talk to the roommates again after we discovered the link, can I just remind you that we've been pretty busy chasing down a lot of different leads in the past few days?"

"It's all just excuses."

"Whatever," she said in annoyance. "Look, Devin, you be angry later, but the time we waste on you mentally kicking yourself is not getting us anywhere."

Kate had a way of delivering a pep talk and a smackdown all at the same time, something he both admired and found irritating, usually because she was right.

He couldn't turn back the clock; he could only move on from here. "I can't figure out how Sam and Baines came into contact with each other in the first place," he said. "Did he reach out to her? Did she reach out to him? And if she did, how did she get to him?"

"I don't know, but the meeting between them at the bar before the fire changes everything. Either Rick lured her to the bar and then to the house, or they were working together in some way."

"They could have been working together," he said slowly, a theory gathering steam in his head. "Baines wanted to be a firefighter, but he'd been rejected. Maybe he wanted to show he was a hero, that he could stop an arsonist in his tracks. I know that sounds a little out there, but it's possible he reached out to Sam."

"I can see the logic to that."

"We need more than logic; we need proof."

"Baby steps."

"I am tired of baby steps," he said with a groan.

"I know. So what's next? We have about ninety minutes before the book signing and fundraiser. Shall we go back to the apartment? Or is there someone else you want to talk to?"

He thought for a moment, his mind racing in a dozen different directions. Should he seek out Malcolm Homer? The other roommates? Someone else?

"I don't know. I need to think," he said. "I need to make a plan. I'm still in shock that Sam met with Baines."

"It's a lot to take in," she agreed. "Why don't we grab some food and talk it out before the book signing?"

"We could do that."

"Do you like Chinese food? I can take you to one of my favorite restaurants in Chinatown."

He nodded. "That sounds good."

Fifteen minutes later, they entered the Golden Dragon. Despite the magnificence of its name, the restaurant was hidden away down an alley and did not look like much from the outside, but it was obviously a local favorite, as it was already crowded at five thirty on a Saturday night.

The host greeted Kate with a smile and a hug and quickly escorted them into the dining room, past the line of people waiting to be seated.

"That was a nice reception," Devin said, as they sat down. "What strings did you pull?"

"None. My father pulled all the strings for the entire family a long time ago. He saved the owner's family in a fire. Ever since then, there's always an open table, or Ben pulls one out of the back room for us. The food is excellent, too, by the way. What looks good to you?"

He glanced down at the menu, but the words were just a blur. "Why don't you order for both of us? My brain is fried."

She gave him a sympathetic smile. "Okay, I've got it." After Kate ordered dinner, she turned back to him.

"It's hard to know what to do next. Do we zero in on Baines and his past relationships? Do we focus on the potential targets? Do we try to chase down security footage of the car you were following?"

"All good questions. I wish I had answers. After the fire, we talked to everyone who had a connection to Baines. About a month later, I made the rounds again and came up with nothing for a second time," he said, once again feeling frustrated by the lack of progress he'd made on the case despite the amount of time he'd put in. "We can go through the list one more time and see if anyone besides Malcolm has had a renewed burst of memory, but that's going to take time, and the arsonist will strike again within a few days." He tapped his fingers restlessly on the tabletop. "I can't decide if it's better to look at the targets and figure out where the arsonist is hitting next or re-interview everyone."

"Since there are two of us, maybe we can do a little of both." She paused. "Putting aside the old roommates and Baines, let's talk about the book signing. We know that Dillingsworth and Gerilyn Connors will probably be there. Can we tie them in any way to Baines?"

"I don't see any connection. They're not close to the same age group." He thought for a moment. "Unless it's the firefighter link."

"Between Brad Connors and Baines or Dillingsworth and Connors?"

"Both." He met her gaze. "It's a stretch, but it's possible that Baines and Connors could have met because of Baines's interest in firefighting. The high school counselor said that Baines shadowed at a firehouse."

"How long ago was Connors fired for substance abuse problems?" she asked.

"Four years."

"The fires started five years ago."

"I know that doesn't match up. But I believe he was a firefighter for over ten years, which would have put him in a firehouse while Baines was in high school." He paused as the waiter set down their food. "This looks good."

"Broccoli beef, cashew chicken, and vegetable chow mein. I hope you like it," Kate said.

"I'm sure I will."

As he ate, his mind continued to process the information he'd gotten at the bar. By the time he'd cleaned his plate, he was feeling full but still restless. "We're missing something," he said to Kate.

"I feel the same way. There's something we're not seeing, but I don't know what it is."

"I should know. I've been thinking about nothing but this case for eighteen months."

"Maybe you're too close, both to the victim and to the case."

"Close, not close enough...what's the difference? I still don't have any answers, and I have one shot left to catch this guy before he goes underground again. He knows someone is on to him, whether he knows exactly who is another question, but there was no doubt that he was aware he was being chased."

"I wonder how that will change his behavior," she mused. "Maybe it's good we're out there, being very visible. If Baines possibly reached out to Sam with information about the arsonist, maybe someone else will do the same thing with us."

"That would be a miracle." He paused. "I know. You believe in miracles."

"I do believe, but I don't wait for them to happen. I try to make my own luck."

"Well, I'd like to think we could shake another Good Samaritan loose, but considering what happened to Rick Baines, I doubt anyone is going to come rushing to help us."

"Good point. There's still a reward, isn't there?"

"Yes. It's still there."

"Maybe we need to publicize it again."

"That's a thought." But he wasn't convinced publicity or a reward was going to be enough. He glanced at his watch. "Let's go to the book signing. We've moved a little away from Dillingsworth and Connors, but I still think it's a huge coincidence that they're both involved in the same event. I'd like to see how they interact with each other."

"And hopefully we can get one or both of them to talk to us."

—➤➤◄◄◄—

Market Lane Books took up the entire first floor of a three-story, turn-of-the-century building whose décor had been inspired by the Gold Rush. While the exterior of the building was gray granite, the interior boasted mahogany walls, porcelain-tiled floors, and carved marble pillars. But the opulent architecture and design was definitely showing signs of age and strain, Kate thought, noting serious cracks in the marble and gouges in the floor, hence the fundraiser to restore the building to its former glory.

"This must have been magnificent in its day," she said to Devin as they wandered around the tall shelves of books. The aisles were crowded with the San Francisco elite, who appeared to be more interested in mingling and sipping on champagne than talking about books. She suspected that most of the attendees were not actually readers but probably more interested in being at the fashionable fundraiser, which was hosted not only by Gerilyn Connors's architectural firm but also the mayor's office.

"It's a cool space," Devin commented, his gaze fixed on the man signing books at the front of the store. "Let's get in line."

"We can't ask Ron Dillingsworth questions in an autographing line," she said. "Let's wait until he's done and catch him then." She glanced down at the program she'd been given. "It says here the signing will go until eight. That's twenty minutes from now."

"He could disappear right after. We might miss our chance."

"We'll block him. Don't worry. We won't let him go without a conversation."

"All right." His gaze swept the room, and he tensed. "Brad Connors is here."

"Really? I thought he and Gerilyn had a bitter divorce. Why would he be here?"

"No idea. At one point, Gerilyn had a restraining order against Brad."

"They look pretty friendly tonight," she said, following his gaze.

Brad Connors appeared to be in his mid-forties. He had sandy brown hair and a thick moustache. His build was sturdy and solid. He looked like a man who'd be comfortable rushing opponents on a football field. According to the bio Devin had worked up on him, that's exactly what he'd done until he was about twenty-five-years old. Then he'd gone into firefighting and had excelled at the job until a growing problem with drugs and alcohol eventually ended his marriage and his career.

"Let's say hello," Devin said.

She had a feeling it wasn't going to be a friendly hello, but she followed Devin across the room. Devin had interviewed Brad and Gerilyn after Sam's death, and judging by the way the couple tensed when they saw Devin, the memory of those interviews was not a good one.

"What are you doing here?" Brad demanded. He then turned to glare at his ex-wife. "Did you know he was coming?"

"No, of course not," Gerilyn said nervously.

Gerilyn was a thin woman with blonde hair and brown eyes. She wore a form-fitting sheath dress with heels and gave Devin a wary look. "Why are you here?"

"I like books about fires," he said.

"You need to leave," Brad said. "This is my wife's event."

"Don't you mean your ex-wife?" Devin asked.

Brad put his arm around his wife's shoulders. "We've reconciled."

"And we don't want any more trouble," Gerilyn added.

"There was another fire last night," Devin said. "At a recreation center. And last Monday, there was a fire at a school. The arsonist is back in business."

"There are fires every day in this city," Brad said. "They don't have anything to do with us."

"Did you know Rick Baines?" Devin asked.

"The arsonist?" Gerilyn asked.

"The man who was killed with my partner was not the arsonist," Devin replied.

"I thought the case was closed," Gerilyn said.

"It's not," Kate said, stepping forward. "I'm Kate Callaway—"

"Callaway?" Brad interrupted. "Are you related to

Jack Callaway?"

"I'm his niece."

"Then you should have more respect for a firefighter."

"I have nothing but respect for firefighters," she returned. "But I'm also a special agent with the FBI. We've reopened the arson case. Devin is helping me get up to speed. That's why we're here. I wanted to talk to you."

"Well, let me help get you up to speed," Brad said aggressively. "I used to be a firefighter. I had a lot of problems with my wife and her job, and that made me do things I'm not proud of. Those things did not include torching the buildings she was working on. Understood?" He didn't wait for an answer. "Now I'm sober, and I have been for the last six months. I'm turning my life around. I'm back with Gerilyn, and we are moving on from the past. I was not guilty before and I am not guilty now. Whatever suspicious fires have occurred in the last week have nothing to do with me."

He sounded sincere, Kate thought. He'd acknowledged his bad behavior and made a point of how he'd turned his life around. It was a solid argument.

"Brad is a changed man," Gerilyn added. "I'm sorry I ever implied that he could be guilty of burning down those buildings, because he had nothing to do with any of that. I know you're just doing your job, but Brad is innocent, and he's working hard on his life."

Gerilyn could be blinded by love, but Kate was inclined to believe her, too. She did, however, have one other question. "It's interesting to me that you're hosting this event with Ron Dillingsworth, a person who is also of interest in the arson investigation. It's an odd coincidence."

"He's a bestselling local author. This is a bookstore. We're trying to raise money so we can save this building," Gerilyn said. "There's nothing more to it than that. I didn't know he was a suspect in the case."

"I'm fairly sure you did know that," Devin said. "We had several conversations about who could be involved, and Mr. Dillingsworth was mentioned more than once."

"Ron is an author. He writes books."

"About fire," Devin reminded her.

"They're fiction," Gerilyn said, a worried look in her eyes. "I don't know why this is still going on. I thought it was over."

"It's not going to be over until the right person is in jail," Devin said.

"Let's go," Brad interrupted. "If you have any other questions, you can speak to our lawyer." He took his wife's hand and led Gerilyn away.

Devin blew out a breath, his expression grim. "I do not like him."

"I don't like him, either, but I kind of believe him," she said.

Devin frowned. "You do? Why?"

"Gut feeling."

"Well, I'm not ready to check him off the list just yet." He paused, his gaze moving toward the front of the store. "Dillingsworth has run out of books. Let's head over there."

Devin was definitely a man on a mission, Kate thought, hurrying behind him as he made a beeline for the dark-haired, bearded author with the glasses.

Dillingsworth was just getting up from his chair when he saw Devin. He froze as if he'd suddenly been trapped, his gaze darting toward the nearest exit.

"Mr. Dillingsworth," Devin said. "Good to see you

again."

"Agent Scott. Wait, that's incorrect. You're no longer an agent, are you?" Dillingsworth asked, quickly regaining his composure.

"He's not, but I am," Kate said. "Special Agent Kate Callaway. Could we speak to you for a moment?"

"I'm afraid I'm just leaving. Any questions you have should be directed to my lawyer."

"There was a fire last night, Mr. Dillingsworth, but you probably already know that, don't you?" Devin asked. "You like to follow fires, show up at them, and watch the firefighters risk their lives."

"That's called research," Dillingsworth said sharply. "Any good writer does his research. But, no, I wasn't at any fires in the city last night. I was in New York. I arrived this morning just before noon. I'm sure the airlines would be happy to verify my travel information."

"We'll be sure to check," Devin said.

"Excuse me, Mr. Dillingsworth, we're ready for a few pictures," a young woman from the bookstore said, interrupting their conversation.

"Of course," he said.

As he walked away, Devin let out a sigh. "If he has an alibi for last night, then he's off the list."

"Anything that narrows down the suspect list is a good thing," she said.

"Mr. Scott?"

Devin turned around as an older, stylishly dressed female joined them. "Mrs. Raffin," he said.

"I can't say I'm surprised to see you here. I heard about the fire at the park on the news this morning. You told us there were more fires coming. Is this what you meant?"

He nodded. "Yes. As you know, the fires come in

threes, and the first two occurred in the past week, which means the third is coming soon."

Her eyes filled with concern. "You're saying that someone is going to go after another one of our historic buildings?"

"I believe so. This is Special Agent Kate Callaway. She's working on the case now as well. This is Eileen Raffin."

"It's nice to meet you," Kate said, shaking hands with the woman. "I understand you do interior design and that you work with Gerilyn Connors."

"I do, and I'm very passionate about our historic buildings. In my spare time, I serve on the Historic Preservation Commission. These fires are very disturbing. I thought they were over, but I guess not." She paused, her gaze darting around the room as if she were looking for someone. "You don't still suspect Brad, do you? He moved back in with Gerilyn, you know."

"I was surprised to hear that," Devin said. "When did that happen?"

"A few weeks ago. She told me he's changed, and he told me the same thing. She's convinced he's sober now."

"It doesn't sound like you're convinced," Kate said.

"I don't know what to think. Brad is a volatile person. I don't enjoy being around him, but I do care about Gerilyn. I want her to be happy. If there is anything she needs to know about Brad, you need to tell her."

"We don't have any evidence against him," Kate said.

"Well, I guess that's good," Eileen said. "Did you come here tonight to talk to Gerilyn?"

"And Mr. Dillingsworth," Devin put in. "I had no idea that Gerilyn knew Mr. Dillingsworth."

"She doesn't know him," Eileen said. "I put the book signing together. We were talking about local authors, and my daughter is a big fan of his books. He's gotten very popular, so I asked him if he would come and give us an hour." Eileen paused, suddenly looking worried. "I know that he was interviewed about the fires, but he's a writer. He's a celebrity. His books are on the *New York Times* Bestseller List. He doesn't set fires; he just writes about them. I had no idea that his being here would cause any problems."

"It hasn't," Kate said.

"We also wanted to talk to you," Devin said. "We're looking at potential targets for the next fire, and you have the most knowledge of anyone I know about the historic structures in the city."

"I am always happy to help. I'll be in my office Monday if you want to come by and go over your list. I have no idea if I'll be able to give you any solid information, but I'll try."

"That would be great," Devin said.

"I should probably go and mingle, try to get some people to open up their wallets, so we can restore this building to its original glory."

"It is an amazing space," Kate said.

"You'll have to come back when it's done. Then it will be truly spectacular. If you'll excuse me..."

As Eileen left, Kate turned to Devin. "Eileen Raffin doesn't trust Brad as much as Gerilyn does."

"I got that impression, too. But she does love Mr. Dillingsworth. She sounded like a big fan."

"So who should we talk to next? Is there anyone else here?"

He looked around the room. "I don't think so. We can follow up on the alibi Dillingsworth gave us. Beyond that, we didn't get much."

"We did get Brad's attention. He knows we've

reopened the investigation, and he's not happy about it."

"Gerilyn isn't, either," he said. "I can't believe she took him back. Actually, I can believe it. Like I told you the first day we met, love is blind."

"I don't think it needs to be. But rather than get into a philosophical discussion about love, let's go back to your apartment and start working up the target list."

"All right," he said, weariness in his eyes.

"Are you okay, Devin? Is your head hurting?" He'd downplayed his bruised head, but she suspected he'd been fighting off a killer headache all day.

"It's fine. Let's go."

As they turned to leave, she realized their exit was blocked. "Oh, no," she said in dismay.

"What's wrong?" Devin asked.

"I'm busted."

"Why?"

Before she could speak, her name rang out, and a pretty redhead and a tall, dark-haired man with blue eyes came up to them.

"Kate, what on earth are you doing here?"

"Hi, Mom—Dad." She looked at Devin. "These are my parents."

Seventeen

‑‑‑►≫◄◄‑‑

He could see the family resemblance. Kate had her father's blue eyes and her mother's warm and curious smile.

"This is Devin Scott," Kate added. "He's a former FBI agent. Sharon and Tim Callaway."

"Nice to meet you both." He shook Tim's hand and then received a hug from Sharon.

"It's nice to meet you, too," Sharon said with a very interested smile. She turned to her daughter. "What are you doing here, Kate? I thought you weren't going to be able to come home until Wednesday."

"Surprise," Kate said a little weakly.

Her mother raised an eyebrow. "What's going on?"

Kate licked her lips, and he could see her hesitation. She hadn't asked for his help, but he decided to throw her a lifeline.

"It's my fault," he said. "I asked Kate to come home early, so I could see her before she got busy with the wedding."

"Oh," Sharon said, her gaze turning more speculative. "So you two are…"

"Dating," he finished, ignoring Kate's warning look. *If she didn't like his story, she should have come up with one of her own more quickly.*

"Why didn't you tell me you were dating someone?" Sharon asked.

"It's new," Kate said. "There was nothing to tell. I was going to call you."

"Where are you staying, or should I ask?" Sharon enquired.

"I'm staying at Ian's," she said. "Don't get mad at him. I asked him not to tell you."

"Why is it a secret? I don't know if I like the way the FBI is turning you into such a cagey person, Kate."

"I told her she should come clean," Devin interjected. "And I'm glad you're here, because I really wanted to meet you. Kate has told me a lot about her family, but, of course, I want to know more."

"We want to get to know you, too," Sharon said. "Don't we, Tim?" She slipped her arm through her husband's.

Tim seemed amused by the entire exchange. "Absolutely."

"So you'll come to brunch tomorrow," Sharon said. "It's at our house this week. The whole family will be there."

"Oh, I don't know…" Kate began.

Her mother waved off her answer. "It's just brunch, Kate. You and Devin will have plenty of alone time before and after."

"But I'm going to see all the family at the wedding, so—"

"So you'll see them tomorrow, too," Sharon said. "Right, Devin?"

He now realized he'd opened a door that probably

should have stayed closed. "Whatever Kate wants."

"That's what I like to hear," Sharon said with an approving nod. "A man who puts my daughter first." She paused. "Are you two sticking around? Shall we get drinks?"

"No, we were just leaving," Kate said quickly.

"Then we'll see you both tomorrow." Sharon gave him a pointed look. "I'm looking forward to getting to know you better, Devin."

"Me, too," he said.

"Why did you say we were dating?" Kate asked as her parents left.

"You needed an excuse for why you were in town early; I gave you one."

"You gave me a lie, and you got us invited to brunch."

"We don't have to go."

"Are you kidding? If we don't go, my mother will hunt us down."

"You can go."

"Oh, no, not just me. You started this. You're going to finish it. When you get swarmed at brunch tomorrow by more than a dozen Callaways, you will remember this is all your fault."

So maybe teasing Kate and making up a story for her mom wasn't the best idea he'd ever had. On the other hand, as her mother had said, it was just brunch. "I think we can get through it. Don't worry, I'll be good."

"I'm not worried that you won't be good; I'm concerned you'll be too good. My mother would love to see me with a boyfriend."

"Really? Even though you just started working a big job?"

"She thinks I can have it all."

"Maybe you can."

She shook her head. "I don't think so."

He found himself wanting to change her mind, which was surprising and disturbing, because her future relationships were not his business.

"Let's get out of here," she said, heading across the room. As they left the bookstore, she added, "Why, oh why, did my parents have to be there?"

"They seemed nice."

"They are nice. They're just really nosy—at least my mom is. I hope you're ready for a grilling, because there won't just be steak on the barbecue tomorrow; there will be you and me and our fake relationship."

He laughed as they got into the car. "I can handle it. I promise to be an excellent fake boyfriend."

"Do you even know how to be a boyfriend?" she asked dryly, as she started the engine and pulled away from the curb.

"Enough to fake it."

"Have you met anyone's parents?"

"I've been in a few living rooms," he said with a smile. "I've talked to some dads. I've made a few promises regarding a few daughters."

"Did you keep your promises?"

"I think so. I tried. Those daughters were never quite as innocent as their fathers thought they were."

"That's probably true," she agreed. "Daughters don't tell their dads a lot, no matter how close they are. Moms are a different story. Even when I try to be more private, my mom somehow gets information out of me. I told her she probably would have made a good interrogator. She has great skills."

"That's because she knows you."

"Too well. Maybe that's the way it is with mothers.

They know their kids better than anyone."

"Not all mothers," he muttered, then wished he'd kept silent, because Kate's gaze swung in his direction.

"I feel like you need to mend that relationship, Devin. Not now," she added quickly. "I know you can't focus on anything else, but after...sometime soon."

"I told you we're fine. Let's get back to your parents. Why do you think they were at the signing? Are they Dillingsworth fans?"

Kate stopped at a light and looked at him. "Good question. I don't think so. My dad doesn't read any fiction, and my mom reads romance. I wouldn't think Dillingsworth's books would appeal to her. I guess I should have asked them." She frowned, then drove through the intersection. "They got me so flustered, I didn't think to ask them questions. I will say they're very well-connected in the city. They both have a ton of friends, and they go to a lot of events, so it's probably just that they knew someone who asked them to come."

"That makes sense." He paused. "There's a parking spot down on the right."

"I see it."

"Is it possible your father knows Brad Connors from his firefighting days?" he asked, as she parked the car.

She nodded. "Very possible. The fire department is a close-knit group. I'll ask him tomorrow." Her expression changed as she turned to face him. "But Devin, I don't want them involved in this case. I can't have my parents mixed up in my professional life."

He understood her reasoning. When he'd been with the Bureau, he'd distanced himself from not just family but friends. There were too many things he couldn't talk about, too many secrets he had to protect, too many bad things that he couldn't share. "I get it, Kate."

"Good." Relief filled her eyes. "It's not that I don't trust them."

"I know. It's that you love them. It's not going to be easy for you," he said, shaking his head. "Not with the kind of family you have. There's so much love, affection, connection between you all. You're going to want them in your life, and they're going to want to be in your life."

"They understand there are boundaries. When it comes to the important things, they won't press."

"Sometimes the boundaries become walls, big ones, hard to get over—no matter which side of the wall you're on. You forget why you built the walls. Was it to protect them or to protect yourself? It gets fuzzy."

Her concerned blue gaze held his. "Is that what happened to you, Devin? Is that why you're so isolated? Why you can't remember the last time you talked to a friend or a family member?"

"Partly that and partly the case," he said, wishing he hadn't been so honest with her, but Kate, like her mother, was also very good at getting information out of people.

"But there's always a case, right? So when do the walls come down?"

"They don't. That's my point. You're just starting out. You think you can compartmentalize, put different parts of your life into different boxes, but eventually you start to realize that can't happen, because everything blurs together. Sometimes your whole life is a lie; the people you meet, live with, talk to. They don't know who you are. Eventually, you can forget who you really are, too."

"Then I'll have to remember to keep people around me who know me, who can remind me, who can see past the lies and through the walls. Who don't let me pretend, because they know I need to be honest with someone."

She wasn't talking about herself anymore; she was

talking about him, and his heart beat a little too fast, which was getting to be a normal occurrence when it came to Kate.

"I'm coming in," she told him.

He looked into her eyes and felt like he was standing on the edge of a cliff. There was a big part of him that thought he should send her away but then another part of him that asked if it was completely insane to think of telling her to go.

Just because she thought she could strip down his walls didn't mean she actually could. He could handle her. He had more years, more experience, more practice at self-preservation.

"Of course you're coming in," he said, opening his car door.

He didn't really remember how they got from the car and into his apartment, because his blood was rushing out of his brain to other parts of his body. But as soon as the front door slammed behind him, they were in each other's arms.

They kissed their way down the hallway, taking only quick second breaks to strip off their clothing. By the time they fell onto the bed, they were completely naked. He ran his hands over her curves—her shoulders, breasts, hips—and down her thighs as he followed the same path with his mouth. He wanted her to take everything he had to give, but Kate seemed to have other plans.

She put a hand against his chest and then pushed him back against the pillows. "My turn," she said.

He swallowed hard at the purposeful look in her eyes. She was definitely on a mission of pleasure, and he had a feeling those walls she wanted to get past were already crumbling. So he'd build them back up later, he told himself, feeling a little desperate at the thought that Kate was getting too close.

But his thinking process evaporated as she kissed her way down his body, as her hands cupped him, as she closed her mouth around him.

Damn the walls. She could have anything she wanted as long as she didn't stop doing what she was doing.

And she did exactly that...until he needed all of her, until he turned the tables, until they came together in a connection so intense and so deep that it blasted away whatever walls were left between them.

Kate hadn't just gotten past his defenses; she'd gotten into his heart.

Soon...he'd have to figure out a way to get her out.

But not now.

Now, she was his, and he was hers...and the outside world didn't exist.

———

Kate woke up wrapped in Devin's arms. She felt warm, safe, protected, and it was weird how much she liked the feeling. She'd been fighting for independence since she came out of the womb. She'd been trying to prove herself her entire life, that she was just as strong, just as smart, just as powerful as anyone else. But this morning, in Devin's soft bed, his hard body pressed against hers, she didn't want to be strong; she just wanted to be herself and to be here.

She breathed in deep, her senses tingling with Devin's scent. Her memories and her body reminded her of every touch, every kiss, that had passed between them.

He was going to be really hard to forget.

Did she have to forget him?

Of course she did. She had a career to go after. She

was just starting her dream. Living out the ambition of a lifetime. She couldn't let a man get in the way.

But as she studied the hard profile of Devin's face, the strength of his jaw, the sexy grizzle of his shadowy beard, the firm lips that could both tease and tantalize, she knew that this man was not just any man.

He was Devin.

He knew her. He understood her. He didn't try to change her.

Not yet anyway.

No, he wouldn't try to change her. Just as he wouldn't try to change himself.

She'd gotten past his defenses last night, but they'd be back up today, probably as soon as he woke up. He'd been guarding his heart since his parents split up, since his dad died, and even more so since Sam was killed.

He'd been hurt many times, and she wanted so badly to take some of his pain away. She'd been able to do that for a while last night, but she was too smart not to know that sex wasn't a long-term answer to Devin's pain. He might not think he needed anyone, but he did. He'd been alone too long. He needed love in his life. He needed someone who cared about him.

But she couldn't be that person.

Devin's eyelids fluttered, and for a moment she thought he was waking up, but then he let out a little sigh.

This was her chance to escape. She could shower, get dressed, put her game face back on before Devin woke up. She could be at work on the computer while he was catching a few more minutes of sleep.

So why the hell wasn't she moving?

She took a deep breath and forced herself to move, but then Devin's arm came down heavy on her waist.

"Where are you going?" he asked sleepily, his brown

eyes now open and on hers.

"Time to get back to work."

His gaze moved to the clock on the bedside table. "It's early."

"We have to go to my parents' house this morning. We should work before then."

"We will. We'll start here—in bed."

The teasing smile on his lips melted her heart and her resistance. "How are we going to work here?"

"You're going to show me again how helpful you can be."

He shifted his body and she felt his arousal. "I don't think you need any help," she said with a laugh.

"Oh, but I do. I need you, Kate Callaway."

She knew he was only talking about a sexual need, but she had the craziest feeling that she wanted the words to mean so much more.

He followed his words with a kiss and whatever lingering protest she'd thought to make completely vanished—because she needed him as much as he needed her.

Eighteen

—⪼⪻—

They left Devin's apartment at eleven, and Kate felt a little breathless and rushed as she got into the car. They'd lost all track of time and had finally gotten out of bed and grabbed a quick shower before heading out of the apartment. Her hair was still damp, and she was quite sure that if her mother saw her now, she'd know exactly what her daughter had been doing for the last several hours.

"You okay?" Devin asked as she made a quick stop at a rapidly changing light.

"Sorry, yes, I'm fine." She tucked a strand of hair behind her ear. "Just wishing we hadn't agreed to this."

"It will be fine. I won't chew with my mouth open or talk about how great you are in bed."

She glanced over at his teasing smile. "You're in a good mood."

"And you're responsible for that. The question is— why aren't you in a good mood?"

"I am. I'm just...I don't know." She couldn't find the right words, and the words that came to mind she couldn't say.

"Well, I think this is the first time you don't know

what to say," he said, giving her a thoughtful look. "Let's talk about your family. Is Emma going to be there today?"

She was grateful to have a question she could answer.

"I don't know for sure. Everyone in the extended family is always invited, but we never know who's coming in advance. We have the brunches every Sunday after Mass. It rotates from house to house. It's a massive potluck. If you come, you bring something."

"Maybe we should stop and get something."

"My mom will have us covered. I'm pretty sure at least a few of my siblings will be there, Mom and Dad, of course, maybe my grandparents. My grandmother Eleanor Callaway has Alzheimer's, so if you see a pretty and elderly blonde woman with somewhat vacant blue eyes, you'll know why."

"Sorry. That must be rough."

"It is. She has good days but not as many as we'd like. My grandfather is devoted to her. He has become quite the caregiver, which surprised everyone a little. He's a gruff, brusque man and he doesn't show much affection for people, but he has a deep and abiding love for her. They've been married sixty-five years now."

Devin whistled under his breath. "That's a long time."

"They've had some trouble over the years, but my grandmother told me once that there has never been a moment in her life when her love faltered or that she considered breaking her vows. She married for life." She paused, realizing that Devin's profile had grown a little tense. "Sorry, I'm rambling, and I'm not being very sensitive. I just remembered that your parents split up when you were little."

"They definitely got over the idea of breaking their vows. In fact, I don't think they gave it a second thought."

"I can't imagine what you went through, Devin. As

much as my parents make me crazy, I really liked having both of them around when I was growing up."

"What's your dad like? He seemed pretty relaxed at the bookstore. He let your mom do the talking."

"He's definitely quieter than she is. He's a rock. He's brave and confident, intensely loyal. He's the kind of man you want around when things are tough." As she said the words, she realized that she was describing Devin, too. They would both go to the ends of the earth for a friend. She glanced at Devin. "What was your dad like? He was an agent, so I'm thinking he had some good qualities."

Devin nodded. "He was a solid guy. He was strict. He had a lot of rules, and there wasn't much gray area for him. I think that's partly why my mother fell out of love with him. He was rigid. And, of course, he put his job first. He believed that he was working for the greater good."

"He could definitely make that case," she said tentatively, not sure her opinion would be welcome.

"He could, and he did—many times. I'm sure it was true. But maybe he shouldn't have gotten married, shouldn't have had a kid."

"Well, I'm glad he had a kid," she said, giving him a smile, and wishing she hadn't brought up his father, because she'd definitely put a dent in Devin's good mood.

But her words did bring a smile to his face. "Glad to hear it," he said. "So getting back to you. Are we going to the house you grew up in?"

"Yes. It's off the Great Highway and across the street from the ocean."

"You grew up at the beach?"

"I did. My brothers did a lot of surfing when they were teenagers, but I preferred to look at the water from the sand."

"I've never been a fan of surfing, either—all that waiting-in-between time. And around here the ocean is cold."

"Exactly. Hawaii, I might get on a board. San Francisco, you need a wet suit and a tolerance for gray skies and really cold water." She paused. "I think we should talk about how we're going to play our relationship."

"What's to talk about? I can handle a few questions from your family."

"You have no idea what you're getting into. They're going to ask how we met, our first date, what you like about me, what I like about you."

"We'll say we met through the Bureau—mutual friends. I like your golden blonde hair and your sparkling blue eyes, your competitive spirit, and you have just enough snark in you to keep things interesting."

She glanced over at him, wondering if that was really what he liked about her or if he was making it up.

"Think they'll believe that?" he asked.

"That I have snark—yes."

He grinned. "I can go into more detail and tell them how much I like kissing you, how passionate you are, how great you look naked in my bed."

She flushed and said, "We're not trying to give anyone a heart attack."

"So what are you going to tell them you like about me?"

She thought for a moment. "I like that you're sharp—a quick thinker. You're competitive and you never let me win, which makes me try harder. Mostly, you're a good guy. You have more heart than you admit to, and I know you'd take a bullet before letting someone else get hurt."

She looked over at him as she stopped at a light. As

their gazes met, something deeper and more serious passed between them, as if they both had suddenly realized just how much they did like each other.

A car horn blared, and she realized the light had turned green. She put her foot on the gas and gave her attention back to the road. "Don't be surprised if my mom wants you to come to the wedding and all the other events next week. I think it's better if we just vaguely go along with her rather than say we won't be there together."

"Fine. Let's get through brunch and we'll worry about the rest later."

A few minutes later, she parked down the street from her parents' house. There were already a lot of cars, so she suspected most of her family was already inside. As they walked down the sidewalk, she saw two of her cousins and their wives get out of a car.

"That's Drew on the left in the sunglasses," she told Devin. "He was in the Navy and is now a pilot for the Coast Guard. The dark blonde is his wife, Ria. The brunette next to her is Sara and her husband Aiden. Aiden and Drew are two of Emma's brothers."

"What does Aiden do?"

"He used to be a smokejumper. Now, he does construction with my uncle."

"Smokejumper?" Devin muttered. "You do come from a family of thrill seekers."

"Aiden is one of the leaders in that department. So is my brother, Hunter. He's never met a mountain he didn't want to climb or jump off of." She slipped her hand into Devin's. "Ready to be my boyfriend? My babe? My snickerdoodle?"

He laughed. "Boyfriend, yes. If you call me snickerdoodle, I will have to blow your cover."

"Fine. Then just smile and pretend you love me,

because it's show time."

                  —➤➤◄◄—

    It wasn't difficult to pretend he was in love with Kate, Devin realized as she introduced him to her relatives and friends of the family. The two-story house was filled to the brim with all ages of people—from the elderly to babies in arms, and everything in between.

    The kitchen counters and dining room table were filled with dishes of food, and it was clear the cooks had made a real effort. There were no bags of chips and store-bought appetizers but casseroles, veggie wraps, gourmet sandwiches, salads, and meat skewers that were hot off the barbecue.

    He couldn't imagine what it had been like to grow up in this big, boisterous family. There was so much love, so much laughter, so much of everything. He felt a little jealous. Even when his parents had been together, life had been a lot quieter than this. And neither of his parents had many relatives, so even extended family had been hard to come by.

    "Are you okay?" Kate asked, grabbing two beers off a side table in the dining room as they made their way toward the back of the house.

    "I'm great."

    "You look a little dazed."

    "It's a lot to take in," he said, taking a swig of beer. "This happens every Sunday?"

    She nodded with a smile. "Not always here, but somewhere. Family gatherings are very important to everyone. No birthday, no holiday, goes by without appropriate celebration. Here comes Mom and Dad."

    She slipped her hand into his, and he tightened his

fingers around hers, thinking that he was enjoying being her fake boyfriend a little too much.

"Kate, you came," Sharon said with delight. "And you brought Devin. I was afraid you were going to make me chase you down."

"I wouldn't do that." She let go of Devin's hand to hug her mother.

Devin shook Tim's hand, seeing the quiet regard in the older man's eyes. "It's nice to see you both again," he said.

"You, too," Sharon said, giving him a speculative look. "So tell us a little about you, Devin. Did Kate say you were in the FBI?"

"I used to be. Now I'm a private investigator."

"Why did you leave the Bureau?" Sharon asked.

"A lot of reasons," he said vaguely. "I like being my own boss, so it's a good move for me."

"Do you investigate for anyone in particular?" Tim asked.

"I'm an equal opportunity investigator," he said lightly.

"How did you two meet?" Sharon asked.

"Through mutual friends," he said.

"FBI friends," Kate added. "We should get something to eat."

"So you live here in the city," Sharon said, ignoring her daughter's comment. "Are you and Kate going to do long-distance?"

"It looks that way," he said lightly.

"I told you, Mom, this is all new," Kate said.

"It can't be that new if you came back early to spend time with Devin, and you didn't want anyone in the family to know you were in town."

Devin smiled seeing the discomfort on Kate's face.

She might be a skilled agent, but when it came to her mother, she was definitely out of her league. "That's my fault," he said. "I wanted to spend some time with Kate before she was busy with the wedding."

"You should come to the wedding," Sharon said. "In fact, I insist. I'm sure you want to spend as much time together as possible. You're welcome at all the events. I'm quite certain that Mia would love to meet Devin." Sharon looked at Kate. "Does Mia know about your new relationship?"

"Not yet," Kate said.

"Tim, Sharon," a man said loudly as he approached the group.

As Devin stepped back, he saw Jack Callaway approaching, an attractive blonde at his side, who was probably his wife.

When Jack saw him in the group, he stopped abruptly, his gaze darkening. "Agent Scott? What the hell are you doing here?"

"He's with me," Kate said quickly.

"Why is he with you?" Jack demanded, his hard gaze swinging to Devin. "Are you using my niece to get to me?"

"No," he said shortly.

"We're dating," Kate said.

"Since when?" Jack asked suspiciously.

"Awhile," Kate said.

"What's going on?" Tim interjected, his gaze growing concerned as the tension grew within the group.

"Devin is investigating a series of arson fires," Kate said. "An FBI agent died in a fire eighteen months ago, and that agent was Devin's partner. He left the Bureau to focus on solving her case."

"I'm sure you're aware that there have been two more

fires," Devin said to Jack. "Maybe now you'll reopen the case that should never have been closed."

"That's already been done," Jack said tersely. "But we're not discussing this here. This is my family. And you don't belong here. You need to leave."

Before he could say a word, Kate stepped up. "He's not going anywhere, Uncle Jack. He's with me. And he's not using me. I know exactly what he's working on."

"You're both staying," Sharon said firmly. "Jack—I don't understand the problem between you and Devin, but you can work it out elsewhere."

The woman next to Jack put her hand on his arm. "Sharon is right," she said. "This sounds like business, and today is for family."

Jack blew out a breath and then said, "Fine. But I'm warning you—if you're messing with Kate, every man in this house will make you pay."

"Got it," he said evenly.

Jack turned and walked away, his wife following.

"Maybe we should go, Mom," Kate said.

"No. I meant what I said," Sharon said firmly. "You'll stay. You'll eat. You'll have fun. I'll catch up with you later."

"And I'll go find Jack," Tim said.

"Sorry about that," Devin told Kate.

She shrugged. "Uncle Jack was out of line. I'm going to talk to him."

"Don't do that on my account."

"I'm not doing it for you; I'm doing it for me. You're my guest, Devin, and my uncle can deal with it."

Her determined expression matched the one her mother had worn a few moments earlier. "You definitely take after your mom."

"I take after my uncle, too. He would go to the ends

of the earth to protect his friends and family. He should understand your motives better than anyone."

"Kate, wait. There's something you should know first."

"What?"

"After Sam died, after everyone closed the case, I went to see your Uncle Jack, and I was out of my mind. I made some nasty accusations about cover-up. He threw me out of his office."

"It's understandable. You were grief-stricken."

"It was unprofessional. I don't blame him for thinking I might be using you to get to him. We had some bad words."

"We both know that you're not using me. And he needs to know, too."

"Hi guys," Emma said, interrupting their conversation. "What did I miss? Colton just told me that Dad tried to throw Devin out of the house."

"Devin will tell you," Kate said. "I'm going to have a few words with your dad."

Emma gave him a questioning look as Kate left. "Should I be worried for Kate or my dad?"

"Maybe your dad. When Kate gets fired up, there's no stopping her."

Emma smiled. "She said the same thing about you when we spoke the other day." She paused. "How are you feeling?"

"I'm fine."

"I'm sorry we haven't been able to find the arsonist. Max is working on it, too."

"I know. I appreciate the help."

"Have you eaten yet?"

"Not yet."

"Let me show you the way. The last thing you want

to be in this crowd is shy."

He laughed. "I've actually never been called shy."

"I'm sure." As they walked back toward the dining room, she said, "I guess Kate decided to tell her family she's in town."

"She was forced into it. We ran into her mom last night. By the way, her family thinks we're dating. It seemed like a good cover story at the time."

She grinned. "And now?"

"I have a feeling we opened Pandora's box."

"Oh, you definitely did. We'll stop at the bar on the way to the buffet. I think you're going to need another beer."

–•➤➤◄◄•–

"Uncle Jack—can I speak to you?" Kate asked, breaking into her father's conversation with her uncle.

"I'll leave you two alone," her father said, moving away.

"Your father said I need to apologize to you," Jack said, not looking too happy with that thought.

"That would be a good start."

"I don't like that guy you brought."

"You don't know him. If you did, you would like him, because he's a lot like you."

"I don't think so."

"Devin told me that he came at you and some of the other fire investigators without a lot of finesse, but his partner—his best friend—had just been killed, and he knew that the wrong guy was being held accountable. No one believed him, but that didn't stop him from going after the truth. He quit his job so he could focus on getting the right person off the streets, and this past week there have been two more fires that fit the exact same pattern as the others."

"As I told him earlier, I'm aware of the most recent fires, and the fire department is investigating."

"I knew you would reopen the case, because you're very good at your job. Just as Devin is good at his. You are also one of the most loyal people I know. I can't believe you wouldn't have done exactly what Devin did if the situation was reversed."

"He's not your boyfriend, is he?" Jack asked.

She shook her head. "No. We're working together. I didn't want to involve the family in my job. My boss assigned me to the case because he knew I was headed to San Francisco. He asked me to give Devin a few days of my time."

"That makes sense. You've grown up, Kate," Jack said, an admiring glint in his eyes.

"I have done that."

"How do you like the Bureau? Is it what you thought it would be?"

"It's not at all what I thought it would be, but I really like it."

"You're doing the Callaway name proud."

"I hope so." She paused. "Are we good? Do I have to worry about you taking a swing at Devin?"

"I never swing first. And we're good. I'm going to check the barbecue. Whenever Aiden is in charge, he turns our burgers into hockey pucks."

As Jack left, she moved towards her father.

"Everything okay now?" he asked.

"Yes."

"You're working with Devin, aren't you?"

"I am, but can we keep what I'm doing with Devin just between you and me for a few days?" Kate asked. "I don't want to worry Mom and get her involved. She has the wedding to work on, and I don't want to take anything away from Mia."

He nodded. "We can do that, for a few days anyway. But don't be surprised if your mom has already figured it out."

He was probably right about that, but she'd deal with her mom when she had to. "I also wanted to ask you why you were at the bookstore last night."

"We went to support Gerilyn. She's had a rough few years."

"You know Gerilyn Connors?"

"Sure. Brad was in my firehouse for a few years before he completely turned his life upside down."

"Drugs and alcohol, right?"

"Yes. He lost his job, and I thought he had lost his wife to his addictions, but apparently he's sober now, and she's found a way to forgive him."

"Brad Connors is a person of interest in the arson fires, Dad."

"I know. Gerilyn was complaining to your mother that the FBI was harassing Brad just because he used to be a firefighter."

"And because he was violent toward Gerilyn, and because several of the houses she worked on were targeted."

"I didn't know the ins and outs of it," her dad said. "Is he still a suspect?"

"I'm not sure, but what do you think about him as a suspect? Is he a man who would start fires?"

"I'd like to say no. I worked alongside him for four years. But that was before he started screwing up his life. The way he treated Gerilyn during the divorce was shocking to me. I guess I can't say for sure that he wouldn't burn down one of her buildings out of revenge."

"Why do you think she took him back? After everything they went through?"

"Hell if I know," he said. "A man shouldn't treat a woman the way Brad treated Gerilyn. There's no excuse. And I don't care if she still loves him; she should love herself more. I wouldn't want any of my daughters to take a man back who didn't treat them well."

"I think your daughters are all far too stubborn," she said lightly. "I better go find Devin. He's probably drowning in Callaways."

"You know, Kate…if you like him, it's okay."

"I do like him," she admitted. "But I've just started my career. The timing sucks."

"It almost always does," he said with a laugh. "Sometimes poor timing forces you to figure out what you really want."

"Or it just drives you crazy."

"That, too."

She hugged her dad and went to find Devin. He was in the dining room, working his way around the buffet.

"I see you got food."

"Yes, and it's all very good. How did your conversation go with your uncle?"

"He apologized for being rude to you."

Devin raised an eyebrow. "Seriously? Jack Callaway apologized?"

"Well, it wasn't exactly an apology, but I made him understand that your behavior after Sam died is not really who you are. He gets it. He's as fiercely loyal to his friends as you are. And he's going to do everything he can to help."

"Now that there have been two more fires."

She understood his cynicism. "Well, yes. I know that

doesn't excuse the inattention over the last year and a half, but it is what it is. I also talked to my father about why they were at the book signing. They're friends with the Connors. Brad worked with my dad."

"That's interesting."

"He had heard that Brad was a person of interest in the arson cases, but he didn't have any further information. I asked him if he thought Brad could be guilty, and he didn't say no, which is hugely significant."

"Why is that?"

"Because the firefighters in this town are brothers. They stand up for one another. The fact that my father couldn't immediately do that said a lot. Firefighters see the devastation of fire every day; the loss of life, the horrific burns, the destruction of families. They don't start fires; they put them out. But after all the drug and alcohol problems Brad had gone through, my father couldn't say for sure that he was innocent." She paused. "We need to figure out where Brad was last night and last Monday."

"I agree. We should get Emma's help on that. She has the power to investigate those fires specifically, and she can bring in the local police."

"Is she still here?" Kate asked, looking around the room.

"She had to take off. She said she and Max were going to take some time for themselves this afternoon. Apparently, they haven't had much of that lately."

"I'll text her the info. I'm sure she'll get to it when she can or tomorrow at the latest."

"In the meantime, we'll keep Connors high on the list," Devin said. "And we'll focus in on the properties on the target list that might have a tie to Gerilyn. She won't be eager to help us, but perhaps we can get the same information from Eileen since they work closely together."

"That's a good move." She paused, seeing her older sister approaching. "Hey, there's Annie."

"Kate," Annie said, surprise flashing across her face. "I thought you weren't coming until Wednesday."

"I got in a little earlier." She gave Annie a hug. Her sister was three years older than her with dark red hair and green eyes like their mother. But today those eyes looked a little tired, and Kate wondered why. "How are you doing, Annie?"

"I've been working a lot."

"Your company must be doing well."

"It is. I just wish there were more people in my company than just an assistant and me. But I can't complain." Annie's eyes drifted to Devin. "We haven't met."

"Devin Scott."

"Annie Callaway." Annie's gaze moved from Devin to Kate. "Is Devin a friend of yours?"

"I'm her boyfriend," Devin said with a grin.

Annie's jaw dropped. "Really? Well, isn't that a piece of news?"

Devin was enjoying his fake boyfriend status a little too much, Kate thought. "It's very recent," she told her sister.

"What do you do, Devin?" Annie asked.

"I'm a private investigator."

"That sounds interesting and a little dangerous. How did you and Kate meet?"

"On a job."

"He used to be FBI," Kate said. "Anyway, what is up with you? Are you bringing a guy to the wedding?"

"Nope. Flying solo," Annie said, more shadows filling her eyes.

"I thought Mom said you were seeing someone."

"That ended."

"Sorry."

"Don't be. It's fine." She paused. "It's good to see you, Kate. You do not keep in touch very well. I miss you."

"I promise to be better. It's been a crazy year."

"I know you need to get your feet on the ground in your new job as a special agent, but don't forget your family, especially your sisters."

"Never."

"Good. I'm going to make the rounds." She started to leave, then stopped. "Did you know that Hunter is planning to climb to Base Camp on Mount Everest in a few months?"

"What?" she asked in astonishment. Her daredevil brother had done some adventures in his life, but he hadn't gone that high or that far.

"Yes. He's training for it right now. He loves a challenge." Annie glanced at Devin. "Kate got the Callaway adventure gene like our brothers. Mia and I did not."

Devin smiled. "Adventure is the spice of life."

Annie groaned. "You're a thrill-seeker, too, aren't you?"

"I haven't climbed Mount Everest yet, but it sounds like a fun challenge."

Annie shook her head in bemusement. "Not to me. But I have a feeling Kate would join you."

"I don't know about that," she said. "It sounds like a lot of work."

"I'll see you two later," Annie said, heading off to visit with some of her other relatives in the living room.

"Annie looks like your mom," Devin commented.

"She takes after her, too. She's very protective when

it comes to family, especially her younger sisters." Kate leaned across the table and grabbed a bite-sized egg salad sandwich off a tray and popped it into her mouth. "My aunt Lynda makes the best egg salad. Did you try these?"

"Yeah, I had about six of them," he said with a laugh.

"I'm glad you weren't being shy."

"Emma told me it wasn't allowed."

"You were fast to tell Annie that we were in a relationship."

"Just trying to do my part," he said with a smile.

"Well, my dad already guessed that I'm working with you."

"Will he tell your mother?"

"Eventually, but I asked him to wait a couple of days. So you still have to be my fake boyfriend for a while longer."

He heaved a mock sigh. "I guess if I have to, I have to."

She punched him in the arm. "It's not that bad."

"How would you know?"

"Because I'm a catch."

He laughed. "You are that, Kate. Just promise me one thing…you'll tell your mother the truth before she starts planning our wedding."

"I promise. But she'll be disappointed. She already likes you."

"She doesn't know me."

"She has a good instinct about people. Her gut is never wrong."

"Well, I like her, too. She stood up for us to your uncle, and he's not an easy man to confront. I like your family, Kate." He waved his hand toward the clusters of family members talking and laughing together. "You're lucky to have so many people in your life who love you.

Don't ever take that for granted. Don't let the job become your whole life. It's easy to do—but this—this is what's really important."

She nodded, thinking that it wasn't only the people surrounding her who were important; it was also the man in front of her.

Nineteen

———⟫⟫⟪⟪←—

They got back to Devin's apartment around three and immediately dug back into the fire data, going through each historical structure fire in as much detail as they could. They were trying to find any small patterns that they could tie together, any detail that would help them narrow down the list of potential targets, which was next on the *To-Do* list.

At six, they stopped long enough to make some eggs for dinner and then got back on to their computers. It was after nine when Kate's eyes started to blur.

She sat back in her seat at the kitchen table and looked over her computer at Devin. He was still focused on whatever file he was reading, and she was once again impressed with his concentration. Tonight she saw the Devin who had made an excellent FBI agent.

He looked up and met her gaze. "Are you done?"

"I don't know about done, but I am tired. We've narrowed down the list to six structures, four of which have an obvious tie to Gerilyn Connors's firm. The fifth one was owned by a former St. Bernadette's teacher; I don't quite know what to make of that. The sixth one is down the street from where Marty Price lives, but we haven't really talked about Marty lately."

"I know. He's fallen lower on the list."

"He was at several crime scenes," Kate reminded Devin. "He also wanted to be a firefighter but couldn't get into the academy. But he's three years younger than Baines and Jenkins, and he did not go to school at St. Bernadette's."

"My gut is leaning away from Price. I don't think he's smart enough to pull all this off. I also don't see a motive nor a connection to Baines or any of the structures, except that he was at a couple of fires."

"I agree. The fire pattern is too precise. This person is acting in a very deliberate manner. They're not just setting fires; they're following a specific plan, and I think it's all tied to anger, resentment, and revenge. It feels emotional to me."

"I want to talk to Gerilyn tomorrow," Devin said. "If we go to her office and catch her away from Brad, we may get additional information. We can also talk to Eileen. She might be willing to provide more insight on Gerilyn and Brad's renewed relationship."

She nodded. "The big problem with Brad is that he also doesn't tie to Rick Baines in any way, which makes it harder to connect him to the fire at St. Bernadette's." With a sigh, she added, "I feel like we're going around in circles."

He gave her a faint smile. "I've been doing that so long I live in a perpetual state of dizziness. Looking away from Brad for a minute, I think I've found a phone number and address for Kristina Strem, one of the females in Baines's yearbook."

"Well, that's exciting." She sat up straighter. "Way to bury the lead, Devin. Why didn't you say that before?"

He laughed. "I just pulled it up. She lives in San Jose."

"So, in the area...that's good. Let's give her a call."

"Why don't you do the honors, Special Agent Callaway?"

"Happy to."

She dialed the number he gave her, then put the phone on speaker. A moment later, a female voice came over the line.

"Is this Kristina Strem?" she asked.

"Yes. Who's this?"

"I'm Special Agent Kate Callaway with the FBI. We're investigating a fire that killed one of your former classmates last year—Rick Baines."

There was silence for a moment, and then the woman said, "I heard about that on the news, but I don't know why you're calling me. I don't know anything about the fire."

"But you did know Rick?"

"I went to school with him for a few years," Kristina said. "I thought that Rick was the one who set the fire, and he died, so what are you investigating?"

"We're just reviewing the case," she said, being deliberately vague. "Did you see Rick after high school, perhaps in the last few years?"

"I saw him once or twice when I was out with my friends. But that was like two years ago now. That was pretty much it."

"Was that at a bar called Rebel, Rebel?"

"Yes, I think it was. We went there a couple of times."

She was happy to hear that they could tie Kristina to the bar. "Were you with other friends from St. Bernadette's?"

"I don't really remember. Maybe."

"Do you know if Rick stayed in touch with anyone else from St. Bernadette's?"

"Alan Jenkins talked to him a lot. Rick worked at the gym where Alan used to go. But Alan moved down south last year."

"So you're friends with Alan?"

"Yes, but we haven't seen each other since he moved."

"Did you ever see Alan and Rick at the bar together?"

"Yes, they were both there one night."

"Do you have Alan's number?"

"I think so, unless he changed it when he moved."

"Can you text it to me?"

"All right. Hang on."

Kate waited a moment, happy to see a text come through a second later with a phone number, but it was the same one she had gotten from the gym, the one Alan wasn't answering. Putting that aside, she said, "Who else was close to Rick during high school? Did he have a girlfriend?"

"No, he was shy and nerdy," Kristina said. "But there was a group of us who hung out together. It was me, Rick, Alan, Lindsay, Julie and Michael."

Kate was thrilled to have someone finally give them a list of people who knew Baines. "Do you keep in touch with any of them?"

"Julie is here in the city. She works at the Delaney Street Bakery. Michael moved to New York. I haven't seen Lindsay in years. She went away to college in Chicago, and I don't know if she ever came back." Kristina paused. "Why are you calling me anyway?"

"We saw a photo of you with Rick in the high school yearbook."

"And why is that important?"

"There was a fire at St. Bernadette's last week. In investigating that fire, we became aware that Rick went to school there."

"If Rick is dead, then you think someone else from St. Bernadette's set that fire and maybe the others? Is that what you're saying?"

"It's a possibility."

"I can't imagine who would do what you're talking about except Rick. He was really into fire. He always wanted to be a firefighter. He talked incessantly about it in high school. I think his grandfather or someone was a firefighter."

"I didn't know that," she said, seeing Devin type something on his computer. He was probably looking up Baines's family.

"Yeah, he was obsessed with getting into the academy," Kristina continued. "That's how he and Alan became friends. Rick started working out all the time, and Alan was a jock; he was always in the gym. Once Rick got into weights, he got obsessed with that, too. When the firefighting thing didn't work out, he got a job at a fitness center, so I guess it worked out."

What Kristina said made a lot of sense and definitely provided a connection between Baines and Jenkins. "Did Alan ever express the same interest in fire that Rick did?"

"I don't think so. There was a fire at the school when we were there. It was set in a trash can. We joked that Rick probably did it just so he could practice putting it out. But Rick always said he didn't do it. I don't know if he was lying or if one of our other classmates was into fire. It's not something I would have ever asked anyone."

"I understand. Would you mind giving me the last names of the people you mentioned were in your group and any phone numbers or addresses that you have?"

"Sure, I can text them to you later. I have to go out right now."

"As soon as possible would be great. We really appreciate your cooperation."

"I hope that no one I know was involved with Rick's death," Kristina said. "You've kind of freaked me out a little about Alan."

"Is there some reason you think Alan could be involved?"

"Well, I didn't until you called. It's just now that I'm thinking about it, Alan was super upset about Rick's death. He even went to the scene. I saw him a few days after the fire, and he was really shaken up by it. But that would probably mean he didn't have anything to do with it, right?"

She thought it was interesting that Alan had gone to the fire scene. Who did that? Only someone who had either a morbid fascination with the scene of a friend's death or someone who wanted to see that burned-out structure and admire his handiwork. But she wasn't going to say any of that to Kristina. "Thanks for your help," she said. "I'll look forward to getting the information from you."

"All right."

Kate ended the call and looked at Devin. "Interesting that Alan went to the scene."

"It is. I just wish he'd call us back. I also wish he hadn't moved, because that makes him less of a suspect."

"I have kind of a crazy thought."

"What's that?"

"What if Alan didn't move? If he isn't in San Diego?"

Devin met her gaze. "Why would you suggest that? It seems to be a story we've heard from more than one person."

"Could it be a cover? Is it possible Alan wants everyone to think he's out of town when he's not?"

"It's a big stretch, Kate."

"Maybe, but Alan was the closest person to Rick in the months before Rick's death. If Rick was talking to anyone, it was probably Alan."

"I'm not going to rule anything out, but that theory is not at the top of my list."

"Okay. It was just a thought. What about Baines's grandfather? Was he in the fire department?"

"Not that I've seen."

"Rick could have made it up. He might not have even known what his grandparents really did. It doesn't sound like he spent much time with them." She let out a sigh and rolled her head around on her shoulders. Her neck muscles were aching. "I've been sitting in this chair too long. I'm going to take a break."

He gave her a vague nod, his attention back on something on his computer. She walked over to the couch and sat down, enjoying the soft leather and the comfortable cushions. It was a nice change from the hard-backed straight chair she'd spent the day in. She flipped on the television, lowering the sound so as not to disturb Devin.

"You can turn it up," he said a moment later. "It won't bother me."

"I feel guilty that you're still working. What are you doing?"

"Just going over stuff. Don't feel guilty."

"Okay, I won't."

He laughed. "That was easy."

She turned up the sound a few notches, still keeping it low. She went through the channels, happily settling on an old James Bond movie. She was already engrossed in the film when Devin sat down next to her a half hour later.

"So it's Bond that has you riveted," he teased. "I should have figured you'd like the handsome spy type."

"How could I not? If only I worked with a few more people who actually looked like James Bond."

"Hey, I'm sitting right here."

She laughed. "You do think highly of yourself. But you're not an agent anymore."

"True."

"Are you a Bond fan?"

"I've seen a few movies," he admitted. "Are you watching for the action or the sexy guy?"

"Both. You know me. I like action and sexy men."

He grinned back at her. "And I like action and sexy women, especially hot blondes with big blue eyes, which I now realize come from your Callaway gene pool. You look like your grandmother, Kate."

"I'll take that as a big compliment. I'm glad you got to meet her and that she was able to talk to you."

"She was sweet. I don't think she knew who I was or why I was there, but she was welcoming."

"We've been really close over the years. She has a ton of grandkids, but she always makes time for everyone. The only thing I wish I'd done was go to Ireland with her. She went when I was in high school, and took some of my cousins, but I had some stupid reason for saying no. That's my one regret. Someday I want to go to where she was born and see the land she's talked about for so long."

"You'll get there."

"I will," she said. "When I set my mind to something..."

He laughed. "I know; there's no stopping you. I

learned that the first day we met when I tried to send you away."

"And I'm still here."

His eyes darkened. "I'm glad you're here, Kate, and not just because you're helping me on the case."

Her stomach fluttered. "I'm glad I'm here, too."

As the action on the television got louder, she turned her attention back to the screen. "This is my favorite part."

He put his arm around her. "A girl who likes chase scenes. I can't believe it."

"What's not to like about a good chase?" she asked in bemusement. "Speed, danger, thrills…"

"Agreed. It has it all."

She snuggled up next to him, happy to be doing something normal for a change. As Bond raced through the streets of London, she put her head on Devin's shoulder. A short while later, Devin pulled a blanket off the back of the couch and covered them both with it. She felt warm and happy but also really tired. Even in the middle of the action, her eyes began to drift closed, and it was getting more and more difficult to stay awake.

"I should go home," she muttered.

"The movie isn't over."

"Maybe a little longer then."

"Stay as long as you want, Kate."

As she drifted off to sleep, she had the foolish thought that she might want to stay forever.

--→➤➤◄◄←--

Kate woke up with a cough. Her chest was burning, and the air was thick and heavy—smoky. A steady, sharp, beeping sound relentlessly played through the air.

She blinked her eyes open. She was on the couch with Devin. They must have fallen asleep during the movie. The television was still on, now running some sort of infomercial, but it was difficult to see through the dark haze.

Something was burning. And the alarm going off had to be the smoke alarm.

The smell was worse now. Not just smoke but also gasoline. And there was a heat building around her. She couldn't see flames, but something somewhere was on fire.

"Devin," she said, grabbing his arm. "Wake up."

"What?" he asked sleepily.

"There's a fire," she said, coughing at the end of her sentence.

Devin sat up, then jumped to his feet as his gaze took in the smoke around them. "Shit! Where's it coming from?"

"I don't know."

"We have to get out of here."

"My computer." She got up from the couch, heading toward the kitchen table. She was almost there when the door on the heating vent on the wall suddenly blew off, and flames leapt out of the walls. The door hit her in the arm, and she stumbled backward, landing on her ass.

Devin ran to her side. "Are you all right?"

"I'm okay. The fire is in the walls."

"Must have started downstairs. We need to go now."

She got back to her feet, throwing her computer and phone into her bag while Devin did the same. As they started down the hall, the heat intensified, and she was suddenly terrified that they wouldn't be able to get out of the apartment.

Pulling the neck of her shirt up over her mouth and

nose, she followed Devin to the front door, keeping a hand on his back so she wouldn't lose him in the smoke.

When they went out the front door, she saw that the entire first floor of the building was ablaze. Sirens filled the air. Someone must have called in the fire.

Devin went down two steps, but as he hit the third step, the wood collapsed, and he would have fallen through if she hadn't grabbed his arm. He pulled out his leg and bypassing that step, they made it down to the sidewalk as a fire truck turned the corner.

The first man off the truck was her brother Hunter. He stopped abruptly when he saw her, then ran over to her. "Kate? What the hell?"

"I was in there," she said, pointing to the house. "We just got out."

"Anyone else inside?"

"No."

"Are you all right?"

"I'm fine. Go. Do your job."

He gave her a hard look, then joined the rest of the crew, while Devin and Kate watched the old Victorian house go up in flames.

"Damn," Devin muttered, staring at the blaze. "I didn't expect this."

"Expect what?"

"That he'd go after us and not the target."

He was right. Devin's building wasn't on the register. And it wasn't in the target zone.

"This isn't the third fire, Kate. This is a warning." He looked back at her, his lips set in a grim line. "We're getting too close."

"Are we close?" she asked in bewilderment. "We have no idea who's warning us."

"They obviously don't know that. Someone we've

talked to recently figured out where I live, and he sent us a message. This could be his first mistake."

Seeing Devin's home destroyed didn't seem like much of a mistake to her. "You might lose everything Devin."

"But maybe we just got our first real clue."

There was no denying the excitement in his voice, but she didn't understand where it was coming from. "What clue? We don't know who did this."

"Not yet. But we forced him to break the pattern. The arsonist got nervous enough to act out of order. Who knows what he'll do next? I'd rather deal with someone who's panicking than someone who's acting with cold-blooded precision."

He had a point. "Okay, I guess it's about time you turned into the optimistic one, especially since it's your home that's going up in smoke. Oh, no. I just remembered—we didn't get the map off the wall."

"We have the photo you took earlier. And I have one on my computer."

"Right. Thank goodness. I didn't want to start from scratch again." She paused. "The first floor tenant is going to lose everything. All those beautiful vintage clothes are gone. The fire must have started in there."

"I'm sure it was easier to break into an empty store. There was no one around." He paused, turning to look at her again. "Thanks for waking me up."

"I keep thinking…what if I hadn't?" She was a little shaken by that thought.

"But you did. That's what matters."

"I'm glad we never got undressed and went to bed. At least we're still in our clothes."

"Yeah, we would have made quite a scene running out naked."

His joke lightened her mood a little. "Especially since my brother was the first one here."

"I didn't meet him yesterday, did I?"

"No, Hunter didn't show up. He's the one who's going to climb Mt. Everest."

"I can't imagine that's a bigger adrenaline rush than running into a burning building."

"I can't, either. I never ever wanted to be a firefighter. I forget how dangerous it is because I don't see it, and the firefighters in the family always downplay the risk. But there's risk. They just don't care. They don't get scared."

"They probably do get scared, but they push past it. You do that, too, Kate. You're every bit as brave as your brothers."

"I don't know about that, but thanks." She looked down the block, seeing neighbors coming out of their homes, gathering on the surrounding streets. *Did they all belong here? Or was someone out there—watching them?* A chill ran down her spine. "Do you think he's here?" she asked Devin. "Do you think he's enjoying this?"

"If he's out there, he's going to see that we're fine, and he's going to know that we're coming for him," Devin said with grim determination. "He's not getting away. He didn't scare me. He just motivated me more."

Twenty

After scouring the crowd for any suspects and talking to both the fire investigator at the scene and to Emma on the phone, Devin took Kate to a nearby hotel just before four in the morning. They checked into a room on the tenth floor, and Devin noticed that Kate made sure to double bolt the door. She was definitely rattled, and he couldn't blame her. They were lucky to have gotten out of his apartment alive.

Kate took a quick shower and stripped off her clothes and got into bed. He showered after her to get the smoke off his skin and out of his hair, and by the time he slid under the covers, Kate was asleep.

He left the light on for a minute, taking a moment to just look at her, to reassure himself that she was all right. The paramedics had offered them oxygen and a ride to the hospital, but while they'd taken the air, they'd declined the hospital trip, and he hoped that was the right decision.

Kate looked fine. Her cheeks were rosy from her shower, her hair still damp from the quick blow-dry she'd done, and her skin was its usual creamy texture. She was a beautiful woman. Sometimes when they were in the middle of things, he forgot that. When he was with her—her fire, her determination, her optimism—were so forceful and bright that all he could see was her personality—all he could see was *her*.

She was one-of-a-kind—the full package. The kind of woman who could kick down a door one second and nurture a baby the next.

The kind of woman he could love.

That thought shook him more than any other, and he rolled over onto his back and stared up at the ceiling.

Seeing Kate with her family had shown him her softer side. He'd watched her try to patiently connect with the autistic Brandon, and hold a sobbing baby while her mother went to get her a bottle. He'd seen her joke with her brother and sister and share confidences with her cousins. It was clear how well loved and liked she was, and he'd been more than proud to be her fake boyfriend.

He just kept fighting the urge to make it real.

But how could he make it real?

There was no way. Their paths were going to split and go in completely opposite directions in just a few days. There would be no more trips to the batting cages, no more dance lessons, no more watching a movie together, no more sex…

Glancing over at her, he didn't know if he could stand the thought of never kissing her, touching her, being with her again. He'd never had such a feeling of panic run through him. But that had to be what was making his heart thud against his chest.

How could he have let this happen?

He knew better than to let himself care too much about anyone, especially someone who had one foot out the door.

But here he was—in the exact place he didn't want to

be.

Except that he did want to be here, in this bed with her. He just knew it couldn't last.

Taking a deep breath, he rolled over onto his side and put his arm around her, burying his face in the silky strands of her hair. She would be gone soon, but for now...

She moved in closer to him, sliding her arm around his waist. He liked how she knew him, wanted him, even in sleep.

So he held her close until the night turned to dawn. The minutes passed both far too slowly and far too quickly. Finally, he couldn't fight the exhaustion, and he fell asleep, hoping she'd still be there in his arms when he woke up.

Devin was just waking up when Kate walked out of the bathroom, fully dressed.

"Hey sleepyhead," she teased. "It's almost noon."

He sat up and ran a hand through his hair. "I feel like I just fell asleep. When did you get up?"

"About ten minutes ago."

"I'm glad you got some rest. You fell asleep fast last night."

"I don't even remember coming into this room." She sat down on the bed next to him. "My clothes still smell of smoke."

"I'm sure mine do, too."

"I'm sorry about your home, Devin."

"It was just an apartment. Nothing in there was too important. I'm glad you weren't hurt."

"Right back at you," she said, knowing he was

making light of his loss. Even if the apartment hadn't held anything of great sentiment, it was still his personal space, and now it was gone. "So what do we do next?"

"Well, I don't believe last night's fire is going to stop the real one that's coming. That pattern is begging to be completed, and, if anything, I think the arsonist is getting impatient. He's going to want it to be done, before he's stopped."

"I agree. I think it will happen within the next two days. He might go into hiding tonight, make sure we haven't found him, and then come back out."

"Or he might be making plans to strike tonight," he said. "Let's talk to Gerilyn Connors. At the very least, we can find out where Brad was last night."

"That's a good idea. I just ordered some room service."

He smiled. "You always know what I need."

"It wasn't a big guess to think you'd be hungry now."

"I'll grab a shower."

As Devin got out of bed wearing nothing but a pair of boxers, she couldn't help but look at him. His chiseled male body was pretty spectacular, and she was more than a little tempted to join him in the shower, especially when he threw her a teasing look and said, "See anything you like?"

"Go," she said, waving him into the bathroom.

"There's room for two."

"But no time," she said firmly. "We have a lot to do today."

She let out a breath when he closed the door, putting temptation farther out of reach.

She pulled her phone out of her bag and saw a dozen messages from numerous members of her family. Hunter had obviously told everyone about the fire at Devin's house. She was just about to call her mom back when her phone rang. It was Mia.

"Don't tell me the news already made it to Angel's Bay," she said.

"If you mean the fact that you were almost killed in a fire last night—yes," Mia said, worry in her voice. "And I've texted you six times. What the hell are you doing?"

"I was sleeping. I was just about to check my messages. I'm fine. Totally one-hundred percent fine. Hunter should have told everyone that. He saw me."

"What happened? Why are you in San Francisco so early? And who is this new boyfriend you're bringing to the wedding who I've never heard anything about?"

She sighed, waiting for Mia to run out of steam on her questions. "Okay, he's not a real boyfriend; I just told Mom he was so she wouldn't ask any more questions. I came to the city early to help a former agent on an arson case. I didn't want Mom to know, but I ran into her, so I let her think we were dating."

"This is the guy you were waiting for in the car when I spoke to you the other night?"

"That's the one. We were at his place last night when the arsonist decided to send us a warning, but we got out in time."

"My dream," Mia said. "I dreamt you were surrounded by bright light. Remember? I told you that."

Her nerves tingled at the reminder. As twins, they'd always been very in tune with each other. "There wasn't actually a lot of fire near me, just smoke."

"To think you could have died last night—"

"Mia, stop. I didn't come close to dying, honestly. I smelled the smoke. We left the apartment. And we came to a hotel. That's the whole story."

"Somehow I doubt that is even close to the whole

story. And what were you doing in this guy's house in the middle of the night? Are you sure he's really a fake boyfriend?"

Her sister's question drew her gaze to the bathroom door. "Actually, I'm not totally sure about that. He's an amazing man. But I'm going back to work after your wedding, and my work is in DC. I don't know what Devin is going to be doing after this case is solved. So I really need to not like him so much."

"Oh, Kate, that's not going to happen."

"It could happen," she protested.

"Not in a million years. Once you give your heart to someone, you don't get it back."

"I can take it back. And I didn't give him my heart…just a lot of everything else."

Mia laughed. "How was it?"

"Better than I have words for."

"Well, that's good. Are you going to bring him to the wedding?"

"I'm sure this will be over by then, and if it's not, I'll leave him to work on things. I'm not going to let you down, Mia. I'm going to be there for you. I will stand up at your wedding. I promise."

"You better. Because we've been together since before we were born, and I am not doing this without you, Kate."

"You won't have to. I'll see you on Thursday."

"Don't get into any more trouble before then."

"I'm going to try hard not to."

As she ended the call, she hoped she could make good on that promise.

—➤➤◄◄◄—

They arrived at Gerilyn Connors's architecture and design firm a little before one o'clock in the afternoon. The office was housed in a brick building with exposed beams and floor-to-ceiling windows. Lush carpets covered the sleek, dark, hardwood floors, and expensive artwork hung on the walls.

The receptionist told them that Gerilyn was still out to lunch, but that Eileen Raffin would speak to them in her office.

Eileen's space was just as pretty as the lobby. In addition to a large mahogany desk, there was a seating area with white couches and chairs around a unique-looking coffee table that appeared to have once been an old steamer trunk.

Eileen got up from behind her desk and gave them a welcoming smile.

"I'm so glad you came by. I got the target list you texted me last night," she told Devin. "And I have to say I was a little troubled by four of the houses on there. They are all places that our firm worked on. I don't want anything to happen to any of them. They're beautiful properties, and I did the interiors for three of them."

She waved them toward the couch and chairs by the window. "Please have a seat. I know that you've told me before that houses we've worked on were targeted in the past, but I really thought it was just a coincidence, that someone just didn't like historic buildings, but now it feels like someone doesn't like us."

Kate saw the worried light in her eyes and felt reassured that Eileen was being so open and honest with them. "It's possible this firm is a target in some way," she said. "We wanted to speak to Gerilyn again, but the receptionist told us she's at lunch."

Eileen nodded. "She had a meeting with a developer.

So it's back to Brad? I was really hoping you could clear him. Gerilyn has been happy since they got back together, although this morning she looked more like her old self."

"What do you mean?" Devin asked.

"She had dark circles under her eyes, like she hadn't slept. She said she just had a bad night, but she didn't say why. She looked that way a lot during her divorce."

"Do you think she's having problems with Brad again?" Kate asked.

"I didn't want to ask. We're close, but I let her talk when she wants to talk. I try not to pry. It's difficult to watch your friend go back to someone who hurt them before. I think that's why Gerilyn isn't telling me much right now. But I hope she'll talk to you." Eileen glanced down at her watch. "She should be back within about fifteen minutes. You can wait here in my office. I actually need to go to one of the properties on your list, the one on Village Court."

"Why?" Kate asked in surprise.

"The owners want to redecorate. I did their original design about six years ago. So it needs updating." Eileen paused. "Would you like to see the house? You could come with me."

"I would like to see the house." Kate glanced at Devin. "You could wait for Gerilyn, and I could take a look at the property. It might give me a better idea of how vulnerable it is, and where we should put it on the target list."

He hesitated, then nodded. "All right. We can meet up afterwards."

Eileen got to her feet as her cell phone rang. "Hello? I'm sorry. I can't talk right now. I'm on my way out." She paused. "I'll have to call you back, okay?" She ended the call and shook her head. "Children. No matter how old they are, they can still be annoying. Do either of you have kids?"

"No, we're both single," Kate said. "Someday. When I'm ready."

"I thought I was ready for motherhood, but it was much harder than I ever expected it to be. I was thankful when my daughter hit eighteen. It felt like a huge achievement. Little did I realize that eighteen was not the end of her needs. Anyway, let me get my bag, and we'll go."

As Eileen moved around the desk to grab her purse, Kate looked at Devin. "Should we meet back here?"

"Why don't you text me when you've seen the house, and I'll let you know if I've connected with Gerilyn yet? Then we'll figure out our next move." He paused. "If you can get Eileen to tell you any more about Gerilyn, that would be helpful."

"She seems pretty chatty; I'll see what I can do." She handed him the car keys.

"Make yourself at home, Mr. Scott," Eileen said, rejoining them. "And let the receptionist know if you need anything."

"I will. Thanks."

Kate followed Eileen out the door. "I really love your offices. It makes me want to redecorate my apartment."

"It's important to live in a place that makes you feel good," Eileen said. "The right décor can change your entire mood every time you walk through your door."

She wondered if that were true. She had a feeling that having a man at home when she walked through the door might do the trick, too.

"Agent Callaway?"

"I'm sorry," she said, realizing Eileen had asked her a question. "What did you say?"

The older woman gave her a thoughtful look. "I asked you how long you'd been with the FBI?"

"Oh, a little over a year."

"Is it dangerous?"

"Not usually," she said, as they took the elevator downstairs and entered the parking garage. "Most of the time it's a lot of talk. But last night got exciting. Someone set fire to Devin's apartment building while we were inside."

Eileen's lips parted in surprise. "Are you serious? Why? Who would do that?"

"It was a warning that we were getting too close."

Eileen stared back at her. "You think it was Brad. That's why you came to the office today."

"We'd like to know where he was last night."

"If he wasn't with Gerilyn, I don't think she'll tell you. She has become very protective of him since he got sober."

"Would she tell you?" Kate asked. "If we weren't around?"

"I don't know."

"Would you ask her?"

Eileen slowly nodded. "When we get back. But maybe she'll be forthcoming with Mr. Scott."

Kate hoped so, but somehow she didn't think it would be that easy.

--->>><<<---

Devin paced around Eileen's office, wondering if he'd made the right decision to wait for Gerilyn Connors. He had wanted to check out all of the target properties today, and there was a good chance that Gerilyn was going to give him nothing but a runaround.

His phone rang, and he was startled to see a San Diego area code. "Hello?"

"This is Alan Jenkins," the man said.

"Mr. Jenkins. Thank you for calling me back." He was honestly surprised at the return call. He'd about given up on the guy.

"I was on vacation for a few days. Why are you blowing up my phone with messages and texts?"

"I need to talk to you about Rick Baines."

"Why? He's dead."

"It's about how he died."

"I thought he killed himself in a fire."

"You were friends with him at St. Bernadette's weren't you?"

"Yeah, we went to high school together. So what?"

There was an angry, antagonistic edge to Alan's voice that was either defensive or offensive; Devin couldn't tell which. But he had a feeling being direct was the only way to go with Alan. "There was a fire at St. Bernadette's a few days ago."

"And…what does that have to do with me? I live in San Diego."

"It's our belief that Rick Baines was not the person who set the fire that killed him. We think it's possible he knew the arsonist. And since that person recently hit St. Bernadette's, it seems likely that that individual has a connection to Rick and the school."

"That's a wild theory," Jenkins said.

"So humor me. Tell me about your relationship with Rick."

"We weren't close friends, but we knew each other from high school, and I went to the gym where he worked."

"Did he talk about wanting to be a firefighter in

recent years? Did he refer to any of the suspicious fires happening in the city? Did he seem to be paying attention to them?"

"He always talked about wanting to be a firefighter. I told him to stop talking and get off his ass and try again. I knew he went after it several years ago and couldn't get in, but it was still his dream, so I encouraged him to fill out another application. He said he did, but the next thing I knew he was dead—and in a fire—I couldn't believe it. I wondered if the guy was living a secret life, because I had no idea he could do something like that. I guess that's always what people say when they're interviewed after someone seemingly normal does something abnormal."

"Was it that out of the ordinary?" he challenged, remembering Kate's conversation with Kristina the night before. "It's my understanding that Rick might have set a small fire when you were at St. Bernadette's."

"Who told you that?"

"Kristina Strem."

"Kristina has a big imagination. There was a really small fire, and we all wondered who did it, but Rick never said he did. It could have been anyone."

"Kristina also told us you went by the scene where Rick died."

"You had a long conversation, didn't you? Yeah, I went by there. I had to see it for myself. Like I said, I thought it was weird that he would die in a fire when he had such a fascination with fire. I still think it's strange. Is that a crime?"

"No. Did Rick keep in touch with anyone else from high school?"

"Probably. I know he saw Kristina a few times. Julie came into the gym with her boyfriend once. Rick mentioned running into Lindsay one day. Oh, and he said

Michael Bennett had come back from New York and was working for one of those ride-share companies. So, yeah, I guess he saw people from high school. But none of those people would set fires. I really don't know what to tell you."

Devin sighed. He was getting nowhere fast. "I appreciate you calling me back."

"No problem. I wish I knew something. Because if someone killed Rick, that's disturbing. Especially if it was someone he knew—someone I might still know."

Was Alan now genuinely concerned? His tone had certainly changed since their call had first begun, but mostly when he realized he wasn't actually being accused of anything. "If you hear anything from any of your friends from St. Bernadette's regarding Rick or the fires, I would love a call," he said.

"You got it. I'm sorry I took so long to get back to you."

"Where did you go on vacation?"

"Oh, um, I was in Hawaii."

"Which island?"

"Maui. Love Maui. Hate Oahu—too crowded."

"I agree," he said, thinking Jenkins was now being a little too smooth. "Maui has some great hotels. Where did you stay?"

Jenkins hesitated. "Sunset Villas. Do you want me to send you a receipt?" The antagonism was back in his voice.

"No, that's fine."

"You think I had something to do with these fires, don't you?" Jenkins challenged. "You are wasting your time if you're going down that path."

"I'm just asking questions. That's all. Thanks again."

"Yeah. Whatever." Jenkins ended the call on that

abrupt note.

As Devin set his phone down on Eileen's desk, he made a mental note to check into the Sunset Villas, find out if he could trace Jenkins to Maui, because his gut told him that Jenkins was lying about something. His behavior had been inconsistent, too. He'd gone from angry to helpful, to frightened, and then to anger again. Was he just being defensive because he thought he was being accused of something he didn't do, or because he was guilty?

"Mr. Scott. What are you doing here?" a female asked.

He turned around to see Gerilyn Connors enter Eileen's office. She looked tired and worried. He wondered if that was solely due to his presence or to her marital relationship.

"I came to see you," he said.

"I have nothing to say to you, and you need to back off, or I'm going to go to the police and ask for a restraining order against you."

"Where was your husband last night, Mrs. Connors?"

His abrupt question took her aback, and in that hesitation he knew that whatever was about to come out of her mouth was a lie.

"He was with me," she said.

The fearful light in her eyes and the pallor of her skin told a different story. "Are you sure about that?" He let his question sink in, then added, "I'm only the first person who is going to ask you that question. The police will probably be next, then the arson investigation unit, maybe some of your husband's former firefighting friends."

"What happened?" she asked tightly.

"Someone set fire to my apartment building. It was a warning, and the only person I can think of who was angry enough to give me a warning is your husband."

"I'm sure there are other people who don't like you," she returned.

"Where was he last night?"

"I told you he was with me. And I'll tell anyone else who asks."

"Why are you covering for him? You once got an order of protection against him."

"He was drinking then; he isn't now. He's better. And I want him to stay better."

"Lying for him isn't going to keep him sober or keep you safe. If he's involved in these fires, you could be in danger. You really need to think about who you're defending, what he's capable of doing."

She stared back at him, and all of the defiance suddenly seemed to go out of her shoulders. "We had a fight yesterday. He left around six, and I haven't seen him since."

He blew out a breath, relieved to have finally gotten past her defenses. "What was the fight about?"

"The fires. I asked him what he thought about there being two more fires, and he asked me if I was accusing him. Things went from bad to worse."

"You have doubts about him, too," he said, seeing the truth in her eyes.

"I don't want to believe that he's been burning down buildings I worked on to punish me, but I can't deny that there's a pattern. I really thought it was over until this past week when they started up again. Now, I don't know what to think. Eileen is really worried, and I am, too. I don't want it to be Brad. I really don't."

He could see the desperation in her eyes. "We need to find him. If he's not responsible, then we can clear him and move on. But disappearing and not being willing to talk will not help his cause."

"I've already called him a couple of times. And I called his sponsor, too. He hasn't heard from him."

Devin did not like the sound of that. "If you talk to him, you need to find out where he is, and you need to call me immediately."

She slowly nodded. "All right. He's not a bad guy, you know. He just has a temper, and he was upset that anyone could suspect him of arson. He gave so much of his life to firefighting."

"If he's not guilty, he doesn't have to feel bad."

"It's easier to say that when you're not being accused of something."

"It's not easier; it's just the truth."

She gave him a long look. "I'll let you know if I find him."

As Gerilyn left the room, he moved back to Eileen's desk to grab his phone. As he reached for it, his gaze caught on some family photographs on Eileen's desk. The girl standing next to Eileen in one of the pictures was very familiar.

He walked around the desk and picked it up to take a closer look.

He could hardly believe what he was seeing. The young woman with the straight brown hair and brown eyes was the same girl he'd seen in the St. Bernadette's yearbook. But that girl's last name had not been Raffin.

With his pulse beating fast, he took the photo down the hall to Gerilyn's office. He walked in without knocking.

"Gerilyn?"

"What now?" she asked, dabbing at her eyes with a tissue.

"Who's this with Eileen?" He held up the picture for

her to see.

"That's her daughter, Lindsay. Why?"

"Is she a stepdaughter? Why doesn't she have Eileen's last name?"

"She has her father's name—Blake. Eileen uses her maiden name."

His heart was beating so hard and so loud, he could hardly hear himself think. He was standing on the precipice of something..." Did Lindsay go to St. Bernadette's Catholic High School?"

"I think so. Why? What's wrong?"

"Where can I find her?"

"I'm not sure where she lives now—somewhere in the city. You can ask Eileen."

Eileen. They hadn't thought Eileen was the target but rather Gerilyn. Had they been wrong?

"What's Lindsay's relationship with her mother?" he asked.

"The usual mother-daughter drama. They've had their troubles over the years. They haven't always been close. Eileen worked a lot when Lindsay was small. Lindsay seemed to resent that." Gerilyn paused. "Why are we talking about Lindsay?"

"Because she went to school with Rick Baines at St. Bernadette's. Because a few days ago, there was a fire at that school."

"Now you think Lindsay had something to do with the fires?" Gerilyn asked in astonishment.

"Not something—*everything*. I think your husband just got off the hook, Gerilyn."

"Where are you going?" she asked as he jogged toward the door.

"To find Lindsay."

As he headed out of the building to the car, he

remembered that Lindsay had called her mom while she was in the office, and she'd been agitated about something.

Maybe about the fire she'd set the night before?

Was it possible that it was Eileen's daughter who was out for revenge? But why? Resentment for her mother working during her childhood? That didn't seem like a strong enough reason.

When he got to the car, he texted Kate. *Ask Eileen about her daughter. Find out where Lindsay lives. Get me the address if you can but try not to make her suspicious.*" He wasn't completely sure that if Lindsay was involved, she was acting alone.

Perhaps Eileen was part of it, too. His gut tightened. Eileen had offered to take Kate to one of the target properties. Wasn't it a huge coincidence that one of the properties on the list he'd sent to Eileen the night before now wanted a remodel?

Was Eileen just trying to get Kate into the house?

Had she done the same thing with Sam?

He felt sick at the thought.

He started the car and peeled off down the street. He knew where they were going. He just had to get there before the unthinkable happened.

Twenty-One

"I'm so sorry," Eileen said, as she searched for a parking spot. "I promise this will just take a few minutes. My daughter gets really upset around the anniversary of her dad's death, which is this week. I just want to make sure she's all right."

"Of course," Kate said. Eileen had gotten a call from her daughter again when they'd gotten into the car. Even from a distance away, Kate could hear how hysterical the girl was, so she'd agreed to stop for a minute so Eileen could make sure her daughter was all right.

As they turned another corner, she frowned, realizing exactly where they were—only a few blocks from Ashbury Studios.

"This is where you live?" she asked.

"No, not anymore," Eileen replied. "It's where I used to live. After my husband died, we moved to Nob Hill. I had this flat remodeled, and it's been a rental for the past ten years. But a couple of weeks ago, my long-term tenant moved out, and my daughter asked if she could move in. I said yes, but now I think it was a bad idea. Even though the place has been completely redone, there are memories there."

Eileen pulled in front of a two-story townhouse, partially blocking the driveway, and turned off the car. "Do you want to come in or…"

"I'll come in," she said, her heart skipping a beat as she got out of the car and looked across the street at the bookstore where a large peace sign hung in the window.

What the hell? This couldn't be a coincidence, could it?

As they entered Eileen's building, she saw some texts from Devin, but she didn't have time to read them.

She texted him the address and a quick message: *Eileen's daughter lives here—across from the peace sign. Going to meet her now. Something weird going on. Come if you can.*

"There are two units," Eileen said, leading her up the stairs. "The first floor is rented to a single man. He's out of town a lot."

When Eileen reached the door, Kate said, "Wait."

Eileen gave her a questioning look. "Why?"

"It smells like gas."

Eileen's eyebrow shot up. "It does smell like gasoline. Oh, God, I hope someone hasn't gone after my daughter because they have a grudge against me." Her hand trembled as she tried to insert the key into the lock.

"I don't think we should go in," Kate said, her gut telling her there was nothing good on the other side of the door.

"My daughter is in there. I'm going in."

Kate was torn, but as the door opened, she felt compelled to follow Eileen inside. The smell of gas was stronger now. There were rags and newspapers strewn around the floor, over the couch and along the far wall. Fuel—ready to burn.

"Lindsay," Eileen called. "Where are you?"

Lindsay? It was the first time Eileen had said her daughter's first name, and Kate's stomach churned. Lindsay was the name of the girl in the St. Bernadette's yearbook.

As Eileen headed toward a dark hallway, the front door slammed shut.

Kate whirled around to see a slender brunette in her mid-twenties, standing in front of the door that she'd now dead-bolted shut. In one hand was a long match. In the other was a box with more matches.

Kate's heart leapt into her throat.

"Lindsay," Eileen said, coming back into the living room. She saw her daughter with the match and froze. "My God, what are you doing?"

Everything suddenly clicked into place for Kate.

Lindsay was friends with Baines.

Lindsay was Eileen's daughter.

Lindsay was the arsonist.

"It was you," Kate said. "You set the fires."

"What are you talking about?" Eileen asked, her gaze moving from Kate to Lindsay. "Lindsay, what is she talking about?" She started toward her daughter, but Lindsay motioned her back.

"Don't move," Lindsay said.

"I don't understand. Lindsay, what are you doing?" Eileen asked.

"I'm going to burn the apartment down. Isn't it obvious? Our beautiful home is going to explode and burn to the ground, and we're going to be in it when it happens." Her gaze moved to Kate. "You escaped last night's fire. You won't be so lucky today."

"Lindsay," her mother said. "This is crazy."

"Well, I'm crazy. And you know why, so you can

stop acting surprised."

"I don't know why." Eileen looked at Kate. "I don't know what's going on."

"Lindsay set all the fires," Kate said, her gaze on Lindsay's stoic, cold eyes. "Why did you do it, Lindsay?"

"Because I had to escape from *him*."

"From who?" Kate asked.

"My father, of course."

"Oh, Lindsay," Eileen said in a pleading voice. "I told you that I didn't know he hurt you, that I was sorry."

"Actually, you never said that, Mother. You said you thought I misunderstood. You said sometimes Dad does things he doesn't mean to when he gets drunk. You said you would have done something if you'd known. But that isn't true. You always knew. You just didn't want to admit it."

"I didn't know. I swear it. I told you that when you talked to me after he died. I wish you had come to me sooner."

"When would I have done that? You were gone all the time. And when you went to meet your clients at night, he would come into my room. He would tell me that I had to make him happy, because you were gone. You liked historical houses more than him, more than me, so we had to take care of each other." Lindsay drew in a breath. "He abused me for years, and no one would listen to me."

Lindsay's wavering voice gave Kate hope. If she could keep the young woman talking, maybe she could distract her and take her down before she could light the match in her hand. But while she had no doubt she could overpower Lindsay, she was worried she wouldn't be fast enough, that the flames would hit the gasoline and injure Eileen and possibly all of them before they could get out.

Devin would come as soon as he got her text. She had to give him time to get there.

"The peace sign," she said, interrupting their conversation. "I saw it in the window of the bookstore across the street. Is that where you got the idea for the fire pattern?"

Lindsay's gaze swung to her. "I looked at that neon sign every night when he was in my room. Peace. I wanted that peace. But I didn't know how to get it. I went to the counselor at school. I told her my father was doing things he shouldn't, and she said she'd call my mother, and she'd call the police. But she didn't call anyone. She left for maternity leave. She went to have her baby while I was being hurt."

"Was that Marion Baker?"

"No, it was the other one."

"Is that why you set the first fire at a school?"

"Yes," Lindsay said. "I knew you were figuring it out when that guy chased me away from the rec center fire. How did you know I was going to go there?"

"We knew it had to be one of a few buildings within that area. Did you try to get help from someone at a community center, Lindsay?"

The girl nodded. "But I couldn't ask them, because there were other kids around, and I didn't want anyone to know. I tried to hint, but they didn't get it. I didn't have any way out of my horrible life. I was burning up inside. And then one day my friend was playing around with matches, and he started a fire in a wastebasket, and in those flames, I saw the papers crumple into ashes, and I thought I could do that, too. I could make that happen. I knew I wasn't going to escape unless *he* went away."

"Oh, my God," Eileen breathed, her hand going to her mouth. "No, Lindsay. You weren't home that night. You were at your friend's house."

"For some of the night, I was. I waited until he got drunk and passed out, and then I came back, and I lit the apartment on fire. I watched him burn, and I felt the most incredible release. Everything was gone. All the pain, all the anger. I was free. And he was dead. It was the best night of my life."

Eileen looked like she was going to pass out. "They said it was cigarettes. He was smoking on the couch."

"He was always smoking on the couch. It was easy to make it look like that."

"Did Rick teach you how to set fires?" Kate asked, stunned to hear Lindsay confess to killing her father. The fires had started much earlier than she and Devin had imagined.

Lindsay nodded. "Rick wasn't supposed to die, but he wanted to be a hero. He figured out what I was doing, and he wanted to stop me so the fire department would let him in. He told that FBI agent where I was going to go next. I had to take them both down."

"So now you're going to kill me?" Eileen asked in shock. "I'm your mother. I love you. I want to get you help."

"You never wanted to before."

"I didn't know," Eileen said in a broken voice. "I swear it. I didn't know."

"You're really good at lying to yourself. All these years, I kept waiting for you to notice that the fires were hitting all your buildings, but you never did. You thought it was Gerilyn's husband."

Kate was beginning to realize that every fire had been a call for help. Lindsay had wanted her mother's attention, and she'd finally gotten it.

"The fires started five years ago," Kate said. "Or is

that not true? Were there others before?"

"I thought I could stop after *he* died. It was better for a while. I went away to school. I thought I could be normal. No one would ever know. But after I graduated, after I came back, and I saw her with another guy, another guy who looked at me the way *he* did—"

"Who?" Eileen broke in. "You're not talking about Jeff, are you? He didn't touch you."

"I didn't give him the chance. Once that house burned down that you were both working on, he left town."

"I think I'm going to be sick."

"You're not going to have time to be sick, Mother," Lindsay said in a harsh, unforgiving voice. "And you don't even know what it feels like to be really sick, to puke your guts out, because your own father is hurting you."

Lindsay lit the match with one quick strike.

"Lindsay, you were abused. You need help," Kate said. "You don't need to set any more fires, or hurt any more people."

"It's too late for me. I killed Rick and that woman. I tried to stop after that, but I couldn't. The pain just got to be too much. The only thing that makes it go away is fire." She lifted the lit match in front of her eyes.

Kate suddenly realized that Lindsay didn't just want to kill her mother; she wanted to kill herself.

"It ends now," Lindsay said. "It ends where it started. Then I'll finally have peace."

"Wait," Kate said. "Tell me about the St. Christopher medal. Why did you leave it at the fires?"

"St. Christopher?" Eileen muttered.

Lindsay looked at her mom. "Why don't you tell her?"

"Someone tell me," Kate said.

Lindsay's gaze swung back to her. "*He* wore it around his neck. It would hit me in the face when he got on top of me." She looked down at the match, the flame nearing her fingers. "St. Christopher never protected me."

Devin's voice suddenly rang through the air. He was in the hall.

"Open up, Lindsay," he said, pounding against the wood.

Kate's heart jumped in relief. *Devin had come.*

"Of course he came to rescue you," Lindsay said. "I watched you together at the book signing. He looked at you like he loved you. But he's not going to be able to get through the door in time. Maybe you can try to stop me, but you won't be able to get out before the fire starts. You should say good-bye. You have about one second."

Kate stared at her, unwilling to accept that outcome.

"Devin," she yelled. "The apartment is flooded with gasoline. Stay back."

"Kate, get to the door."

"I can't," she yelled. "Go outside. Let me handle this."

"So touching," Lindsay said. "I thought Rick liked me like that, until he turned on me." She looked back at her mother. "I should have killed you with Dad, but I wanted you to suffer. I knew that the only thing you cared about were the houses you decorated. They were your family. But now it's your turn."

Eileen was sobbing now. "Lindsay, I love you. You're my little girl. If you want to kill me, kill me, but don't kill yourself. Don't kill Kate. Walk out of here. Set the fire on your way out—I won't stop you. Maybe if you get rid of me, you'll be free—you'll have that peace."

Eileen's maternal speech was passionate enough to actually make Lindsay waver.

Kate saw her chance and rushed forward.

As she tackled Lindsay, the match flew out of her hand and the flame sparked the gasoline-soaked rags and carpet. The burst of fire threw them both against the wall. Dazed, she saw Lindsay getting to her feet, grabbing the box of matches that had fallen to the ground, throwing another one into an open can of turpentine.

The can exploded and Kate was knocked back off of her feet. Her head bounced off the floor.

The front door flew open, and Devin rushed in like a wild man. He ran to her first as walls of flame leapt up the apartment walls.

"Kate, thank God." He yanked her to her feet. "Are you all right?"

"We have to get them out." She saw both Eileen and Lindsay on the other side of the fire. The explosion had knocked them unconscious.

"You first," he insisted.

"Devin—"

He wouldn't listen. He pushed her through the doorway and into the hall. Then he ran toward Eileen.

She wanted to stop him from going back in. The fire was exploding everywhere it reached new fuel. There was no way he could get them both out on his own and then get himself out. But there was also no way he was going to leave them inside.

She ran back into the room to help.

"Dammit, Kate," he said, as he dragged Eileen toward the door.

She grabbed Eileen's arms. "I've got her. Get Lindsay."

He turned away, but neither one had gone one more foot before the fire exploded again. Parts of the ceiling came crashing down on her head. She shoved boards and nails and plaster off of her head, struggling to her feet, trying to get Eileen free as well.

Thankfully, the fire department was now on the scene. One of the firefighters grabbed Eileen and put her over his shoulder, while the other helped Kate down the stairs and outside.

When she got to the sidewalk, she saw Devin coming out of the building, and she breathed a huge sigh of relief.

She ran to him, throwing her arms around him, as the terror of what had almost happened became very, very real.

He hugged her tight against his chest for a long minute, and then he pulled back to look into her face. "God, Kate, when I couldn't get in that door...when I smelled that gas...and then the burst of fire..."

"I'm okay. We're both okay."

"Your face. It's cut."

She put a hand to her stinging cheeks. "The glass from the windows."

"We need to get you to the hospital."

"I'm okay. Eileen is the one I'm worried about." She looked over at the paramedics who were working on Eileen.

"She was knocked out, but I think she'll be all right," Devin said. "I couldn't get to Lindsay, Kate." His voice was tight. "The firefighter pulled me out of there before I could get to her."

"You tried," she said, looking back at him. "You did everything you could. They'll get her out." But as their gazes turned to the building, there was no sign of Lindsay. "It's taking longer than I thought it would."

"The fire is bad," he said grimly. "She knew what she was doing. But then I guess she had a lot of practice."

She blew out a breath as she turned to face him. "I

can't believe Eileen's daughter was the arsonist. We came here because Lindsay called and said she had to see her mom right away. I had a bad feeling when I smelled the gasoline, but Eileen was going in no matter what. She thought someone was after her daughter, that they'd set her up. I wasn't sure, so I followed her inside. And then Lindsay locked the door and blocked our way out. I was stupid."

"You weren't stupid. You were trying to protect Eileen. Lindsay wasn't on my radar, either. Not until I saw her photo on Eileen's desk, and I realized she was the girl from the yearbook picture."

"Their names weren't the same."

"Eileen uses her maiden name."

"That explains that." She paused, licking her dry, parched lips. "Lindsay was abused by her father. Her mother didn't know about it or said she didn't know. Lindsay asked for help, but no one seemed able to give it to her. She started setting fires with Rick. She liked how it felt to watch something burn. Then she decided to see how it would feel to watch her father burn. She killed him when she was sixteen years old. I can't believe Eileen never told us that her husband had been killed in a fire."

"She killed her father?" he echoed in shock.

"Yes."

"Damn. This started a long time ago."

"Ten years. I guess that's why Eileen never mentioned it. She also thought her husband fell asleep while smoking, and that's what caused the fire. It was never believed to be suspicious."

"Was Lindsay there?"

"She was sleeping at a friend's house that night, or at least that's what she told her mother. After her father died, Lindsay felt better. She said it was a tremendous relief.

She thought she could be normal again, and for a while she was. She went away to school. She tried to live a normal life, but when she came back to San Francisco, she saw her mother with another man and it triggered all the memories."

"Another man went after her?"

"No, I think it was just the fact that this man was in her mother's life, that her mother was giving all her attention to him and not to Lindsay. She said his name was Jeff and that he was working with her mom on a house, but once it burned down he left town. I'm guessing he was a contractor or someone who had something to do with a remodel in that first house fire."

"He definitely wasn't the owner, but there was construction going on at the house. So that's why the fires started five years ago," he said. "What about Rick? Were they working together?"

"She told him what she was doing, or he figured it out. Lindsay said that Rick told the agent. Sam didn't figure it out. She didn't have some clue that we didn't. Rick took her to the house to stop Lindsay. He wanted to be a hero so the fire department would take him on. But Lindsay killed him and Sam. And today she was going to kill her mother and herself. I was going to be an added bonus. She knew we were getting close. That's why she tried to take us out last night. She didn't want us to stop her before she lit her final fire." Kate paused. "The peace sign in the bookstore—she could see it from her bedroom window. She looked at it every night when her father came in."

He let out a heavy breath. "It all makes sense."

"She was hurt, and she hurt a lot of people in return." She stopped abruptly as the firefighters brought Lindsay out of the building and put her on a stretcher. She could see it wasn't good.

"Don't," Devin said, tightening his arms around her. "Don't go over there. Don't look at her."

She felt a rush of emotion. Lindsay had killed three people, had injured others, had destroyed millions of dollars in property and had had an enormously devastating impact on the lives of many people, but she'd also been a victim. She felt compassion for that little girl who had been abused, but she felt nothing for the woman who had cold-bloodedly gone out for revenge.

"I'm okay. I don't need to see her," she said, looking into his eyes. "Lindsay did this to herself, and I hope she finally found the peace she wanted." She paused. "I hope you can find peace now, too, Devin. It's over. You know the truth. And Lindsay isn't going to hurt anyone again."

He nodded, his face tight, as if he were desperately trying to hang on to his control.

He pulled her back into his arms, and she closed her eyes as she rested against his solid chest. She could hear his heart beating hard and fast. It was the most reassuring sound she'd ever heard. She wanted to stay right where she was, but the paramedics insisted on looking at her, and then Emma arrived, and one of her cousins, and her mom and dad, and the distance and people between her and Devin grew greater.

He told her to be with her family. He needed to tell the Parkers what had happened to their daughter.

She wasn't ready to say good-bye yet, but Devin was gone before she could ask him to wait. And maybe that's the way it had to be. She'd done everything she could do to help him close the case. The last of it was up to him.

—➤➤◆◆◆—

Tuesday morning, Devin skipped his run and went to the cemetery just south of the city. It was a beautiful piece of land that overlooked the ocean. He put a bouquet of flowers on Sam's grave and then knelt down next to her gravestone.

"It's over, Sam. The person who killed you is dead. I know what happened now. I wish I could say that looking back I can see what we missed, where we went wrong, but I can't. Lindsay was clever. She didn't fit the profile, just as you said. I guess Rick must have told you about her before you left me that message. Anyway, Lindsay had a grudge that none of us could have figured out. Not even her mother knew what was going on in her head." He paused. "I just wish I would have been with you when Rick called you. Maybe I could have saved you. Or maybe not. You were good at your job, Sam. Hell, you were better than me. I just wish I'd gotten to you before the fire did."

He breathed through the last lingering waves of pain.

"But it's done. Justice is served. Your mom is going to be better, I think. The uncertainty and the doubts were making her life difficult, and I was to blame for that. I was the one who kept pushing for the truth. I was right, of course," he said, smiling to himself, thinking Sam was probably smiling at his cockiness—wherever she was. "But I made things harder on your family. I'm sorry about that. I hope they can heal now."

He looked out at the ocean, then back at the gravestone. "You're probably wondering what I'm going to do about Kate. I don't know. What can I do? She has a life to lead, a life I want her to lead, because it's her dream. I can't stand in the way of her dreams."

For a moment he thought he heard Sam's voice, asking him about his dreams, but maybe that was just his subconscious talking.

"I don't know what I want anymore," he said. "For the last year and a half, it's only been about this case. I haven't thought past it. Now, I guess I have to move on. I'm going to miss you, Sam."

The wind lifted his hair, and he felt as if Sam was answering him back.

And that whimsical thought probably came from having spent way too much time with Kate and her idealistic view of life.

He stood up. "Rest in peace, sweet Sam."

He walked away from the grave and paused on the edge of the bluff, looking out on the shimmering blue water of the Pacific Ocean.

The infinite horizon opened up his head. There was a bigger world out there than the one he'd been living in.

So what was he going to do now?

Twenty-Two

"I'm not sick, Mom," Kate protested, as her mother delivered a tray of her favorite breakfast foods to her bed. She'd finally gone home after the fire the day before, and her mother had been spoiling her ever since.

"You're recovering from a traumatic event, and I get to take care of you for a little while, so suck it up."

She smiled and took a bite of the chocolate chip pancake. "Oh, my God, still as good as ever. But I feel like I'm five years old again."

"I wish you were five years old, and I could know where you were every second of the day. I could make sure you were safe."

"You have to trust that I can take care of myself, that you raised me right—which you did, by the way."

Her mother shook her head. "Why do you have to do such a dangerous job?"

"It's not usually dangerous, and it's because I'm a Callaway. I was raised to serve and protect. I want to do my part to make the world a better place."

"I'm proud of you, Kate, but I still don't like to see you hurt."

"I just have a few scratches. A little makeup, and I'll be fine for the wedding photos."

"I'm not worried about that. I just know that you don't always tell me when you're hurting."

"I'm not hurting. I'm fine."

"Then why are there shadows in your eyes?"

"I'm still a little tired. I didn't sleep well last night."

"Were you thinking about the fire, or were you thinking about Devin? Your father told me it was all a ruse, but I saw something between you and Devin when you were here together. So fess up. Is it a fake relationship or a real one?"

"I like him, Mom," she admitted.

"Why do you make that sound like a bad thing?"

"Because I have to leave after the wedding. I can't quit my job because I like some guy."

"He's not some guy, and do you have to leave your job? Have you talked to him about moving?"

She shook her head. "No, we've been focused on the case. In fact, Devin has thought of nothing else the last year and a half. I'm not sure what he's going to do with his life now that the obsession is over."

"It sounds like you both have some decisions to make. I know you don't want my advice..."

"I actually wouldn't mind your advice," she said.

"Really?" Her mom looked pleased at that thought.

"I do value your opinion."

"Good. I know you like to make your own decisions and that you treasure your independence, but I also know that love and family are just as important to you as a career. I've always told you that you shouldn't settle for less than everything you want, and I still believe that. That's how I got your dad."

"You and Dad were living in the same town and

wanted the same things."

"Your dad was a hotshot firefighter when I met him. He was brash and cocky and quite the ladies man. But once he met me, that changed. Well, he was still brash and cocky at times, but he was all mine. If Devin is the right man for you, then everything is going to work out."

"How do I know if he's the right man?"

Sharon smiled. "You already know. You just have to be honest with yourself. Now eat your pancakes."

"Thanks, Mom—not just for the pancakes—for everything." Her thoughts drifted to Lindsay and Eileen and how troubled their relationship had been. She'd been fortunate to have such a wonderful mother. "I want you to know I appreciate you so much. I was lucky to have you as a mom."

"Well, that's very nice to hear, and you're welcome. And since you're done with your case now, we could use your help with the wedding. So when you finish eating, come downstairs and I'll put you to work."

"I thought you were going to spoil me awhile longer."

Her mom laughed. "Like you said, you're fine. See you soon, honey."

―――――

When Kate got downstairs, she found her mom sitting on a couch in the living room, and she wasn't alone.

"Look who's here," Sharon said with a knowing smile, tipping her head toward Devin.

"Devin, I was going to call you. I know we need to wrap things up," she said.

"I'll leave you two to do that," Sharon said, as both she and Devin got to their feet. "Devin, don't forget what I said."

"I won't," he promised.

"What was that about?" Kate asked suspiciously, as her mom left them alone.

"Nothing. How are you?"

She sat down on the couch, and he took the seat beside her. "I'm good. What about you?"

"Same."

"Really?" She searched his face for the truth, but she couldn't quite read his expression. "How did it go with the Parkers?"

"It was difficult," he admitted. "There were a lot of tears, a lot of questions, but I think it was healing."

"For you, too?" she asked quietly.

"It's still sinking in, but yes, I feel like a big weight is off my chest. I just wanted to get justice for Sam. I didn't want her to have died while the arsonist was still running free. I didn't want anyone else to get hurt."

"I know. I saw that from the first time we met. Your motives were never in question for me."

"I'm glad." He paused. "I went by the hospital last night; I saw Eileen. She has a concussion, and she's devastated and heartbroken, but she will recover."

"Physically maybe; I don't know about emotionally. Lindsay really hated her, and perhaps for good reason. Maybe Eileen did know about the abuse and just pretended it wasn't happening."

"I don't know. She told me that Lindsay had only mentioned something about her father touching her inappropriately after he died, and she didn't know what to make of it. She thought Lindsay was acting out in her grief. But that could just be the nice story she told herself so she would feel better. Anyway, she was released this morning, and she's going to her sister's house. I'm sure all the agencies will be following up with her."

"Are they going to have a funeral for Lindsay?"

"She wants to have a small service, just the immediate family. Lindsay was still her daughter." He put out a hand and gently touched her cheek. "I hope these cuts won't scar."

"They're not very deep."

"That explosion took ten years off my life. When I couldn't get to you, I went a little crazy."

"How did you break down the door?" she asked curiously. "There were two deadbolts on it."

"Fire extinguisher. I rammed the door. I was getting in no matter what."

"I knew you'd come. I tried to keep her talking long enough for you to get there. It wasn't that difficult. Lindsay wanted to speak her truth. She wanted her mom to know everything. It was sad." She paused, wagging her finger at him in warning. "And don't tell anyone at the Bureau that I said that it was sad. I don't want to sound like a girl."

"I thought her story was sad, too," he admitted. "But it didn't excuse what she did."

"No, it didn't. I spoke to Agent Roman last night. I told him everything that happened, although I still have to fill out a lot of official paperwork."

"I'll bet," Devin said with a small smile. "I don't miss that. What did he say about the rest of it?"

"He said you were right all along, and he never should have doubted you."

"Easy to say now."

"He also asked me to pass on a message to you. He said if you ever want to come back to the Bureau, the door is open. All you have to do is walk through it." She paused, not seeing much of a reaction in Devin's expression. "What do you think?"

"I don't think I want to go back."

She felt a little disappointed at his decision, but she could also understand it. The FBI had let him down. It would be difficult for him to ever get past that. And in truth, it would probably be difficult for the people who had let him down not to second-guess themselves on any future cases they worked on. "So private investigation?"

"I've worked with a couple of law firms. They've made me some lucrative offers for full-time work. I'm considering hiring myself out at a higher level."

"That could be interesting. Criminal law?"

"Yes."

"Right up your alley. And you'll get to call the shots."

"At least some of them. The more money I take, the more strings that come with it."

"It sounds like you're going to stay in San Francisco." She tried to hold back the wave of pain that came with that thought. DC was a long way from San Francisco. She'd never been that good at relationships even when they were in the same city. Long-distance might be impossible. But her mom had told her to go for everything she wanted, and she wanted Devin.

"I do like the city," he said.

"Do you like me more?" she challenged.

He stared back at her in surprise. "What are you asking, Kate?"

She took a breath for courage, knowing she was about to put her heart on the line. "I'd like to explore what's going on between us. And I was thinking that there are law firms in DC, too."

"There are," he agreed.

"I want you in my life, Devin. I think you want me in yours. I don't want you to work at a job you don't like, and

I don't want to work at a job I don't like, but maybe there's a way we can be together and still do what we both want."

"That's very optimistic thinking," he said lightly.

The teasing glint in his eyes brought forth a wave of relief. "I am an optimist. I've told you what I want. What do you want?"

He didn't answer for a very long minute. Then he said one simple word. "You."

Her heart stopped and then started again. "Really?"

"Yes. I am crazy about you. You came into my life like a hurricane force wind, and you blew out all the bad stuff. You knocked down my walls. I have no armor left. I'm afraid I just can't go on without you. I love you, Kate."

Her eyes blurred with tears. "Really?"

"Stop asking me that."

"I can't quite believe what you're saying. It's all very fast."

"Life is fast. And I don't want to miss any minutes with you. One of the law firms I was talking about has a branch in DC. They would be happy to have me work out of that office. I'm sure I can find other jobs. If you need to go somewhere else, then I'll follow you. And don't say *really* again," he warned.

"I can't believe you'd change your life for me."

"I want you to be happy, Kate. You're just starting your career. And as you told me many times, you are good at your job. You need to have your chance to live your dream. I don't want to stand in the way of that."

"But I want you to be happy, too. I want you to have your dream."

"These days my dreams all have you in them." He leaned over and placed a lingering kiss on her lips.

She smiled back at him, her heart as full as it could

be. "I love you, too, Devin."

"Good. That will make what your mother asked me to do much easier."

"What did she ask you to do?"

"Be your date at your sister's wedding."

"Oh, my God! Mia is going to go crazy when she finds out I'm in love."

"She's your twin. Doesn't she already know?" he teased.

"Actually, she probably does. I can't wait for you to meet her. You know this means you're going to be an unofficial Callaway."

"I can't wait. Your family is crazy but amazing. I can see why they inspire you, and I think they've inspired me a little, too. I want what your parents have. What my parents should have had but didn't. I want a family. But most of all I want a partner, someone I can love and trust to have my back."

"Always," she promised.

"And I'll always have yours." He gave her another smile. "Why don't you show me your bedroom? I didn't see it the last time we were here."

"Devin, my mother is in the house."

"She told me she was going to run some errands, and we'd be alone until noon. She was very specific about the time."

"I can't believe she told you that."

"I think she likes me."

"I think she wants to plan another wedding," she said with a laugh.

"Well, she might just get her wish," he said. "But I'm not going to ask you to marry me now. I don't want to hear another *really*."

She punched him in the arm. "Maybe I'll ask you

first."

"Maybe we'll just see." He kissed her again. Then they made their way upstairs and into her bed.

Epilogue

—➤➤◄◄◄—

Devin had been welcomed into the Callaway clan with more warmth and enthusiasm than he'd ever imagined. So far he'd been to two wedding dinners and an impromptu bachelor party, where he'd gotten to meet Jeremy, Mia's groom, and also gotten to know Kate's brothers and male cousins a little better.

Today was the big day—the wedding day—and he was standing outside the church in the Presidio while the crowd took their seats, and Kate handled her maid-of-honor duties behind the scenes.

Ian walked up to him and gave him a nod.

Out of Kate's three brothers, Devin related the most to Ian, who seemed quieter, more thoughtful, more observant than Hunter and Dylan. Ian also played his cards close to his chest. Devin suspected that Ian had a life away from the family that they probably knew little about. They wanted to know. They tried to pry and tease information out of him, but he was a vault, and Devin was curious what was in that vault, because he knew a little about putting his heart under lock and key, but he'd had a reason. His parents had split up. His dad had died. Every time he loved someone, they disappeared. What was Ian's story?

Somehow he didn't think he was going to find out today.

"How's it going?" Ian asked. "You tired of the family yet?"

"No, but I'll be excited to spend a little more time with your sister when this is over."

"I hear you're moving out to DC. Is that just for Kate?"

He wasn't surprised to get the question. He'd already gotten it from Dylan, Hunter, Annie, Mia and Kate's parents. "I'm in love with her," he said simply. "I can work anywhere."

"She's lucky."

"No, I'm the lucky one."

"Well, don't tell her that," Ian said with a grin. "Kate is already too cocky."

"It seems to be a family trait."

"You're right, it is. Have Dylan and Hunter been giving you a hard time?"

"A little, but I like that you all want to protect Kate. That's what I want, too."

"Then you're going to fit right in." Ian slapped him on the shoulder, then headed into the church as Kate came outside in her silky teal dress.

She looked beautiful today, her blonde hair pulled back in a loose, wavy ponytail, her makeup enhancing her long black lashes and full pink lips. Her blue eyes sparkled as she walked up to him.

"Hey, babe." She pressed her hands against his chest and gave him a kiss. "I feel like it's been forever since I saw you."

"Well, you were the one who wanted to spend last

night with your sisters."

"It was fun. I can't remember the last time Annie, Mia, and I had a slumber party. But I still missed you."

"You can have me tonight."

"Oh, I intend to," she said purposefully.

He laughed at her candor. "I like that you never play games. You say what you want when you want it."

"How else will I get what I want? I'm just glad you want what I want. Otherwise, it would be a little embarrassing."

"You don't have to worry about that. I always want what you want."

"I have to get inside. We're almost ready to start."

"Of course." He paused, looking into her gorgeous blue eyes. "One day we're going to do this, too, Kate. You know that, right?"

"Real—" She stopped herself just in time, then grinned. "Yes, I know that. I love you, Devin."

"I love you, too. Now go get your sister married."

"And then we'll start working on our life," she said, giving him one last kiss to savor before she headed back into the church.

He followed her inside, feeling over-the-moon optimistic about just what kind of life they were going to have.

THE END

The next book in the Callaway Series:

CLOSER TO YOU

will be released in 2016

———→≫≪←———

Keep on reading for an excerpt from

the first book in Barbara's new series

Lightning Strikes

BEAUTIFUL STORM

Excerpt – BEAUTIFUL STORM

From #1 NY Times Bestselling Author Barbara Freethy comes the first book in a new romantic suspense trilogy: Lightning Strikes. In these connected novels, lightning leads to love, danger, and the unraveling of long-buried secrets that will change not only the past but also the future...

When her father's plane mysteriously disappeared in the middle of an electrical storm, Alicia Monroe became obsessed with lightning. Now a news photographer in Miami, Alicia covers local stories by day and chases storms at night. In a flash of lightning, she sees what appears to be a murder, but when she gets to the scene, there is no body, only a military tag belonging to Liliana Valdez, a woman who has been missing for two months.

While the police use the tag to jump-start their stalled investigation, Alicia sets off on her own to find the missing woman. Her search takes her into the heart of Miami's Cuban-American community, where she meets the attractive but brooding Michael Cordero, who has his own demons to vanquish.

Soon Alicia and Michael are not just trying to save Liliana's life but also their own, as someone will do anything to protect a dark secret...

Chapter One

-→≫←←←-

The clouds had been blowing in off the ocean for the last hour, an ominous foreboding of the late September storm moving up the Miami coast. It was just past five o'clock in the afternoon, but the sky was dark as night.

Alicia Monroe drove across Florida's Rickenbacker Causeway toward Virginia Key Park, located on the island of Key Biscayne. Most of the traffic moved in the opposite direction as the island had a tendency to flood during fierce storms. According to the National Weather Service, the storm would bring at least six inches of rain plus high winds, thunder and lightning.

Alicia pressed her foot down harder on the gas. As her tires skidded on the already damp pavement, a voice inside her head told her to slow down, that a picture wasn't worth her life, but the adrenaline charging through her body made slowing down impossible.

She'd been obsessed with electrical storms all her life. She'd grown up hearing her Mayan great-grandmother speak of lightning gods. Her father had also told her tales about the incredible blue balls of fire and red flaming sprites he'd witnessed while flying for the Navy and later as a civilian pilot.

Their stories had enthralled her, but they'd been an embarrassment to the rest of the family, especially when her father had begun to tell his stories outside the family. Neither her mother nor her siblings had appreciated the fact that a former Navy hero was now being referred to as *Lightning Man.*

A wave of pain ran through her at the memories of her father and the foolish nickname that had foreshadowed her dad's tragic death years later in a fierce electrical storm.

She'd been sixteen years old when he'd taken his last flight. It was supposed to be a typical charter run to drop a hunting party in the mountains and then return home, but after dropping the men at their destination, her father's plane had run into a massive storm. When the rain stopped and the sun came back out, there was no sign of her father or his plane. He'd quite simply disappeared somewhere over the Gulf of Mexico.

Everyone assumed he'd crashed. They'd sent out search parties to find him or at least pieces of the plane, but those searches had returned absolutely nothing. How a man and a small plane could completely vanish seemed impossible to accept, and she'd spent years trying to find an answer, but so far that hadn't happened.

What had happened was her increasingly obsessive fascination with storm photography.

Her sister Danielle thought she was looking for her dad in every flash of lightning. Her brother Jake thought she was crazy, and her mother Joanna just wanted her to stop challenging Mother Nature by running headlong into dangerous storms. But like her dad, Alicia didn't run away from storms; she ran toward them.

While she worked as a photojournalist for the *Miami Chronicle* to pay the rent, her true passion was taking photographs of lightning storms and displaying them on her website and in a local art gallery.

It was possible that she was looking for the truth about her dad's disappearance in the lightning, or that she just had a screw loose. It was also possible that she was tempting fate by her constant pursuit of dangerous storms, but even if that was all true, she couldn't stop, not yet, not until she knew…something. She just wasn't sure what that *something* was.

Her cell phone rang through her car, yanking her mind back to reality. "Hello?"

"Where are you?" Jeff Barkley asked.

"Almost to the park." Jeff was the weather reporter at the local television station and had become her best resource for storm chasing.

"Turn around, Alicia. The National Weather Service is predicting the possibility of a ten-to-fifteen-foot storm surge, which would make the causeway impassable, and you'll be stranded on the island."

"I'll get the lightning shots before that happens. How's the storm shaping up?"

"Severe thunderstorms predicted."

"Great."

"It's not great, Alicia."

"You know what I mean," she grumbled. She didn't wish ill on anyone. But the more magnificent the storm, the better her pictures would be.

"You keep pushing the limits. One of these days, you'll go too far," Jeff warned.

"That won't be today. It's barely drizzling yet. The island is the perfect place to capture the storm in two places—over the ocean and then as it passes over Miami. Don't worry, I'll be fine."

"You always say that."

"And it's always true."

"So far. Text me when you get back."

"I will."

Ending the call, she drove into the parking lot. The attendant booth was closed, and a sign said the park was closed, but there was no barrier to prevent her from entering the lot.

She parked as close as she could to the trail leading into the park. She'd no sooner shut down the engine and turned off her headlights when lightning lit up the sky. She rolled down her window and took a few quick shots with her digital camera. She didn't have a great angle, so she would definitely have to find a higher point in the park to get a better picture.

Putting her digital camera on the console, she grabbed her waterproof backpack that held her more expensive film camera and got out of the car.

The force of the wind whipped her long, brown ponytail around her face. She pulled the hood of her raincoat over her head. It was just misting at the moment, but the sky would be opening up very soon. With tall rain boots and a long coat to protect her jeans and knit shirt, she was protected from the elements, not that she worried much about getting wet. She was more concerned with keeping her equipment dry until she needed to use it.

This was her second trip to the island, so she knew exactly which path to take, and she headed quickly in that direction. While the trails were popular with walkers, hikers, and bikers on most days, there wasn't another soul in sight. Anyone with any sense had left the park to seek shelter.

She was used to shooting storms in dark, shadowy places, but for some reason her nerves were tighter than usual today. The air was thick, almost crackling, and the atmosphere was dark and eerie. She felt a little spooked, as if someone were watching her.

A crash in the trees behind her brought her head around, and her heart skipped a beat at the dancing shadows behind her.

A second later, she saw two raccoons scurry into the woods, and she blew out a breath of relief. The animals were just looking for shelter. Everything was fine.

Ten minutes of a rapid jog had her heart pounding and her breath coming fast as she traversed the hilly section of the park, finally reaching the clearing at the top of the trail. Instead of thick brush and trees, she was now looking at the churning waves of the Atlantic Ocean. But it wasn't the sea that sent a nervous shiver down her spine; it was the towering, tall clouds that the meteorologists called cumulonimbus clouds. These clouds were associated with thunder and lightning storms and atmospheric instability. Alicia felt both terrified and entranced by the potential fury of the stormy sky.

She pulled out her film camera. While she used digital more often these days, there was still nothing like capturing a storm on film.

She took several quick consecutive shots as lightning cracked over the ocean. She checked her watch, noting the lapse of fifteen seconds before the thunder boomed. That meant the lightning was about three miles away.

Eight seconds later, lightning split apart the clouds, jagged bolts heading toward the beach. The storm was moving in fast—the lightning less than a mile away now.

She had a feeling she knew where it would strike next.

Dashing down the adjacent trail, she headed toward the old carousel with the shiny gold decorative rods that would more than likely attract the lightning.

As she moved through the thick brush, the rain began to come down harder, but she didn't slow her pace. She just wiped the water from her eyes and kept going.

When lightning lit up the park in front of her, she raised her camera and snapped two more photos before venturing farther down the trail. The carousel was just ahead.

The thunder was so loud it almost knocked her off of her feet.

She stopped abruptly as another jagged streak of lightning hit the carousel, illuminating the area around it. Captured in the glaringly bright light were a man and a woman engaged in a struggle.

The man raised his hand, something metal glinting between his fingers. A knife?

The woman screamed.

Alicia took a step forward, but the light disappeared and everything was dark again. She juggled her phone, trying to turn on the flashlight so she could see where to go.

Another boom of thunder.

Another flash of lightning.

She saw more dancing shadows. Then heard a long, penetrating scream. Closer now. The woman seemed to be running toward her.

She needed to help her. She moved down the path, stumbling over some rocks, and then the lightning came again. The tree next to her exploded from the strike. A heavy branch flew through the air, knocking her flat on the ground. She hit her head on a rock, feeling a flash of pain that threatened to take her under.

She battled against the feeling, knowing she had to get away from the fire that was crackling around her.

Where the hell was the rain now?

It was still coming down but not enough to smother the fire.

She got to her feet, ruthlessly fighting her way through the flaming branches.

Finally, the skies opened up, and the rain poured down, putting out the fire and allowing her to get free.

She grabbed her backpack from under a branch and moved down the trail.

Using her flashlight again, she walked toward the carousel, her tension increasing with each step, but there was no one around. No man, no woman, no knife, no struggle. What the hell had happened? Where had they gone?

She looked around in bewilderment. It had only been a few minutes since she'd seen them—hadn't it? Or had she lost consciousness when the tree had knocked her down?

She didn't think so, but her mind felt hazy and her head ached.

Despite the fuzzy feeling, she couldn't forget the image of the tall man towering over the smaller woman. She could still hear the woman's scream of terror in her head.

She turned slowly around, seeing nothing of significance in the shadowy surroundings. Then something in the dirt brought her gaze to the ground. She squatted down and picked up a shiny, rectangular military ID tag.

Her stomach turned over. She had a tag just like this in her jewelry box at home, the tag that had belonged to her father.

But it wasn't her father's name on this tag; it was a woman's name: Liliana Valdez, United States Navy, blood type O positive, religion Catholic. Her birth date indicated that she was twenty-eight.

The name didn't mean anything to Alicia, but she still felt an odd connection to the woman who'd lost it. Had it been the woman she'd seen fighting for her life? Had that woman been wearing a uniform?

She couldn't remember. She had the sense that the woman had worn a long, dark coat, but the details escaped her. Maybe she'd caught them on film. That thought took her to her feet.

She needed to get home and develop the photographs. She walked quickly back to the parking lot, pausing for just a moment to get a few more shots of the lightning now streaking across the Miami skyline.

Then she got into her car and sped toward the causeway, hoping she hadn't waited too long to cross before the storm surge made the bridge impassable.

When she reached the bridge, water was splashing over the rail, but she made it back to Miami without incident. She felt relieved to be in the city, but the pain in her temple reminded her of what she'd seen by the carousel. Who were those people? Had something terrible happened? Had she been a witness to...what?

Alicia's gaze dropped to the ID tag sitting on her console—to the name Liliana Valdez. She needed to find Liliana; not just to return her tag but also to make sure she was all right, that she was still alive.

- ⇒⇒◄◄ -

Alicia lived in the Wynwood Art District, a neighborhood just north of downtown Miami and known for its art galleries, boutiques and charming cafés. She lived on the second floor of a two-story building, and the bottom floor housed the art gallery where she displayed her storm photographs.

The owner of Peterman Art Gallery, Eileen Peterman, had leased her the apartment a year earlier, and Alicia was happy to be close to the gallery and in a neighborhood filled with artists and designers. She'd always been more comfortable among creative people who thought outside of the box, colored beyond the lines, and who put their emotions on display, whether it be in a sculpture or a painting or a photograph. She'd never been able to trust anyone who hid their emotions. It always made her wonder what else they were hiding.

After entering her apartment, Alicia dropped her backpack on the floor, set her keys and the ID tag on the side table, and then took off her wet raincoat and hung it on a hook by the door. She kicked off her boots and walked into the bathroom to grab a towel.

After drying her face, she pulled out the band from her hair and ran the blow-dryer through the damp dark tangles of her unruly mass of dark brown waves. Her hair was thick and long, drifting past her shoulder blades, and it was a constant battle to straighten the rebellious curls, which had gotten more out of hand in the wind and the rain.

As she stared at her face in the mirror, she was a little surprised at the size of the bump on her throbbing forehead. It was turning a lovely shade of purple and black and definitely stood out against her unusually pale skin. A dark-eyed brunette with olive skin, she usually had a vibrant, exotic look about her, but today was not one of those days. What little makeup she'd put on earlier that day had washed away in the rain, and the pain of her aching head injury had put strained lines around her eyes.

She set down the dryer, grabbed some ibuprofen from the medicine cabinet, took two capsules, and told herself she'd feel a lot better in about thirty minutes. Then she walked back to the living room.

She picked up Liliana's ID tag and took it over to the kitchen table. Opening her laptop computer, she typed in Liliana's name, age, and birth date. The Valdez surname would be common in Miami, a city made up of thousands of Cuban and Puerto Rican immigrants, so she was expecting her search to be complicated and long.

Surprisingly, it was neither.

The headline of the first article jumped off the page: *JAG attorney missing in Miami.*

As she read through the news story, she discovered that Liliana Valdez, a Navy lieutenant and attorney with the Judge Advocate General, had gone missing while visiting Miami in late July for the wedding of her sister. She'd last been seen in the parking lot outside of Paladar, a popular Cuban restaurant in Little Havana. The vehicle she'd been driving had been recovered from the parking lot, but there was no sign of a struggle or any other clues to her whereabouts.

Alicia let out a breath and sat back on the couch, staring out the window where rain now streamed against the panes.

Liliana Valdez had disappeared two months ago, and no one had seen her since.

Alicia picked up the ID tag, still a little damp and gritty with dirt, and ran her fingers over Liliana's name, feeling the same sense of connection she'd felt earlier.

She had a clue to a missing woman. She needed to take it to the police.

Jumping to her feet, she paused, struck by the thought that she might have more than one clue. Retrieving her camera, she took it into the walk-in closet off her bedroom that she'd turned into her personal darkroom.

Unfortunately, as the pictures developed, Alicia's enthusiasm began to fade.

The couple she'd seen by the carousel did not appear in any of the shots. The lightning was spectacular, but it was so close, so bright, it was impossible to see anything but shadows beyond the light, certainly nothing that clearly defined a person, which meant she had no other clue besides the military tag. Still, it was something. Hopefully, it would be enough to help find the missing woman.

END OF EXCERPT

About The Author

Barbara Freethy is a #1 New York Times Bestselling Author of 50 novels ranging from contemporary romance to romantic suspense and women's fiction. Traditionally published for many years, Barbara opened her own publishing company in 2011 and has since sold over 6 million books! Twenty of her titles have appeared on the New York Times and USA Today Bestseller Lists.

Known for her emotional and compelling stories of love, family, mystery and romance, Barbara enjoys writing about ordinary people caught up in extraordinary adventures. Barbara's books have won numerous awards. She is a six-time finalist for the RITA for best contemporary romance from Romance Writers of America and a two-time winner for DANIEL'S GIFT and THE WAY BACK HOME.

Barbara has lived all over the state of California and currently resides in Northern California where she draws much of her inspiration from the beautiful bay area.

For a complete listing of books, as well as excerpts and contests, and to connect with Barbara:

Visit Barbara's Website:
www.barbarafreethy.com

Join Barbara on Facebook:
www.facebook.com/barbarafreethybooks

Follow Barbara on Twitter:
www.twitter.com/barbarafreethy

CPSIA information can be obtained at www.ICGtesting.com
Printed in the USA
BVOW08s1506310316

442425BV00002B/2/P